LOOKING FOR THE AARDVARK

BY THE SAME AUTHOR

Death for Old Times' Sake
Death and the Dogwalker
A Little Neighborhood Murder

A. J. Orde

A JASON LYNX MYSTERY

A Perfect Crime Book

D O U B L E D A Y

New York   London   Toronto   Sydney   Auckland

Looking

for the

Aardvark

A Perfect Crime Book
PUBLISHED BY DOUBLEDAY
A division of Bantam Doubleday Dell Publishing Group, Inc.
1540 Broadway, New York, New York 10036

DOUBLEDAY is a trademark of Doubleday
a division of Bantam Doubleday Dell
Publishing Group, Inc.

Library of Congress Cataloging-in-Publication Data

ISBN 0-385-41942-2
Copyright © 1993 by A. J. Orde
All Rights Reserved
Printed in the United States of America
August 1993
First Edition

1   3   5   7   9   10   8   6   4   2

AUTHOR'S NOTE

The Spanish spoken in the Southwestern United States is not the Spanish of Spain or the Spanish of Mexico. Even within the Southwestern U.S., many usages differ from area to area as words mate with similar words in English to acquire new syllables or new vowel endings. Spanish words used in this book are those used by some Spanish-speaking people near Santa Fe. The author makes no claim as to their "correctness."

LOOKING FOR THE AARDVARK

One

TROUBLES, so the old wives say, come in threes. The general category "trouble" no doubt includes abandonment, murder, and mayhem. And since I'd lived through that triplet, I'd decided the trouble quota for my particular life had been fulfilled, and now was time for tranquillity. Or at least for that sort of comforting quiescence which counterfeits tranquillity well enough to be an acceptable second best.

Consequently, so I told myself, I listened for no distant trumpet; I coveted no unclimbed peaks; I woke to no visions of far places or strange quests. The exotic and illicit paled beside peace, so I assured me in the mirror as I shaved each morning, luxuriating in the calm as I did in the sybaritic steam of the shower. The fact that in the space of a few months I'd become much inclined to wallow in pointless ruminations and fruitless activities, I put down as a temporary and totally justifiable phase. I suppose at my age it could be called a midlife crisis, but since my recent life had contained little but crises, I chose to think of it as being becalmed while sirens sang softly, if at all. Only habit, and big-white-dog Bela's need for twice-daily exercise, kept me from growing fat. Fatter.

My police detective friend Grace Willis—not my fiancée, for though I had asked, she had not as yet answered—put it more succinctly though no less precisely:

"Jason Lynx, you're no fun anymore!"

"Was I ever?" I asked in a jocular tone, trying not to be deeply offended. Hurt, that is. While I've never thought of myself as the life of the party, any party, still I've considered myself capable of a quiet sort of charm.

She disillusioned me.

"Yeah. You used to be fun. In a sort of quiet way. No big barrel of laughs, but nice. We used to go dancing. We used to go to movies and museums. We used to have talks. You used to nibble my ear. We used to get involved in stuff. Hear me? I'm saying used to! What about now?"

When animated and involved, Grace looks rather like a banty hen. A seductively silver-blond banty hen, but peckish and determined nonetheless, going after every worm with beak and both feet. She weighs next to nothing because she burns calories as though they were lawn sweepings, great bonfires of energy going on all the time. Merely watching her eat can be exhausting—like watching six muscular men stoking a ship's boiler. Would to God I had her metabolism. Eating one tenth as much, it still takes that twice-daily trot around the park just to keep the fit of my trousers.

"I've just been enjoying . . . you know," I said weakly.

"I do know! Believe me I do, but it's not worthy of you. A few weeks, okay. Even a couple of months would have been all right, but even considering what you've been through, this languishing around has to stop!"

I, a middle-aged orphan with no habit whatsoever of derring-do, had lost my foster father, had several encounters with near death, and had acquired a new family and a new spot in professional limbo, all within the space of a few weeks. This was what "I'd been through," but Grace obviously wasn't going to let me use it for an excuse any longer. So, here was my midlife crisis come upon me without my looking for it. Accusations. Rejection. A challenge to my manhood! En garde! Trumpets blown deafeningly in the wings. *To horse! To horse!*

Mark McMillan, my assistant, had an answer, of course. Mark has answers for most things.

"You need to get involved in something."

He didn't mean professionally. Mark had been virtually running Jason Lynx Interiors for some months and doing an excellent job of it with very little contribution from me. I was still thinking of selling him the business. Getting him hooked by having him run it was part of *the plan*. Not that I'd told him about *the plan*, conceived in despair and brought to term in total misery, but even under improved conditions, selling was a viable option. It's just that nothing had happened to make me decide, one way or the other.

And that was really the problem. Looking back on my life, something I'd done a lot of lately, a good deal of it seemed to have been spent reacting to what other people had done. Except for my marriage to Agatha—very much my own idea—I'd been pushed into most everything else: by my foster father, Jacob Buchnam; by the people who killed my wife and child; by people who had tried to kill me. I'd once joined the Navy to get a perspective on life, only to exchange one set of shoves for another, rather more forceful, set. All those little pushes had resulted in a man who knew art, sort of; knew antiques, pretty well; knew how to blow up things from underwater, how to shoot pistol or rifle with reasonable accuracy, how to pick a lock, how to solve puzzles of various kinds; but not how to get Grace to marry me.

"If you'd marry me, we could decide what to do," I told her plaintively.

"How do I know I want to marry you until I see you moving around," she snorted. "When I was in California once, I went to that big zoo in San Diego. I went to see the aardvark, because I'd never seen one. He—or maybe she—was all rolled up inside this cave, with red lights on and a glass pane in the cave wall. All I could see was this hairy thing, breathing, but I couldn't watch it be an aardvark, because it does that at night, when nobody's looking. I think that must be what you're doing, Jason, being an aardvark when nobody's looking. I sure don't want to marry somebody all I can do is watch him breathe!"

And if that wasn't quite enough:

"What are you doing?" Eugenia Lowe, the showroom manager asked me snappishly one Wednesday mid-morning not long after Grace's ultimatum. Pelion piled upon Ossa, to my increased annoyance.

"Being an aardvark," I said nastily from my position behind

my desk, where I'd been since nine, busy doing absolutely nothing. The morning's crossword wasn't even completed! "I didn't know aardvarks stared out windows," she said. "I didn't know they had windows to stare out of."

"According to Grace, they do," I snarled. "Windows, and red lights, and interested though disappointed observers. Is something on your mind, Eugenia?"

"As a matter of fact, yes. There's a person downstairs who says he's an old friend of yours. Bruce Norman."

"Bruce?" I couldn't believe it. Though there had been letters and cards and occasional phone calls, I hadn't seen Bruce in . . . fifteen years or so. "We were roommates in college," I crowed. "What's brought him here!"

"I suggest you ask him, if you can tear yourself away from whatever fascination the back window of the house next door has for you!"

I made a face at her back as it departed, rigid as a drum major's, then got up and went out after her, through Mark's office to the hallway and balcony overlooking the spacious entry hall of 1465 Hyde Street. When I yelled, the man below looked up, grinning. "Jase! How the hell are you!"

I gestured toward the curving stairs, and he came up, passing Eugenia on the way with murmured thanks. He'd changed hardly at all! There were specklings of gray in his great brush of stiff black hair and a few white hairs in the brooding eyebrows that made a horizontal line all the way across his face, almost ear to ear. He'd grown mustaches off and on when we'd been in school together, but the one he wore now had the appearance of a longtime installation, very stiff and thatchy, making a protruding little roof above his upper lip. He threw both arms around me and pounded me on the back. Still effusive, Bruce.

I took him back through the offices into my living room. The second floor of 1465 Hyde is completely given over to my office, Mark's office, and my living quarters. The living room is decidedly more comfortable than the office.

"What brings you here?" I asked him as soon as he stopped bouncing around on the couch uttering war cries and old recognition signals and gave me a chance to say something.

"Ah . . ." He threw up one hand. "Kind of a long shot, Jase. I need to talk to somebody here. Well, I took a chance you'd be here, and if you were, I thought maybe we could have lunch."

"You need to talk to someone *here*? Here in Denver?"

"Here . . . hereabouts. The thing is, you remember my half brother, Ernie?"

I nodded soberly. How could anyone forget Ernie. "Could I forget anyone so determined to save my soul?"

"He tried for years, didn't he? Every time you came home with me for a weekend."

I nodded, remembering Ernie. Not Ernie Norman, but Ernie Quivada. As I recalled the details of the relationship, Bruce's mother had been married to a man named Ernesto Quivada, who had been killed in an automobile accident when she was seven months pregnant with Ernesto Jr.—Ernie. Immediately following Ernie's birth, she'd married an old sweetheart, Harry Norman, and in the absolute minimum necessary time thereafter had given birth to Bruce, to the great annoyance of her former in-laws.

"Mom got remarried rather sooner than the elder Quivadas thought proper," Bruce had explained.

Proper or not, Harry Norman had tried to do his best for Ernie, which wasn't easy. Although Ernie Quivada was Bruce's big brother by less than a year, that slight seniority convinced Ernie he had all the answers for Bruce's life and Bruce's friends' lives, including mine. His solution for all of life's mysteries and confusions was to be converted into the fundamentalist sect to which Ernie had been early dedicated by his paternal grandparents.

"Mom tells me she wishes she'd moved a thousand miles from the Quivadas and taken Ernie with her," Bruce said now, "but they'd lost their only child, and she didn't feel it was fair for them to lose their only grandchild as well."

"I was always surprised that your mom had married someone from that kind of background." I remembered Phyllis Norman very well. A humorous, forgiving, down-to-earth woman who was also a marvelous cook. Except for Ernie's intrusive presence, weekends at the Normans' had always been high points in my young life.

"According to Mom, Ernesto had no truck with what his folks believed in. Mom would never have married him if he'd been like that. He humored his folks, but he kept their religion at a distance, so Mom never really knew what they were like until after Ernesto was dead. Anyhow, by the time Mom realized what they were doing to Ernie, it was too late."

He nodded to himself, rather sadly. "Poor Ernie."

I'd always thought Ernie's victims deserved all the sympathy. "Why poor Ernie?"

"He's been murdered."

"Murdered!"

Bruce sighed, sat back, and stared at the ceiling. "I came here just to tell you about it. Do you have time?"

Of course I had time.

Bruce settled himself. "A couple of years after I married Lindsay, Ernie married this really sweet woman—girl, really. At the time she was only about seventeen. Margaret, her name is. Not Peggy. Margaret. He'd have been about twenty-four, twenty-five. For a while there, we thought she'd kind of . . . mellowed him down. Made him quit being quite so . . . well, you know."

I did know. When I knew Ernie, he had felt called upon to pray, frequently, lengthily, loudly—and publicly. He did it before restaurant meals, with sufficient volume to override all conversation at other tables. He did it at other people's weddings and funerals, often disrupting the ceremonies. He did it upon visiting the sick and the bereaved, including some who knew him only slightly, if at all, and who weren't up to being prayed over.

Bruce went on, "Anyhow, soon after they were married, Ernie and Margaret had a daughter, Felicia. She's their only child. Then, about ten years ago, they moved from Maryland to Texas, and from there to Oklahoma, and finally up to Santa Fe. Ernie had churches in each of those places."

"He was ordained?"

"Well," Bruce shrugged. "Bible college. If you remember Ernie . . ."

" 'The word of God is the only necessary study,' " I said, quoting one of Ernie's most frequent sayings. "So then what?" "Ernie kind of gave up on me and Mom. Mom got to the point where she wouldn't talk about religion with him, and since he never wanted to talk about anything else, relations got kind of strained. We always remembered them on birthdays and at Christmas, and though we hardly ever heard from him, Margaret wrote to us every now and then. Mom and I got the feeling she liked Santa Fe. It's an arty place, and Margaret likes to paint."

"Did he make a living as a minister?"

Bruce shook his head, doubtfully. "I think not. Each place they went, Ernie got a job to make ends meet. He did that in Santa Fe, too. And of course, Margaret always had a job of some kind, at least part-time."

"And?"

"And now, Ernie's dead. Murdered."

"When you say that . . . I can't believe it. Murdered!"

"Well, hell, Jase, I wanted to murder him often enough. I suppose you did, too."

Right! But one couldn't really have done it. Ernie was exasperating, infuriating, but . . . not a worthy target. It would have been like beating to death some small dog that was noisy but not actually threatening. I said, "Well, yes, we did want to murder him often enough, but . . ."

Bruce snorted, "Somebody wanted to who didn't say *but,* that's all."

"What do the police say?"

"Not much. Ernie's body was found in his church. His church is on pueblo land, which means it's the pueblo police who are investigating. . . ." His voice trailed off.

I knew much of the land around Santa Fe was Indian land, but I'd never visited the pueblos or considered the implications of their having their own government and police force. Something about it had Bruce annoyed.

"You're not sure they're getting anywhere?" I asked.

"We're not sure they want to get anywhere." He shook his head. "Lindsay and I've been there with Margaret since late Monday, the day after he died. You remember Lindsay."

I remembered Lindsay. Bruce's college sweetheart. Mother of his three children. We had, after all, exchanged Christmas cards and letters.

"Lindsay doesn't think they care much. They think he was . . . a peculiar man. They as much as said somebody was going to kill him, sooner or later. I don't think they want to know who."

"And you do."

He made an abortive gesture. Weariness. Frustration. Annoyance. All the emotions Ernie had always raised in us.

"Hell, Jase, he was my brother. He was Mother's eldest son! She cares about him. She cries over him. It was Mom who suggested you, if you want the truth. Mom remembered how you were always the puzzle solver, and she told me to call you, but the phone's no good for something like this, so I drove up here on the off chance. I told myself if you weren't here, I'd at least have had some time to think.

"The worst of it is, Mom's not well. She's housebound with arthritis. When she frets it makes the pain worse. . . ."

"Damn. That shouldn't happen to someone like your mother. What about your dad?"

"Died. Last year. That's part of it, of course. Mom's lonely. She feels like she's losing too many of us."

"I didn't know."

"Well, Dad was fifteen years older than Mom. He was in and out of the hospital over the last five years, and for the last two years, it was only a question of when."

"So, you came up here. . . ."

"To beard you in your den. To take you to lunch. To talk. See if you've got any ideas. Besides, you've done murders before."

"How did you know that?" I couldn't recall ever mentioning it to Bruce.

He waved vaguely. "The word gets around. Somebody told somebody. Maybe it was Bill Sandiman. Probably it was. He and mother have been friends since they were kids."

William Sandiman was still with the Smithsonian, and I did talk to him every now and then. "Your mom still live in D.C.?"

He nodded. "In the old house. So, can we have lunch?"

We had lunch. I called Grace, who was free for lunch, remarkably. She met us at one of the constantly metamorphozing restaurants on Seventeenth Avenue that had recently changed hands yet again. The new owner, by virtue of prices so reasonable he was foreordained to bankruptcy, was achieving transitory success with his version of a British pub. Bruce and I ordered ale and steak and kidney pie. Grace opted for iced tea and a double cut of prime rib. Bruce told us about the insurance business, in which he was a middling high mucky-muck, and I told him about the antique business, in which I am middling small potatoes. Grace declined to talk about the cop business because, so she said, it's mostly one thing or another. As is bound to happen during diligent let's-catch-up-on-the-last-decade conversations, we found points where our interests coincided. Bruce had had a recent case of insurance fraud, furniture insured for high amounts because it was represented to be several hundred years older than it actually was.

"The amount was too high even if they'd been genuine," I told him. "Even for real antiques, the market's down. Everything I bought last year is worth eighty percent of what I paid for it."

"Retail?"

"Of course not retail. Retail it's worth maybe a hundred sixty percent of what I paid for it. Maybe." Overhead ate up much of that. Lately, net profit was something I'd avoided thinking about.

We gloomed at each other.

Grace laughed at us. "Two pathetic failures if I ever saw any," she said, reaching for the dessert menu.

While Grace ate two portions of raspberry trifle, Bruce and I sat back over coffee while I filled Grace in on the story thus far. Then Bruce took up where I left off.

"I mentioned Felicia, Margaret and Ernie's daughter. She's about sixteen now. According to Margaret, Felicia left home a couple of years ago."

"A runaway, hmm?" asked Grace.

He frowned. "I don't really think so. Margaret doesn't say, 'Ran away.' She says, 'Went to live somewhere else.' Anyhow,

Ernie and his grandparents blamed it on the devil. Satanism. Rock music played backwards putting ideas in her head."

I gasped. "You're not serious!" Even for Ernie, that was odd.

"I am. Ernie was a lot better there for a while, but when he moved to Texas, the Quivadas moved there to be near him, and they followed him to Oklahoma and then to Santa Fe. He got in with a bunch of true believers before he left Oklahoma, and over the past couple of years, he'd . . . regressed. He'd become very fearful, his theology had become paranoid, with devils everywhere. Margaret didn't take it seriously, but I guess Felicia couldn't stand it."

"I sympathize," I said, nodding.

"Me, too. Anyhow, Felicia's living in a kind of street kids commune or . . . a group home, I guess you'd say. It's supported by a couple of staid foundations, and it's a decent place, with good adult supervision. She sees Margaret two or three times a week. She's not mad at Margaret, only at her dad. No, I'm not even sure of that. Margaret didn't indicate Felicia was mad at him, just that she couldn't live with him, or with the Quivadas, needless to say, which makes the whole thing sort of explosive because the old people live not far away from Margaret and Ernie. Felicia's not in any trouble. She's doing well in school. She'll graduate next year."

He stared out the window at the street, falling silent for a long time. I decided to jostle him.

"So, Ernie and Margaret have a house in Santa Fe?"

"Not in. Near. They bought a kind of fixer-upper. Ernie never knew one end of a hammer from the other, but he's put a lot of work into it. It's not a place either you or I would want to live in, but I guess it's shelter. Three bedrooms, a few miles from Santa Fe, not far from where Ernie had his church."

"Which is on pueblo land."

"Right. He wanted it there because he felt the Indians needed saving worse than other people, which was his grandma's idea. She has all kinds of interesting notions. She's decided she's descended from the conquistadors, but they were wrong to convert the Indians to Catholicism. Since she's a descendant, she has a duty to remedy the wrong committed by her forefathers. She'll convert them to the right faith this time."

Grace snorted. She had little patience with evangelists.

"She must be at least eighty," I mumbled, to show I was listening.

"Eighty-four. Old Eduardo is two years older. He's become quite feeble and disoriented. Anyhow, last Sunday morning after services, say noonish, the congregation left, all half dozen of them, including Margaret and Ernie's grandparents. The old people went home. Margaret went to this little place somebody loaned her where she keeps her painting stuff. Did I say she paints? Ernie evidently either stayed at the church or went back there, because when Margaret went home to fix supper, he wasn't at the house. She went looking for him at the church and there he was, on the floor, neck sliced through, blood all over everything."

"She called the police?" Grace asked, suddenly alert.

"She went to their office. There's no phone in the church, and the police office or station or whatever is in the pueblo shopping center, just a few hundred yards away. According to the police, Ernie had been dead about two hours."

"Alibis?" she demanded.

"You mean family? I suppose you'd have to ask that. It usually is family, isn't it? Well, Margaret was in her little painting place until about five, then she went home to fix a meal, and when he didn't show up about six, she went looking for him. From what I know about Margaret, she'd find it difficult to kill a mosquito. Felicia might have had a motive, I suppose, but she was with the other kids in her group home. I was in Maryland and Mom was in D.C. That's it, so far as family goes."

"Ernie's grandparents? The Quivadas?" She actually put her fork down and waited for the answer.

"Feeble. At least . . . yeah, feeble. Tottery. They went home after church, had lunch, took a nap. So they told us, between cries of fury at the devil for having taken their good, God-fearing boy."

"Any other suspects?" I asked.

"Well . . . there's this pueblo situation. The way I understand it is this: The highway goes through the pueblo, so the pueblo people built this little shopping center as an income source. They rent the commercial space to various businesses—a grocery, a hardware store, a branch bank, a doctor's office—and they use the income for the welfare of the pueblo. The building they rented to Ernie was an old one, separated from the new structures. It has electricity but no plumbing, so it isn't suitable for full-time occupancy. The pueblo people probably figured people would be in the building on Sundays and maybe prayer meeting night, and that was it, right? Anyone who needed to make a pit stop could go out behind a cactus. Ernie's lease made him responsible for maintaining the building, and it should have worked out for everyone."

"So what went wrong?" Grace asked.

"What went wrong was, Ernie worked as a deliveryman for a Santa Fe furniture store. The hours were irregular. So, whenever he had time off, he'd drive out to the pueblo shopping center where his church was, any time of the day, any day in the week, and pray over the customers. The pueblo got a restraining order on him, served on him by the same pueblo police now investigating his murder." He shrugged. "So then, he stood out in the parking lot and prayed over people as they left or got into their cars. So, the pueblo tried to evict him, but they couldn't do that. He had a cast-iron ten-year lease. So, you could say no love lost between him and the pueblo officials or the store owners."

Grace shook her head at me, wonderingly. She'd never met Ernie, so it probably sounded unlikely. "Anybody else?" she asked.

"There's this friend of Margaret's who was married recently, big garden wedding with a judge officiating. After promising Margaret he wouldn't, Ernie stood up during the vows and prayed."

"Oh, Lord," I mumbled.

"How did you guess?" He glanced at me sideways. "That's how he started out, at least. Margaret said the bride's mother threatened to sue."

"On what grounds? Misprision of prayer?"

He grinned at me ruefully. It was sad. I knew how Bruce felt. I felt the same way. Sorry, pitying, but not at all surprised. As far back as college, we'd told one another that one day Ernie would go too far because he'd never been able to comprehend another person's reaction to him. Usually, he seemed not even to notice it. If someone rejected his praying, it was the devil doing it, not the person. The devil was horridly strong and people were pathetic and weak, and Ernie was endlessly forgiving of their rudeness and rejection, which was one of the most infuriating things about him! Being rude to Ernie was like being rude to a tick. The only way you could get him off you was to physically remove him —though, come to think of it, I'd never tried applying a lighted match.

Bruce cast an apologetic glance at Grace and said, "I thought if you weren't busy, maybe you'd come down to Santa Fe?"

I leaned back and thought about it. Of course I wasn't busy, as everyone in my life had pointed out recently. On the other hand, I wasn't at all sure that another murder was what everyone had in mind. Including me. Of course, this was my old friend Bruce, but no, I really didn't want to get involved in another murder. . . .

"Of course he'll go," said Grace. "It's just what he needs."

What could I say? On the way back to the shop, I asked Bruce, "Do you believe in midlife crises?"

"Sure." He nodded comfortably. "I've had one about every three years since I was thirty. Every time I get started on a good one, though, Lindsay blows it up on me."

"I suppose it was meant to happen," I told Grace that night, after we'd all had dinner together and Bruce was settled into my guest room—the room my wife, Agatha, and I had once shared. He'd mentioned that he and Lindsay had been staying in a hotel in Santa Fe, and that Lindsay was heartily tired of three meals a day in restaurants. It had seemed odd to me that they'd have been eating in restaurants if sister-in-law Margaret had a house with a working kitchen, but that was none of my business. Where we stayed was, so I'd called my friend and former client, Mike Wilson, to see if one of the guest houses at Los Vientos was available. Mike rents them summers and sometimes during ski season, and he lets friends stay there if they're not otherwise spoken for. Even if we rented, it would be less expensive than two hotel rooms and three meals a day in restaurants. Mike did have a two-bedroom house we could use, so that took care of that.

"All right," I told Grace. "You're sending me off into the wilds of New Mexico, are you going to come with me?"

Grace said she might join me later, but right now was not a good time for her to try and get time off from the cop shop because they were shorthanded with a lot of people on long-planned summer vacations.

"You won't be angry if I have to stay awhile?"

She snorted. "I'll be angry if you don't stay awhile! It's time you got involved in something. Your blood is turning to sludge!"

Though Grace often slept over at my place, or vice-versa, on this occasion she decided to leave me to packing and early rising. I suggested to Bruce that he turn in his rental car at the airport and we'd drive down to Santa Fe together in the morning, Thursday. He was agreeable. Since we'd be at Los Vientos, Bela, the hundred-twenty-pound Kuvasz dog, and Schnitz, the twenty-pound Maine coon cat, could go along. Mark is always willing to do pet duty, but I didn't like to ask him when he already had total responsibility for running the business. Besides, I miss them when they're not around.

Bruce called Lindsay; I gave her directions to the place we'd be staying; and we all agreed to meet there between three and four the following afternoon. It's a seven-hour drive, more or less, not counting stops. I figured we'd leave at eight and allow half an hour for lunch and refueling. No need to pack the animals' stuff; it was all in a prepacked travel kit in the garage: food dishes, folding litter box, leashes, kibble, water bottle. Grace had taught me a neat trick with the water: fill a gallon plastic milk bottle with the water the animals are used to; then each time you pour a little water out for the animal, refill the gallon from the tap wherever you are, mixing it with the home water. By the time they get pure vacation water, they're accustomed to the change in chemical content and are less likely to have stomach upsets. I'm told it works with people, too.

At any rate, we left almost on time the following morning, delayed only slightly at the rental car place. By nine-fifteen we

were circling Colorado Springs, and by ten we'd left Pueblo behind us. Bela lay in the backseat, head up, watching the scenery.
Schnitz was in the pet carrier, where he felt secure. He hadn't
been in the car often enough to be totally accustomed to it, and
when something startled him, he was likely to end up yowling
under my brake foot.

In Walsenburg, we stopped at George's for a hamburger. Everyone who makes that trip more than once stops at George's for
a hamburger. Bruce took over the wheel, and I drowsed over La
Veta Pass and down the wide sun-dazzled San Luis valley, green
fields and tan fields and dirty gray sheep and miles of gray-green
sage distantly rimmed with crumpled blue mountains. Outside
Taos we stopped for stretching and other necessary functions,
and I did the driving from there. All along the way, Bruce ex-
claimed over each new vista as Easterners are wont to do. Lots of
trees in the east, blocking the view, hiding the ugliness, too. Few
trees out here. Everything is right out in the open, visible. Other
than that we didn't talk much. Once one leaves the citified clut-
ter behind, there's something almost hypnotic about that trip.
I've felt it before. One gets lost in it. Day-to-day subjects seem
trivial.

Los Vientos ranch is north of Santa Fe and, as it turned out,
only about five twisty miles from the pueblo where Ernie had his
church. His house was on a different road, but only about seven
miles away. Bruce had suggested to his wife that she do grocery
shopping before we got there, and when we drove down the
long, winding driveway into Los Vientos, we found her carrying
grocery bags into one of the larger guesthouses. Though I hadn't
seen her in years, I recognized her at once. She was still very
much the angular, quizzical-eyed redhead Bruce had married,
though I didn't recall her hair being quite so fiery in those years.
Art improving upon nature.

She leaned in through the open car window and planted a kiss
on my cheek. "I'm glad to see you," she said. "It's good Bruce
brought you to us."

Her voice was level enough, but it had an undercurrent of
weariness and trouble. I wasn't the only one who heard it.

"What's the matter?" Bruce asked.

"Ernie's grandparents! They visited me at the hotel this morning. I don't know who brought them." She made a helpless gesture.

Bruce asked, "What did they want?" His voice was sharp and angrier than I'd heard it at any time during our visit.

"I'm not sure I know," she laughed bitterly. "It had something to do with Satan. And something to do with the worm that dieth not. And something to do with Felicia and Margaret doing right by them."

"The worm that dieth not?" he asked.

"Don't ask me, Bruce. I'm not up on fundamentalist theology. Mostly they talked about the devil."

"And God, no doubt."

"Well, God played second fiddle. The devil was doing the conducting!" She sighed. "I'm just glad to see someone who'll be on my side."

"Did you tell them we were moving from the hotel?" he asked her as he got out of the car.

Lindsay shook her head, giving her husband a look of sheer panic. "Tell them where to find us? Bruce Norman, are you out of your head!"

I turned around and let Schnitz out of his cage, climbed out with him under one arm, and went to fetch a leash out of the pet travel kit. Bela was by this time climbing the window, wanting out. When Schnitz was leashed and Bela was out, the dog went off on a sniffing expedition while the cat found himself a spot of bare earth and began an excavation. When annoyed, Schnitz flattens his ears sideways, making an absolutely straight line from ear tip to ear tip, and glares at me from beneath this uncompromising brow. It wasn't unlike the line of Bruce's eyebrows, but I didn't point out the resemblance for Bruce was completely occupied with Lindsay, hugging her close, rocking her back and forth while he muttered no doubt sweetly uxorious words. It reminded me of things long past, and I caught myself blinking. Envy. Pure envy.

As soon as Schnitz would move, I wandered off, giving the couple a little time alone and me a little time to get the kinks out of my legs. It was early summer in New Mexico, several weeks ahead of Denver. Iris were in bloom, great yellow and white and blue eruptions of them, as well as some large bushes of blazing red flowers—peonies, Lindsay told me later when I asked her what they were. Snowball bushes were loaded with their clumsy-looking bouquets. I've never paid much attention to gardening or flowers; it isn't something Grace is particularly interested in either; but Mark has planted bulbs and perennials in front of 1465 Hyde, to keep the old house from looking gloomy, he says, and I've learned to recognize a few of the commoner kinds.

"Hey," Bruce called. "Where you going?"

"Nowhere. Just getting the kinks out."

"Lindsay's provided for cocktail time! Come on."

It was warm, in the high seventies, but the warmth would last only for an hour or two, until the sun dropped. We carried our suitcases into the house, a long old adobe with a living room at one end, then a kitchen, then a long paseo with two bedrooms and a bathroom opening off it. I took the smaller bedroom for me and the animals. Schnitz would sleep on the bed, Bela beside it on his traveling cot, a thick old blanket permeated with comforting home smells. Mike had thoughtfully provided a "pet run" on the place, where I could leave the critters for a few hours during the day if I had to.

After we'd partially unpacked and settled ourselves, we went outside to the covered porch or "portal," brushing blown blossoms from the chairs—a change from city soot! Lindsay had provided chips and salsa and guacomole along with gin and tonic. We nibbled and drank, not saying much, while the sun sank slowly toward the far mountains behind the great mesa to the west, its face riven into complicated folds. We sat there while great bastions of shadow piled themselves in the canyons, turning them black and mysterious, and it was only after some time of this pleasant aimlessness that Lindsay set down her glass and asked:

"Enough of this! What's our agenda, Jason?"

I suppose it startled me, because she laughed at my expression. "You're our fearless leader. Didn't Bruce tell you?"

"I didn't volunteer to lead anybody," I said.

"Well, don't lead if you don't want to. I just figured, whatever you're going to do, you can use some help."

I thought about it for a while. "Who are we doing this for? You guys?"

"Mom," said Bruce, without hesitation. "I think I can live with the ambiguity of not knowing who and why, but Mom can't. She'll fret."

I shifted uncomfortably, trying to think of what to say next. If I'd been home, I'd have talked with Grace and Mark about the matter. Well, they weren't here, but Bruce and Lindsay were, so treat it as a similar situation. I cleared my throat, sounding rather pompous.

"I'd usually begin by finding out everything we can about everyone involved. Felicia: where was she, who was she with, had she had any recent arguments with her father. Margaret: the same, what was her situation. . . ."

"Peculiar," said Lindsay, emphatically. "Every time I talk to her, I find out something else strange. Her situation is peculiar, to say the least."

"In what way?"

"She's got people living at her house. Bruce and I thought it was odd she didn't invite us to stay with her, or even to have a meal with her. We wouldn't have stayed, but you'd have thought she'd ask. Well, she didn't, and the reason she didn't, which I didn't know until last night, is that there's another family living there."

"Another family?"

"Don't ask me. It doesn't make sense to me either, but that's what she said. There's another family there."

I made a mental note. Talk to Margaret. "Someone needs to talk to the old people, the Quivadas. I suppose that'd better be me."

"Rather you than us," said Bruce.

I shrugged. "Then we need someone to follow up with the police, find out what they know. I'm not family, but you are. You have a right to ask, so that one is yours. Also, we need to look at this church, see where it happened."

"Busy, busy," said Lindsay ruefully. "How long will it all take?"

"Until we find something out, or until you get tired of chasing about and give up and go home," I said.

"No guarantees, huh?"

"Absolutely none, Lindsay. Quite frankly, I think Bruce gives me more credit than I deserve—"

"Getting you involved was Mom's idea," he interrupted, grinning at me. "Blame her."

I ignored his caveat. "I've solved a few little things, but I've flubbed on a few, too. This may be one that goes nowhere. I want you to understand that."

She nodded soberly. "The last thing we want is for you to feel obligated, Jason. It's just . . . we, Bruce and I, feel helpless. It's as he says: *we* can live with that, but his mom feels . . . guilty." She cast a quick look at Bruce and he nodded, agreeing with her. "As though it's *her* fault Ernie was the way he was. God knows she tried with him, but he was always that way. You know that! If we find out why this happened, it may make her feel better . . . no, no, not better, but more accepting, that's all."

"He may simply have gotten into an argument with someone who slashed him and ran," I told her. "People carry guns, people carry knives, there's a lot of violence going around. Did the police find a weapon?"

"They didn't say anything about finding a weapon. In fact, all they said was that his throat had been slashed, no other marks at all. No marks on his hands where he'd put them up to protect himself. Nothing."

"I'd like to see the place," I said.

"Tomorrow morning?"

"What about tonight?" I asked. "Why not now? Bruce says it isn't far. I'll put the animals in the run with some food and water. They'll do fine there while we have a quick look around."

They looked at one another, shrugging. I took Bela and Schnitz down the hill to the run, told them I'd be back soon, and climbed into Margaret's rental car for the trip to the church.

The building was perhaps less lonely and starved-looking in the ruddy light of late afternoon than it would have been at midday, but it was still quite desolate enough: a shedlike building with paint-peeling plywood sides, a door at the northwest, stingy double-hung windows on the southwest, and a lopsided cross tacked to the ridgepole. It bore a handpainted sign: CHURCH OF JESUS TRIUMPHANT. A hundred yards to the east, the earth fell away into an arroyo, almost a canyon, that ran down from the north, opening on the plain to the south, toward Santa Fe. On the opposite rim, the windows of houses glimmered red with reflected sunset, like feral eyes waiting for the night. Two hundred yards from the church door, the fake adobe cloisters of the pueblo shopping center fronted the north-south line of the divided highway, high arched portals shading the storefronts. Despite the nearness of stores and busy road, we stood in real desert, bare pinkish gravel dotted with cactus and choya and chamisa —so Mike had previously identified the ubiquitous growths for me—with a few ragged junipers holding on for dear life. The only driveway from highway to church was the set of ruts we had followed. When it rained, they would be mudholes.

We stood for a moment beside the car, staring wordlessly at all this, then Bruce and Lindsay wandered off to look at a shrub that had blossomed whitely to one side, seeming almost to blaze in the evening light—Moses' bush, alight but unconsumed—while I went up the three tottery wooden steps to the much cracked church door. It stood half open, but I turned my back to it for the moment, examining the site.

At the corner nearest the door, a chunk of tree trunk served as a chopping block amid a scatter of sticks and chips. Aside from the wood, there was no litter. No aluminum cans. No blown paper. Either someone had kept the area clean or the police had collected everything lying about as possible evidence.

The door shrieked against the plywood panel floor as I pushed it until it balked against an iron stove standing in one corner, an empty wood-box beside it. This time of year the last thing anyone needed was heat. The panels had been nailed directly onto inadequate joists, which creaked and sagged in protest as I walked down the strip of threadbare tan carpet between short rows of assorted metal folding chairs in various shades of olive and tan and brown, all chipped, all dented, all dusty. The short aisle ended at a dark-stained plywood lectern across from a battered upright piano, the two separated by a painting that was spotlighted by long, diagonal rays from the west window. The sight caught me in the pit of my stomach, and I stopped, unable to move.

The painting was of a Madonna and child. A glowing, loving, persuasive Madonna and child.

The painted eyes fixed mine with compassion and understanding and humor and acceptance, a familiar expression, though I couldn't place it. The naked baby looked up at her, smiling. I would have said eighteenth century, seventeenth perhaps. European, probably Italian. And if the effect was any measure of value, worth its weight in thousand-dollar bills. I stepped forward, craning, trying to see the signature.

"Margaret," said Bruce from behind me. "Margaret painted it."

"Margaret?" I said stupidly. They had said she painted, in the way one says such things. He writes. She paints. They had not said she was an artist. A fine . . . maybe a great artist.

"This *is* a Protestant sect?" I asked, gesturing at the ugly building. "This painting looks . . . Catholic."

He nodded. "I had the same reaction. Margaret says Ernie asked her to paint a Jesus for his church. She told him she would. She painted him as a baby, that's all."

"She's good," I said inadequately. She was not merely good. "Is this a copy of something?"

"Margaret told Lindsay she copied the style. It's different from her usual style. She's more of an impressionist. But the picture is her own. She used a photograph of Mom as a model."

"Your mom?" Of course it was. I recognized her!

He nodded. "My mom. And Ernie's."

I went on staring. "How long has it been here?"

"Just since Sunday morning. Margaret says she brought it over and hung it before services on Sunday."

"Ah." I gestured at the floor beneath the painting. "And what are those?"

"What's what?"

He came around me to look at the dozen or so candle stubs

and votive lights on the floor beneath the painting, burned down now to mere puddles of wax.

He shook his head. "They weren't there when Lindsay and I were here with Margaret on Tuesday."

I turned away from the Madonna, my eyes drawn to an area that had been shadowed until the sun slipped away from the painting to light the floor near the lectern. There the customary investigatory outline taped to the raw wood showed us where Ernie had fallen, legs bent, one arm outstretched. The area near the head was darkened by a bloodstain already covered with blown grit. In addition to the open door, two of the windows were open to admit the dust-laden wind. Every step crunched beneath our shoes, like walking on sugar.

I went down each row of folding chairs, three to the row, a dozen each side of the center aisle, and no room for more. Room enough, however, if his congregation had numbered only six. The chairs, too, were dusty and unused-looking. About half of them held battered hymnals, covers faded and pages stained from long use elsewhere. I leafed idly through one of them, reading first lines. *On a hill far away. I came to the garden alone. Let the lower lights be burning.* One of the hymnals stood open on the piano. *Oh Lord and Master of mankind, forgive our errant ways.*

On the front of the lectern was a sheet of white cardboard, lettered in felt-tipped pen with the numbers of the hymns and the day's text, something in the gospel of Mark.

"Sometimes I'm glad Mom and Dad reared me to be an agnostic," Bruce commented. "Jacob was Jewish, wasn't he?"

I nodded, yes. "Not observant," I said. "And he never made any effort to convert me to Judaism."

"You know who your family is now. What about your grandmother's religion?"

"Catholicism?" I shook my head, no. It had never crossed my mind. My newly acquired grandmother had never mentioned it, which was hardly surprising. Olivia blamed religion for most of the unhappiness in her life, including the death of her daughter. Perhaps not religion per se, but the repression that had ridden in on its coattails.

I moved around the perimeter of the room, not looking for

anything in particular, the crackling cereal noises accompanying each step. A fiberboard wardrobe in the corner nearest the door held a broom, a rusty-looking parson's robe, and one shelf. On the shelf were a dust pan and dustcloth. The dustcloth and the robe were about the same color.

"I hate to leave that painting here," I said, lowering one of the open windows and attempting to latch it. "There's no lock on the door."

"Margaret said it didn't matter. She says she painted it for Ernie, and if he's gone, any reason for painting it has gone with him."

"Damn it!" I stared at the Madonna. "I could sell that for her, Bruce. Doesn't she need money?"

The two exchanged glances, and Bruce shrugged at his wife. "As Lindsay and I have been discussing lately, she certainly does."

"Well then, at least let's take it with us. If she doesn't want me to sell it, I won't. If she wants to burn the thing, she can, but it's sacrilege to leave it sitting here in this filthy wind!"

"Someone didn't think it was sacrilege," he said, indicating the candle stubs, which, even in their puddled state betokened veneration on someone's part.

He was right, of course. Someone hadn't minded the location. Still, I couldn't leave the painting in that dust-grimed and unlovely building. We put it in the trunk of the car, padded with the parson's robe to keep it from being scratched, and I left a note tacked to the wall giving my name and the guest house phone number at Los Vientos, just in case anyone cared enough about it to worry.

The phone in the guest house rang about midnight. My room was nearest, so I got up and went out into the kitchen to answer it. Someone spoke rapidly in Spanish, and I got about two words. *"Mas lento,"* I begged. *"Por favor. . . ."*

The words that came pouring out were, by their tone, perjorative. Then whoever it was hung up. At first I'd thought it was a wrong number, but one word had been understandable. *"Madonna. La Madonna."* Someone must have copied down the number I'd left at the church. Whoever it was had been very emotional about the whole thing. I turned on a lamp in the living room and looked at the painting, which we'd hung on a hook previously occupied by a framed Howell poster of Indian hair. The Madonna had power. It had feeling. Longing. Yearning. Something.

I turned off the lamp and went back to bed.

After breakfast the next morning, we took a few moments to make beds and straighten up, then Bruce and Lindsay went off to talk to the police and I went to talk to Margaret, taking Bela and Schnitz along on the theory that animals are disarming. People of bad character do not go about with dogs and cats. Pets are a guarantee of principled behavior.

Bruce had phoned to ask Margaret if I could talk with her, and he'd given me a map on the back of an envelope, so I could find the house. One turned off the highway well north of the pueblo shopping center and went east, and then southeast, down the other side of the arroyo we had seen the night before. It sounded simple, but it still took several tries. Around Santa Fe, some roads look like driveways, and some driveways look like roads, and there are often no signs where one would expect signs to be. Considering that most of the trees are no taller than ten or twelve feet, I should have been able to see the place from a considerable distance, but the rolling ground is deceptive, hiding all sorts of little surprises in its folds. I encountered goats, pigs, cows, a line of six-year-olds on ponies, and an enormous and ostentatious Spanish-style gate, with gatehouse, marking a paved driveway that wound down into a wooded river bottom and out of sight. The river bottom told me I was on the wrong side of the mesa.

Part of the difficulty in finding places is created by the uniform style either imposed on or accepted by ninety-eight percent of homeowners in the Santa Fe area. Every building is much the same color as the next. Every building is much the same style. Virtually all have flat roofs, adobe walls (real or fake), protruding vigas, and so on and so on. Cecily (Cees) Stephens, a Santa Fe resident who runs an architectural firm called Habitacion, decries the uniformity. There are other idioms, says she, suitable for adobe or arid land construction. She points to North Africa, which is full of beautiful and fanciful mud structures, some of which are more sensible than the Santa Fe style, and says that Santa Fe might be more interesting for its residents (though perhaps not its visitors) if it tried a few of them.

At any rate, by dint of much going back and rethinking, eventually I turned down the right set of ruts and passed the right set of houses, coming at last upon Ernie and Margaret's "fixer-upper." In my eyes, it remained unfixed. If it had been any less fixed when they bought it, I could not imagine why they'd done so. I pulled up, got out of the car, leashed the animals and got them out, and we turned around to confront a woman who had walked soundlessly up behind me.

"Jason," she murmured. "Bruce's friend?"

I shifted a leash and took the proffered hand. Whatever I'd expected, this wasn't it. She looked so young! She appeared to be in her early twenties. A perfect oval face, features so cleanly understated that I didn't immediately identify them as collectively beautiful. Her eyes were huge, a greenish hazel, softly lashed with perfectly curved brows. Her nose was classic, a uniform barrel to the tip, the nostrils delicately carved at either side. Thick pale brown hair fell loose and straight on the left and was fastened back on the right with an oval of tooled leather anchored by a long silver pin with a turquoise ornament at its end. She wore a high-necked white shirt, severe as a nun's garb, and paint-spattered jeans.

"Margaret?" I managed to get out. Who else could it have been? And where had my voice gone?

"I'm Margaret," she murmured. Her voice was perfectly audible, yet it gave the impression of being overheard from several rooms away. I felt the very act of hearing her speak intruded upon her.

I took hold of myself, found my voice somewhere near my ankles, and hauled it up where it belonged. "Is there somewhere we can sit down and talk?" I asked, trying not to be put off by the aura of privacy and untouchability she spread like a perfume.

"Inside."

"The animals. . . ."

She laughed, a low burble of sound, like a bubbling spring, becoming in that instant a real person. "It won't matter. Believe me. Bring them."

She led me around the corner of the house and into a two-story annex that was obviously newly built. We went down several wobbly railroad tie steps into a sunken area, about fifteen by twenty, with a stone floor covering about half the space. One of the short walls had a narrow balcony about eight feet up, reached by steep ladderlike stairs. The balcony was supported by vigas set horizontally into the sidewalls, the logs tapering from some fourteen to sixteen inches thick at one end to around eight inches at the other. As a result, the balcony floor—made up of boards nailed directly to the treetrunk rafters—was about eight inches higher at one wall than the other.

I turned to see her eyes fixed on me in amusement.

"Sometimes people see it, they know something is wrong, but they can't figure out what," she said.

"You wouldn't dare drop anything round up there, would you?" I asked rhetorically.

"Or spill anything," she agreed. "Or if you were sleeping there, set your bed in the wrong direction. All the blood would go to your head."

"I've seen roofs with less slope," I agreed. "Who did it?"

She shook her head ruefully. "Ernie. I tried to tell him he needed to build one wall a little higher than the other one, to level the floor, but Ernie was being guided by God at the time. He didn't even realize it slanted until he'd almost finished the floor and he dropped a screwdriver that rolled all the way to the far wall."

I couldn't take my eyes off it. "Guided by God," I murmured. "Does God have something against using a level?"

She spoke as if to anyone who might be present, not looking at me, not seeming to care whether I listened. "Well, Ernie says . . . said . . . if you have God, you don't need anything else. He used to ask people for things. He'd start praying over people, asking God to make them see their way clear to donating this, or that, or some other thing. If he prayed long enough, people did give him things. He got the vigas, the logs, that way. They'd have been fine as roof rafters. A roof should slope. But for a balcony, you need vigas that are pretty much the same diameter at both ends. Either that, or walls that compensate."

"Why did he want a balcony?"

"He thought the room would hold more people that way. When the church really caught on."

"He intended to hold services here?"

She shrugged. "He called it the chapel." She sat down on a wooden bench and patted the space beside her. I lowered myself onto the unyielding surface. If I had to sit long, I'd need a cushion.

She took a quiet breath and was silent, looking at the sun falling through the window, paying no attention to me. I could have been a squirrel on a branch, or a bee. Part of the scenery. Her lips were curved into a sensuous arc, lovely as the curve of a Greek amphora. Her eyes glistened, the lids dropping now and then, not in a blink, the way normal people blink, but in a shutting, as though purposeful, to reflect on what the eye has seen.

I felt myself falling, as though under some kind of spell, so I took a deep breath and looked away, taking the opportunity to give the room another looking over, the plywood paneled walls, the wood stove in the corner, the stump beside it which obviously served as a chopping block, the small pile of unsplit logs in the corner. The stove pipe went up to a hole in the wall, about ten feet above the floor. Evidently Ernie had decided it was easier to heat the room with a wood stove than to hook on to the house furnace. If I'd been doing it, however, I'd have put some insulation between the stove pipe and the wooden wall.

Margaret's eyes followed mine. "It caught fire last winter," she said. "When we had the stove burning."

"Yes, I imagine it did," I said, hearing the words come out one by one, as though unwillingly.

"Luckily, I was in here. I got a pail of water." She fell silent once more.

I swallowed. "Mrs. Quivadas . . ."

"Margaret."

"Margaret, I don't want to intrude, but . . ."

"That's all right," she murmured. "Bruce said you'd have some questions."

I did have questions, but first I wanted to sort out the matter of the painting I'd taken from the church. I told her what I'd done. "I couldn't leave the painting there," I said. "It's too good, Margaret. If you don't want it, at least let me sell it for you. You and Felicia can use the money, I'm sure."

Her eyes were focused across the room, through the window, over the hills, noticing something farther away than I could see, communing with something at some great distance, not at all in any hurry about it.

"All right," she said at last. "I don't care. But you must ask Ernie's mother first. It's a picture of her. Of her, and of Ernie as a baby. I had photographs of her, and she'd given me some of Ernie when he was little. It wouldn't be right to sell her likeness without her permission."

She looked into my face, seeing my confusion. She cocked her head, figuring me out, trying to determine what it was that bothered me.

"You're wondering why I painted Ernie as the Christ Child?" she asked.

I nodded. Oh yes, I wondered that. Among other, more personal things.

"The Quivadas kept saying such awful things to Ernie about his mother. I think his mother is very nice. She's always been kind and generous to me, and to Felicia. So, when Ernie asked me to paint a Christ for his church, I painted it that way. A mother, a child. His own mother. Himself as a child. Christ in them." She was silent for a long moment. "The way goodness is in people. People aren't all evil. They're not all possessed by devils. Most of us are just the kind of people God might work in and care about. Do you understand?"

I nodded. I thought I did. "What did Ernie say?"

Her lips curved into a tiny, ironic smile. "He didn't recognize her. He said . . . well, he didn't think it was suitable. He wasn't going to leave it there. Afterwards I realized he'd probably never really looked at his mother. Sometimes Ernie . . . didn't see things. Sometimes people don't. They don't recognize what's inside other people."

She was right. Bruce and I had commented about Ernie never really seeing other people or their reactions. Why would he have seen his mother any differently? Or his wife?

"Do you want to ask me questions?" she reminded me gently.

Bela ceased his explorations of the room, came around behind us, crawled under the bench where we were sitting, and collapsed with a groan. Schnitz, who had been lying on my shoulder, decided to join him. I dropped Bela's leash but kept Schnitz's at hand, just in case, as I bent my attention to questions.

"About Sunday," I said. "Tell me everything that happened."

She gave me a long, serious look with sadness in it. "Everything that happened?" She laughed. "I couldn't possibly. Sometimes . . . sometimes more happens in a minute than you could ever tell anyone, don't you think?"

I nodded, lost in the depths of her eyes. "Tell me what you can." I gulped, getting my Adam's apple back in position.

"Well, let's see. We got up in the morning. I fixed breakfast for me, and for the Bobbisons. Ernie never ate anything before services. He was too nervous about his sermons."

"The Bobbisons?"

"Oh, they live with us."

"I didn't realize you had that much room," I said.

"I suppose there was room." She got up and beckoned me to join her. "Leave the animals here. They can't hurt anything."

I followed her through the door into an L-shaped room, the longer arm of the L with space enough for a small couch, two mismatched chairs, two cribs against the far wall, and a small, empty television table. The shorter arm held a cramped kitchen with a plastic-topped table and four chairs pushed tight against the wall, leaving barely space to move among the stove, refrigerator, and sink. Halfway down the long arm of the L, a door led into a narrow hallway, and Margaret guided me down it, two doors on either side. To my left was a tiny cluttered bedroom, eight by eight, with bunk beds. To my right was a five by eight bath, basin, toilet, shower. Then to the right and left two more bedrooms, each about eight by twelve, one with a queen bed, one with twin beds pushed tight against opposite walls. The room with the queen bed was neatly made up, the other was squalid with twisted and stained sheets, discarded clothing, aluminum cans, paper plates.

"I wish they'd clean up a little," she murmured as she turned to lead me back the way we had come. Her face was tranquil, betraying no anxiety about the mess. "I wish they'd tell me when they're going to be gone."

We moved back into the kitchen, where Margaret pulled out one of the chrome and plastic chairs for me. "I'll make some coffee and we'll take it back out into the . . . chapel. It gets very close in here."

I couldn't breathe either. It was all I could do to wait until she'd boiled water and poured it over two spoonsful of instant coffee. She didn't offer milk or sugar. Normally, I'd have refused the stuff, but Margaret offered it in the manner of one offering the quintessence of hospitality, not a cup of bad coffee but a symbolic gesture. Rather like a tea ceremony. I felt myself genuflecting when I took the cup.

We went back out into the chapel, resuming our former seats. "Tell me about the Bobbisons. Who are they," I asked her, sipping at the dreadful stuff.

"Some people Ernie invited to come live with us. A couple and their twelve-year-old daughter and two little boys."

"Where could you put them all?"

"Well, Mr. and Mrs. Bobbison are in the room I used to paint in. One bed was Felicia's and Ernie got the other bed from somewhere. Felicia had the room where the bunks are now. Ernie found the bunks and then told Felicia she'd have to share with Bobbi Kay, the little Bobbison girl. The two little boys have the cribs in the living room."

"How long have they been with you?"

"Oh, they've . . . shared our lives for almost two years. Well, not Felicia's. Felicia . . . departed. She says she felt crowded. I understand. . . ."

I stared at her in disbelief. "Who does the cooking?"

"Usually I do. Mrs. Bobbison has fainting spells when she stands up for too long."

I dropped my voice. "Where are they now?"

She gave me a vague, distracted look. "I don't know. They were here Sunday, all day. Sunday night, when I was fixing supper, they were here, I remember that. Then after it . . . after it happened, after I came home later that night, they were here then. And in the morning, Monday. But you know, I think they've been gone since Monday afternoon. Though it might have been Tuesday. I was . . . I wasn't paying attention." She looked down at her hands, a child caught in a naughtiness. She thought she should have paid attention. Or thought someone else expected it of her.

"Do you think they're coming back?"

"Oh, they've gone off before. To visit her parents. Twice. They were gone for two weeks each time. The first time they didn't tell me, but then when they got back, I'd moved all their things out. So, the next time, they told me they'd be back."

"But this time?"

"They didn't say a word. Isn't that odd? And they took the television. And some jewelry Bruce's mother had given me. It was supposed to be for Felicia." She gazed at me in wonderment, as though she'd seen something far past belief.

"Did the Bobbisons have a car?"

"They have an old van. It breaks down all the time, but when it doesn't run, they get their relatives or friends to take them places."

"Have you reported the theft of the TV and your jewelry to the police?"

"The television wasn't much. I never watch it. The jewelry . . . I remember Phyllis without it. The jewelry was the least important thing she gave me. Of course, now I don't have it to give to Felicia. That was the importance of it. Passing it on."

I digested that. "You have a place where you paint?"

"I couldn't do it here anymore," she explained. "Not with all the interruptions, the noise. . . . So this friend of mine has a garage he wasn't using, and he let me have it to paint in. And this wonderful thing happened." She smiled radiantly, silent glory pouring from her.

"Wonderful thing?" I prompted.

"Oh, yes. My friend owns a gallery in Santa Fe. And he's going to give me a show! A show, all my paintings. Isn't that wonderful?"

I agreed it was wonderful while she basked in the idea, like a rabbit basking in the sun, nose wrinkling, beaming pure contentment.

I took another tiny sip of the coffee, wishing there were somewhere in the room I could dispose of it. "Do you have any idea where the Bobbisons went?"

She shook her head. No. She didn't know. It was clear she didn't care, that they did not interest her at all.

I cared. It seemed to me that a Bobbison, a thieving Bobbison, as yet an unknown quantity, might turn out to be a suspect.

Two

SINCE I NO LONGER completely trusted Bruce's back-of-the-envelope maps, I asked Margaret how to get to the Quivada house. She pointed the direction, south down a little hill, and east around a bend. A little over a quarter of a mile.

"They won't welcome you," she said.

I smiled, telling her I'd assumed as much, shook her hand, and went away with my animals, leaving her staring after me but not at me, seeing things I didn't see. I had an eerie feeling that she spent most of her life seeing things other people didn't see. My hand, the hand she had shaken, rested on the steering wheel, and I found myself looking for some mark on it, some indelible evidence of her touch. The fingers gripped the wheel quite normally, all neatly intact, no flaming brands or instant tattoos. Still, they tingled. I told myself to stop being fanciful and get on with the job.

The Quivada dwelling was another fixer-upper, but no attempt had been made at fixing anything. It had originally been a trailer (not a mobile home) that someone had built walls around and added a room on to, but several holes in the walls allowed the original aluminum container to show through. The thin stucco was cracked in a dozen places and the two by four headers above doors and windows sagged like hammocks. The minuscule porch was just large enough for Mrs. Quivada's rocking chair, which swayed in unvarying rhythm, seemingly without volition, as though the motive power came from somewhere else. Incuriously, she watched me drive in, not changing position, expression, or tempo.

I parked in the shade of a dilapidated garage a short distance from the house, rolling down the windows partway to give the animals air. The lady of the house didn't look welcoming even of people, much less four-legged critters. Bela often whines to get out when the car stops, but today he merely stared at the rocking woman, making a troubled sound low in his throat. I strolled slowly toward the porch, stopping politely ten feet away and adopting a posture suggestive of hat in hand. At the porch's corner post a vine struggled up from the parched soil, the only green thing in sight, wrinkled little leaf hands begging water.

"Mrs. Quivada?" I asked.

"Who're you?" she demanded.

"A friend of Bruce's and Lindsay's. They've asked me to join them here, to see if we can throw some light on what happened."

"That's rich, that is," she crowed, her head level and still, gyroscopically poised, her eyes glaring past me while her body went on with its endless motion. To and fro, jiggle joggle, back and forth. "That's rich."

"What's that, Mrs. Quivada?"

"Well, they killed him, didn't they. Killed him dead. They did."

"Not Bruce and Lindsay. They weren't even here."

"Devil doesn't have to be here. Doesn't have to be nearby. He can stretch out his hand and a man dies, a thousand miles away. He can stretch out his hand and bring sickness, bring evil, like he did on Felicia, like he did on Margaret."

"What evil was that?"

"Went from her family into the houses of the wicked. Stopped cleaving unto her husband and took the path of evil. . . ."

"What path is that, Mrs. Quivada? Margaret didn't seem evil to me."

"Evil is as evil does, and she did it. Turned her body from him, turned her face from him, turned her hands from their duty, disobeyed him. Went on following the devil, making graven images. Oh, if thine eye offend thee, and thine hand, making graven images. . . ."

I was silent for a moment, surprised at this reference to Margaret's painting. The old woman mumbled and chewed at her cheeks, hardly seeming to know I was there, lost among her demons in her own little hell. When I took a step closer, I detected a smell both sour and charred, like some furious fermentation boiled over and burned. It could have been the smell of an old, unbathed body, but I sensed it as something else: the seethe of anger and the stench of the pit.

I balked, shocked at the idea. The morning seemed rife with fancies.

"Did Ernie object to her painting?" I asked.

"Got rid of the room she did it in. Filled it up with charitable works. Off she went, found someplace else. Some devil's place."

"I understand it's just a garage. Belongs to a friend."

"Man friend," she spat. "Pure married woman's got no business having man friends! That tells you right there, don't it? I say, don't it?"

She was glaring at me, eyes wide, the pupils shrunk to pinpoints, pale coronas lost in orbs of yellowed ivory, like the eyes of some ancient and faded idol.

I decided to push the matter a little farther. "The painting she did for the church was very nice, I thought. A lovely Christ Child."

"That woman!" she spat again. "Was a picture of that whore my son married. Didn't even grieve for her husband. Didn't even take time to have his baby and raise him up to remember his daddy. Went whoring after men. Got herself married again, pregnant again. . . . That whore!"

Ernie hadn't recognized his mother in the painting, but it was obvious Mrs. Quivada had.

I pretended shock. "What woman is that?"

"Her that bore our Ernie. She's the one should have died. She's the evil one. But the devil had to kill my Ernie. Had to. He was doin' God's work, so the devil had to kill him."

"Vangy. . . ." came a querulous voice from inside.

"Hush," she cried vehemently. "You hush. It's not lunchtime yet."

"Vangy. . . ."

"You want anything, you get it yourself!"

Silence.

"When did you see Ernie last?" I asked.

She rocked, rocked, angrily. "This mornin."

I looked up at her, catching a glance both spiteful and victorious.

"This mornin!" she insisted. "Early. He came to the side of my bed, askin' vengeance. He said I had to avenge him. Avenge him against that woman!"

"Which woman?" I whispered.

"That one," she said. "All of them like that."

I couldn't tell if she meant Margaret or Felicia or both, or maybe even Phyllis Norman.

"Vangy. . . ." came the cry again.

Her mouth worked.

I decided it was time to leave. One question more. "When was the last time you saw Ernie *alive?*"

She thought about this. "After services," she said. "He brought us home. Me and his daddy. Dropped us off, then took them Bobbisons on home with him, then come back for a spell."

"Margaret wasn't with you?"

"She got out down the hill. At that devil's place she has."

"At the garage where she paints," I said impatiently. Mrs. Quivada was having the same effect on me that Ernie had often had. His lexicon of good and evil had often led me into a mood of baffled fury.

"Decent woman would have gone on home, fixed a Sunday dinner for people depending on her. Decent woman would have gone on home. Not her. She was paintin', she said. She'd be home to fix supper later, she said."

She hawked and spit, missing me by very little. I got up, nodding what I hoped would pass for thanks.

"Them your animals?" she asked, jerking her chin in the direction of the car.

"Yes," I said. "Mine."

"You got to watch *them,*" she said. "Familiars. Satan can take control of 'em. They don't have souls, you know. Cats in particular. I wouldn't have a cat. Satan can take control and bring harm on you."

I went back to the car and spun the wheels on the road leading out, needing desperately to be gone. How had Margaret kept her sanity?

By not seeing, I told myself. By not hearing, not smelling, not being aware. By looking at other things, listening to other voices. By letting the Quivadas talk at the shell of her but never letting them reach her core.

On the way back, a different and more direct way than the one I had come, I passed a spacious adobe-walled complex set between the road and the canyon edge, with a garage facing the road. It had old-fashioned double doors, one of which stood open, and inside I saw Margaret, her back to me, a canvas beyond her, both lit from above. Her pose betokened absolute concentration. I didn't stop. I did, however, mark the place in my mind, slowing to read the name on the mailbox.

Xavier Fortunato, neatly spelled out in firm block letters on the side of the mailbox. Xavier Fortunato, number 54, Paseo de Santos.

Margaret painted at a house on the Street of Saints.

Bruce and Lindsay and I had agreed to meet back at Los Vientos. We sat outside in the portal, making a lunch of the Schlotsky sandwiches Lindsay had brought for our lunch: ham and cheese and lettuce and ripe olives. Bruce and Lindsay had Negro Modela beer. Beer with lunch always makes me sleepy, so I'd poured myself a glass of milk. Bela and Schnitz joined us to beg bits of meat and cheese. Bela was yearningly patient, as is his nature, but Schnitz's big tufty paw repeatedly snaked up from under my chair, claws extended, to snatch a bit of sandwich or spear a finger if it got in the way. Schnitz is a demon on cheese. A familiar, Mrs. Quivada would no doubt say. I told Bruce and Lindsay about Mrs. Quivada.

"She's gone round the bend," Lindsay remarked around a mouthful of sandwich.

"No, she's right where she's always been," Bruce contradicted. "She was always like that, Linny. Just not quite as vocal as she is now, that's all."

"What did you find out from Margaret?" Lindsay asked me.

I gave the gist of my conversation with Margaret, trying to

convey the atmosphere as much as the actual words. Perhaps I conveyed more than I intended, for Lindsay gave me a curious look as I reached the end of my tale.

"Though I meant to ask, I didn't find out where the Bobbisons came from," I confessed. "Margaret said Ernie invited them to stay. Mrs. Quivada said Ernie got rid of the room she painted in and filled it with charitable works. How do you interpret that?"

Bruce leaned back in his chair. "I can't see Ernie paying any attention to Margaret's painting. He probably didn't even see it. He simply invited the Bobbisons to live with them because he thought it was the religious thing to do."

"Ernie wanted to have more children, didn't he?" murmured Lindsay. "I heard some talk about adoption."

Bruce shrugged. He didn't remember.

"Are you saying Margaret can't have other children?" I asked. If Margaret had been only seventeen or so when she married, if she'd had Felicia right away, she was probably only thirty-four or -five, though she looked ten years younger. Certainly she was young enough to have another child if she wanted to.

Bruce said, "I don't remember anything being said about more children. I certainly don't remember any talk of adoption."

"Margaret might have told your mom," Lindsay said. "I'm certain someone mentioned it to me."

"Does it matter?" he asked me impatiently. "Do we care?"

"At this point, I don't know what matters," I admitted. "At this point we're just collecting data—what people did, how people felt. I'd like to know why Ernie took the Bobbisons into his house. I'd like to know if he wanted other children and Margaret refused or couldn't or whatever. Mrs. Quivada said something about Margaret not cleaving to her husband, not doing her wifely duty. To me, that implies some kind of strain between Margaret and Ernie, and I'd like to know about that."

"The Ernie I knew never paid much attention to anybody's feelings, his own or anyone else's," Lindsay commented. "Whenever he talked about himself, it was always in reference to what he called his 'personal relationship with God.' That preoccupied him to the exclusion of other people, except as subjects for conversion."

Bruce nodded his agreement. "Ernie wasn't long on sensitivity, Jason. You remember that."

Schnitz sneaked a paw up between my knees and snatched the last bit of sandwich from my hand, put it firmly under one foot to keep Bela from taking it, and ate it in small, satisfied bites, purring between swallows. I poured the last of my milk into the empty plate and set it down beside him. Bela looked at it longingly, so when Schnitz had had some, I moved the plate over for Bela to finish.

The Bobbisons remained a nagging enigma. "I'd like to find the Bobbisons," I remarked. "Margaret doesn't know whether they're coming back or not."

Bruce said, "It's unlikely they'll come back if they stole Margaret's jewelry. Damn it, Mom gave her that! Pearls, weren't they, Lindsay. And a brooch and a couple of rings."

Lindsay nodded. "Mom gave some of her jewelry to Margaret and some to me, for our daughters to have when they got married. Couldn't we have these Bobbisons arrested?"

"Margaret didn't seem terribly interested in pursuing the matter." I thought it unlikely Margaret would charge anyone with anything.

"Was it Ernie's death that made them decide to leave just now?" Lindsay asked.

That was a matter we could pursue. "It surprised me a little that Margaret isn't even sure when they left. She thinks they left on Monday. Is she normally that vague?"

They shared a doubtful glance. "It must be when she's painting," Lindsay said at last. "I noticed it for the first time during this visit. When she's painting, she goes off into some other world. Other times we've met her, she's been quite . . . normal. Quite nice. I should think she'd be more concerned with Ernie's death just now."

I said, "I get the impression Ernie and she were emotionally quite distant from one another. His moving other people into their house without even asking her would indicate a considerable chasm between them. And she doesn't have time to grieve.

She's totally concentrated on the upcoming show of her paintings at one of the Santa Fe galleries."

Astonishment. I listened while they babbled at each other, that kind of puzzled familial babble, part surprise, part pleasure plus an inevitable undertone of affront because they hadn't known, hadn't been told. No matter what I'd said, neither of them realized just how good Margaret's painting was.

"How wonderful for her," breathed Lindsay, when she'd exhausted her surprise. "Bruce and I were talking about her just this morning, how we could help her. I had no idea. . . ."

"Do you think she can earn a living with it?" Bruce asked. Bruce the ever-practical.

"Lots of painters earn a living at it who are far less talented than she is," I said. Unfortunately, it was true. Margaret's talent was unquestionable. Her marketing skills might be something else again. In that regard, art is like publishing is like architecture is like decor is like theater and films. The junk is often more successful than the good stuff because it panders to the lowest common denominator. The motivating question is not, "What's beautiful, true, or lasting?" but "What sells?" In most fields, it's the sentimental slosh and the quick thrill that sells.

Now was no time to talk about that, however. "Did you two find anything out from the police?"

"They're sticking with their earlier estimate as to the time of death," Bruce remarked. "They still say an edged weapon of some kind. He was killed where Margaret found him, but the pueblo police believe he was killed over his religion."

"What reason do they give for believing that?"

"Their reasoning seems to be historic." Lindsay made a rueful face at Bruce, who nodded at her, telling her to go on.

She sat back and expounded. "Essentially, without all the flourishes, what they told us went like this: The Spanish came here in the sixteen hundreds, forcibly converting the pueblos to Catholicism. Then the Americans took over and tried to wipe out the Indian religions and languages that had survived the Spanish. Then, when the government quit persecuting them, various religious sects descended on them, the Mormons and the Adventists and this one and that one. The man who spoke to us was very bitter about this. He said that during all this missionizing, brother was turned against brother, kinfolk against kinfolk. Whole pueblos were divided or even lost over religious matters. Now they have had enough. They will not stand for disrespect, and no holier-than-thou Anglo has the right to cast dirt on their religion! End of lecture."

"Ernie disrespected their religion?"

"We assume that's what they were talking about. They never mentioned him by name," said Bruce.

Lindsay shook her head. "They were trying to be nice about it, Bruce. They were keeping in mind that Ernie was your brother."

I thought about it for a while. "If religion was the motive, and if the killer is one of the pueblo people, it's unlikely we're going to find out anything about it. We have no entrée at all into the pueblo, and we're unlikely to get one."

"What about the candles on the floor of the church?" asked Lindsay. "That didn't look like traditional Indian religion."

"I think it does in a way," I said, trying to remember things I'd read or been told by Mike. "You've just said it yourself. The Spanish added an element of Catholicism to the Indian beliefs, so all those candles could be reflective of both. The emotion that motivated the candles probably wouldn't have motivated murder, however!" I got up and stretched. "Don't push it, Lindsay. It's too early for us to try making a pattern out of things. At this stage we'd just be forcing things to fit. We need a lot more information."

"What's our schedule this afternoon?" Bruce asked.

"I thought we might go see Felicia," I said. "She can probably tell us a good deal about the Bobbisons."

While we had been eating, the sky had clouded over and a cool breeze had come up, which meant we could take the animals with us. I hate seeing animals left locked in cars on sunny days. The temperature inside can get up over a hundred thirty or forty, animals can die more quickly than you'd think possible. In fact, rescuing dogs (and in one case, a baby) in parking lots had helped make me an expert in the wire coat hangar school of breaking and entering. It has become dangerous lately, with all the car alarms. I've considered other tactics, like throwing bricks through side windows after spray-painting I AM A CRUEL BASTARD, on the windshield. All in all, it's easier just to call the local humane society. They have license to break and enter when needed.

The group home where Felicia lived was down a curving side street in Santa Fe, one lined, so Lindsay pointed out, with huge old lilac bushes and vasty clumps of hollyhocks. I took her word for it. Since neither was in bloom, the leaves were anonymous humps of greenery so far as I was concerned. We found the home: part cinder block, part pseudo-adobe, part wood frame, stretching back along an alleyway from a tiny low-walled courtyard on the street. When we drove down the alley, looking for a place to park, we found it ended in an abrupt drop at the edge of yet another of the ubiquitous arroyos.

Arroyo or no, the alley seemed a safe enough place to leave the car, so we backed almost to the street and parked tight against the house wall beneath a line of high windows. I rolled the car windows down two inches, let Schnitz out of his crate, locked the car, and told them both to have a nice nap.

We went through the courtyard to the front door, which was answered by a Hispanic youth, the picture of an idealized matador—broad shoulders and chest, whip-slender waist and hips, snapping dark eyes, a dangerous grin, and a splint on the third finger of his right hand. He introduced himself as Hector and went to find Felicia for us.

She came running down the brick-floored corridor, and while she was hugging Bruce and Lindsay, I took note of the fact that she was unmistakably her mother's daughter. She had her mother's build, her mother's face, her mother's gorgeous eyes. For all the evidence of Ernie's parentage, she might have been born by parthenogenesis. She lacked her mother's beauty, though not by much, and I suspected it would come upon her in her twenties, surprising everyone else and astonishing her. She wore jeans and a loose T-shirt with a message so faded I couldn't read it.

"Felicia," I acknowledged Bruce's introduction, giving her hand a firm shake. "It's nice to meet you."

"Mr. Lynx," she greeted me in her mother's voice. "Come on in the living room. Nobody uses it much this time of day."

"Where are the other residents?" Lindsay asked curiously as we went into a comfortably shabby room full of saggy furniture and thriving pot plants.

Felicia gestured us toward a grouping of couch and chairs, each a different color and style. I lowered myself gingerly and found the chair to be surprisingly comfortable. Broken in, one might say.

"Most of the kids have jobs," Felicia said. "I do. I'm a stocker at the supermarket, but it's only part-time. And some of us are going to summer school, to catch up, you know."

"I'm sure you don't need to catch up," Bruce said fondly as he seated himself beside Lindsay. "Your mother says you're doing great."

"Well, I am," she admitted. "Pretty good. Better than when I was home. But I'd really like to go back home if those people are gone for good this time."

"That's one reason we came," Bruce admitted. "We want to know about the Bobbisons. What can you tell us?"

She sat down with a thump, then rooted around in the pocket of her jeans for a half stick of gum, which she unwrapped, folded once, and popped in her mouth. Masticatory memory. When the jaw moves, the brain functions. I know people who have smoker's memory, and drinker's memory. I myself have a coffee memory. It works best when fed large quantities of freshly roasted and ground caffeine. Early in the morning, that's the only way it works at all.

"The Bobbisons?" I prompted her when she'd chewed silently for a minute or two.

"Dwight and Vera and Bobbi Kay and the two brats," she said unemphatically. "The whole fam-damly. I honestly don't know much about them. Nobody warned me they were coming, and I didn't stick around long after they got there."

"Suddenly?" I asked. "They came suddenly."

"I came home from school one day and there they were." She waved her hand like a magician, materializing them out of nothing. "Daddy and Dwight were moving my bed and another bed into Mom's painting room. Vera was sitting in front of the TV. I don't think she ever moved after that, except to go to the toilet. I know she ate there. I think she slept there, too."

"Didn't she take care of her two little boys?"

"Mom did that, mostly. When she was home. And the first time Mom left the house, Vera told me to do it. I told her they weren't my kids, they weren't my family. She made a stink about how I wasn't polite; Daddy got all over me. That's when I started thinking about leaving. A few weeks later, I did."

"Why should you take care of her kids? Why not Bobbi Kay?" Bruce asked.

"Bobbi Kay was too busy."

"Doing what?" Lindsay asked.

"Her hair." Felicia wrinkled her nose and made a gesture, throwing something away. "That took her about two or three hours every day. Longer than her homework did. And she did her fingernails. That took an hour or so every day. Daddy put bunk beds in my room. I got the top one, because Bobbi Kay was company. I'd clean up the room, and she'd trash it. I'd clean it, and she'd trash it. I yelled at her, and her mom yelled at me. Even if Vera hadn't wanted me to take care of the little boys, I'd have moved out. There wasn't any room for me there anymore. There wasn't a single place in that house I could go and shut the door and be by myself to do homework or anything!"

"You didn't just go out on the streets?" Bruce asked, brow furrowed.

Felicia made a face at him. "Uncle Bruce, I've got more sense than that, and if I hadn't, Mom would have. I already knew about this place. I'd seen about it on TV. I came here. They called Mom. She came down and told them my situation was . . . unten. . . ." She fumbled for the word.

"Untenable," I offered.

"Right." She chewed reflectively for a moment. "Mom knew what it was like. It was untenable for her, too. But when she's painting, nothing else is even real."

"You don't seem angry," I said softly. "At your father."

She shrugged, her face creasing. "Oh, I was."

"But not now?"

"What's the point? He's dead."

"You're not grieving, either."

Stung, she cried, "That's what Great-Grandma said. That I'm not grieving. But I said, hey, a father is somebody puts his own family first, right? But he put the Bobbisons first, so let them grieve." She turned a furious face on me, like a mask. She couldn't hold it. It collapsed to let the pain and tears come leaking through.

Lindsay put her arms around the girl and they rocked together. "It's okay, Licia. Your father did love you. He was just a little strange, you know. Kind of mixed up."

The girl hiccuped with laughter, wiping at her wet face. "Oh shit, that's the truth, Aunt Lindsay. He was really weird. . . ." Her voice ran out into a tiny sob, like the tail end of a long sorrow.

"We'd like to find the Bobbisons," I said when she'd calmed down and let go of Lindsay. "Do you know anything about them that might help us locate them? Anything at all?"

She shook her head. "They used to live in Florida, or at least that's what Bobbi Kay said."

"What did they live on?"

"They got welfare sometimes. Disability something. I asked Dwight once why he didn't get a job, and he said they didn't need much, so as long as they had shelter, they could get by without working. He said the 'guvvamint' owed him housing. The 'guvvamint' owed him that, and health care, and food, so all he needed money for was beer and video rentals for him and Vera, chewing tobacco for him, and hair stuff for Bobbi Kay. And burgers and fries and pizza."

I gave Bruce a look, and he turned to stare out the window, avoiding the issue.

"You're telling me they lived at your house for free?" I asked.

"That's right. Daddy gave them free room and board, and Mom cooked for them, and cleaned up after them, and everything. For most of two years. Until Saturday, that is."

"Until Saturday. What happened Saturday?"

"That's when Mom found out for certain about the show. Xavier, the man who owns the gallery, had been hinting at it for weeks, but on Saturday he said she was ready. She came down here to tell me. We went out for ice cream, to celebrate! I was so proud of her!"

"What did that have to do with the Bobbisons?" Lindsay asked.

"Well, she had to get at least thirty paintings ready, and she only had about twelve or fifteen. So she had to spend all her time painting. She told me she couldn't get enough paintings ready if she went on cleaning up after them and cooking for them. Right?"

We all nodded like Chinese dolls, agreeing.

"Saturday night she told them the same thing. That she couldn't do it anymore. That they'd have to cook for themselves and do their own laundry and stuff."

"Did that apply to your father, too?"

"Oh, no, she was going to go on doing for him. His laundry and meals and stuff. But see, Vera and Dwight had to have separate meals cooked. Separate shopping and everything. They couldn't eat what Dad ate. Because of their sensitive stomachs. They had to have special things fixed."

"Like?" asked Bruce.

She looked at the ceiling. "Oh, like pork chops with cream gravy and grits and pot roast with sour cream and stuff like that. Daddy mostly ate vegetables. You remember, Uncle Bruce. Daddy was mostly a vegetarian. Before the Bobbisons came, Mom and I usually had a little something in the kitchen before dinner. An egg, maybe, or a hamburger. And whenever Mom sold a painting, we'd splurge on steaks when Daddy was gone."

I'd forgotten that Ernie had been mostly a vegetarian, sometimes eating eggs or chicken or fish, but more often contenting himself with a salad or a dish of rice. "Giving in to your body," was what he called eating meat. It was not giving in to his body, however, to eat sugary doughnuts, candy, ice cream, or pastries in quantity. Such things could be eaten freely, "For energy, to do the Lord's work." Ernie had been dead set against giving in to any appetite except as it expedited the Lord's work. News of his marriage had come as a real surprise to me. Wasn't sex giving in to his body? Unless he saw marriage less as gaining a bedmate than as getting a housekeeper, laundress, and cook.

"What did the Bobbisons look like?" I demanded. My mental picture of these people kept wobbling around.

"Vera weighs about three hundred pounds," said Felicia. "Dwight weighs less than me. Bobbi Kay is skinny, and she has pimples. I know that isn't her fault, I'm just telling you. Great grandma says its because she plays with herself, but Mom says that doesn't cause it."

Stifled merriment from Bruce.

"Well, it doesn't!" Felicia said.

"I know," said Bruce. "I just didn't know anyone worried about masturbation these days. I thought people only worried about AIDS."

"Believe me, Great-Grandma worries about anything to do with sex," Felicia said. "Satan uses it to snare you, according to her. Nice women don't have any feelings at all down there. She says when she was a girl, there was a doctor in their town who used to cut girls clits off if they masturbated."

"Oh, Lord," said Lindsay. "Return to the Dark Ages."

None of the others seemed at all disconcerted by this conversation, though I found myself more than a little embarrassed. Bruce and Lindsay have teenagers of their own, of course, and I suppose sex and pregnancy and AIDS are now so freely discussed on TV and so openly talked about in school that young people aren't at all abashed by what I think of as intimate details. We boys in the Home, where I grew up, talked about sex the way boys do, using the words we all used, at first out of bravado and then out of habit. When I started living with Jacob, he put an end to what he firmly identified as dirty talk. He wouldn't tolerate any kind of sexual or racial epithet. On the few occasions when he heard me use questionable language, he sat me down and talked at length about dignity. The greatest sin one could commit, according to Jacob, was to destroy dignity because it was a kind of rape. "You are not a rapist," he said over and over again. "Do not use rapist's words."

Jacob had been ahead of his time.

"You were telling me what the Bobbison family looks like," I reminded Felicia, hoping to get away from uncomfortable subjects like sex and back to comfortable ones like murder.

She scrunched up her eyes in concentration, half closing them, visualizing the Bobbisons. "He's bald. She has sort of sh—ah, dirt-colored hair, and it's always up in pink curlers. I don't think she ever takes them out. And she wears a kind of tent all the time, with flowers on it, and he wears black trousers and a white shirt with the collar torn off and glasses. And bedroom slippers and no tie. And Bobbi Kay has hair like her mom's, only she dyes it blond, real blond. Silver. And she has one ear pierced three times and the other one pierced four times, and she wears these studs up the sides. Red and green and gold. And the two little boys aren't potty-trained yet. Their names are Carleton and Overby."

"How old are the little boys?" I asked, appalled at the picture she painted.

"Vera was pregnant with Overby when they came, and she had him practically right away, so he's about two. Mom thought she'd lose some weight when she had the baby, but she just got fatter. Carleton's about three. And Dwight is not Bobbi Kay's father, according to Bobbi Kay. And that's all I know about them, except that Bobbi Kay was flunking school when I left and probably still is. All she wanted to talk about was boys and doing it."

I didn't ask doing what. It had to be sex or drugs, and either was depressingly inappropriate for a twelve-year-old girl. "We really wanted to find them, but they probably didn't tell anyone where they were going. . . ."

"Unless they went back to the homeless shelter where Daddy found them," offered Felicia. "The nice one on Calle de las Tortugas. Bobbi Kay used to say it was nicer than our house, and I'd say, why didn't they go back?"

"Are you going home?" Lindsay asked the girl. "I'm sure your mother could use some familial support."

"If she's moved them out, sure. I mean, they've gone away before and come back. But if she's really moved them out, I'd go back home just like that! I told her. She knows. I mean, I like it here okay. I like the kids and the Romeros are great, and Hector's a hunk, but I'd rather be home if it is home and not some trashed-up Bobbison pen."

Lindsay gave her a final hug, the perfect model of a solicitous aunt. She seemed to have a special feeling for Felicia.

We found the car as we'd left it, both animals curled up on the back seat. Bruce eased Bela over and took Schnitz on his lap. I crawled across the front seat to the driver's side, and Lindsay came in behind me. We just sat for a few minutes, all of us thinking one thing or another.

"Calle de los Tortugas?" I asked.

"We can try," said Bruce in a doubtful voice.

Lindsay got the city map out of the glove compartment and looked up Turtle Street. Once I had the route in mind, we set out southwest on Cerrillos Road, trying to keep an open mind rather than feeling cynical and disapproving of so-called "shelters" for the homeless.

Back in Denver, eight or ten so-called shelters had been built over the past decade, most of them by religious groups, all in the same section of town. The area is conveniently close to bars and pawnshops, so the alcoholic homeless have easy access to liquor, and those minded to theft have a convenient market for the loot. Since they're all crammed into one area, homeless women and homeless mentally ill are conveniently set up, unprotected, for muggers and rapists.

They're unprotected because the so-called shelters are closed except at night, which means all the homeless are thrust onto the streets during the day, where they're forced to use the alleys as toilets and sleep off their substance abuse in doorways and fight off their attackers under bridges. Meanwhile, except for the owners of the bars and liquor stores, longtime residents of the area (including some good friends of mine) are in despair over the change in their neighborhood. Many of them had sunk everything they had into rebuilding housing and businesses. Their distress has not moved city hall, however, which seems determined to create a ghetto where none had existed before.

The shelter on Tortuga Street, which had been built to house only families, was a different matter. It was set away from bars and liquor stores on a considerable tract of land with a fenced playground for children and a dining hall where, so said the sign, three meals a day were served. The same sign identified an office at the front of the complex as a hiring hall.

Seeing people moving around inside, Bruce went in to ask about the Bobbisons. He returned shaking his head.

"No room at the inn," he said. "They showed up here last Monday night, but the place was full. Evidently everyone knows them; the guy shook his head when I asked about them. This place specializes in getting jobs for people and getting them rehabilitated. Dwight, so says the guy in there, isn't interested in being rehabilitated, so they're reluctant to let the Bobbisons in. The man in there referred them to one of the other shelters, but he said he was willing to bet they'll show up here within the next few days because almost all the other shelters have a three- to five-day limit."

I turned to Lindsay. "Any suggestions?"

"I'm depressed by this whole business," she said. "I'm tired of thinking about it! Let's, for God's sake, do something else this evening. It's already after four."

"I'm willing," said Bruce, getting in beside me once more. "Let's go change, and I'll buy us all dinner."

It sounded like a good program to me. When we got back to the ranch, I left Bruce and Lindsay to their showering while I took Bela and Schnitz for a run, figuring by the time I got back, the bathroom would be available. It was steamy but empty on my return. I showered, wrapped myself in a terry robe, and went into the living room to phone Grace.

No answer at her house. I try not to call her at the cop shop unless it's an emergency. I tried Jason Lynx Interiors and got Mark.

"What're you doing there," I asked him. "It's past closing time."

"Getting out a few bills," he said. "How's the investigation going?"

I told him how it was going. When I'd finished, there was silence at the other end.

"Hello?" I said.

"You're very taken with this Margaret person, aren't you?" he said.

My mouth dropped open. That wasn't the way I'd have put it. "Well, it's a little like discovering Marc Chagall lives next door," I mumbled. "Ernie's wife should have been a dowdy little woman who crochets afghans or does flower arranging."

"Mere appreciation for art, is it?"

"So far as I know, yes," I snapped.

"Be careful," he said in a cheery voice. "That's what you'd tell me."

It is what I'd tell him, under certain circumstances, none of which fit the current situation.

"Myron called today," he said, changing the subject. "He's found a Queen Anne drop-leaf breakfast table he thinks we might want."

"How much might we want it?"

"He says he can get it for ten, and it's worth twenty-five. He says it's perfect, all original wood, built maybe 1760. Mahogany and pine. Iron hinges."

"Cabriole legs?"

"Cabriole legs with claw and ball feet."

"You asked him for pictures."

"Right. I thought of it for your farmhouse job, but it's a little pricey."

"It's way too pricey for the Bonifaces," I grumbled. Celia and Bill Boniface were the very pleasant owners of an oldish farm house outside Littleton, which they'd been remodeling for some months. "What we need for them are some nice Colonial Revival pieces, in good shape, for not too much money. They aren't collectors or antique lovers, they just want their place to look nice."

"Don't we all?"

"I saw someone today who didn't." I told him about the ramshackle Quivada house, and about Mrs. Quivada's preoccupation with the devil."

He said it again. "Be careful, Jason."

"I don't think I'm in mortal danger," I said snappishly.

"Probably neither did your old acquaintance, Ernie," he replied. "There's something about this whole business that makes my hackles rise. Whenever religion and passion mix it up, watch out."

"Passion?" I asked, dumbfounded.

"You should have listened to yourself describing the painting at the church, Jason. And the woman who painted it. If you could feel it, so could someone else."

I snarled something by way of goodbye, only to have him stop me.

"Hold on a minute. Remember that guy you did the Southwestern decor office for a couple of years back? He wants to upgrade."

"Upgrade?"

Mark chuckled. "Evidently someone told him the furniture he had was not authentic."

"I told him that at the time! It was within his budget."

"Well sure, Jason, he knew it. But he didn't expect his friends to know it. So, he wants to upgrade. I told him you were in Santa Fe. He wants, I'm quoting, 'Navajo rugs, some of those expensive prehistoric pots, and real furniture.' "

"Did you tell him what all that would cost?"

"I did. I'm sending you down a memo with his signature on it. Just something to keep you busy when you need a break from detecting."

I gave him the number of the phone in the guest house, asking him to pass it on to Grace. Then I sat on the couch and stared at the wall, thinking about Navajo rugs and "prehistoric pots." They weren't exactly floating around loose. Ten thousand maybe. Twenty. He didn't really want something pre-Columbian. He wanted something authentic, gorgeous. San Ildefonso or Santa Clara pottery maybe.

My mind slipped sideways, away from pots. Mark had used the word "passion," and now that he'd mentioned it, I could agree there was passion in the Madonna painting. Margaret's passion. Perhaps that's the emotional undercurrent I'd been subconsciously aware of all day, her passion for her painting. Her passion, *probably* for her painting. She might feel passion for something, someone else? What about Xavier Fortunato?

I was still sitting there brooding when Bruce emerged from

the bedroom looking freshly pressed and brushed in crisp trousers and a white guayabera, ready for a night on the town. Lindsay was right behind him, in a flouncy dress, woven leather sandals, silver and turquoise jewelry—very Santa Fe. There is a Santa Fe look, but Mike tells me almost no one local dresses that way. Tourists do, the ones from California and the East, particularly. Texans dress like Texans, wherever they go.

I got dressed while Bruce put the animals in the run and Lindsay called Casa Sena to see if they had room for us. We could be seated around eight, which was good enough. We could while away the interim in the cantina.

It was a twenty-minute drive back to town and a ten-minute search before we found a parking place on Marcy Street. We strolled south to Palace, then turned west, toward the Plaza. I remember the Plaza of twenty-five years ago, when it was a multicultural marketplace, interesting in its diversity. Now the rents are so high that only the ostentatiously upscale can afford them and there has even been discussion of eliminating, in a mercantile sense, the Indians who sell jewelry and crafts in front of the Palace of the Governors. The family that plays Andean flute music in the Plaza was recently threatened with suppression. Heaven forfend that anyone should just come to the Plaza to stroll, or dicker with an Indian artist or enjoy the ambience. Any time not spent shopping in the stores is wasted, according to the merchants. Soon the Plaza will be just another Aspen, all its historic interest supplanted by price tags.

We went down one of the little alleys that leads through a streetfront building and into a spacious central courtyard shaded by large trees and surrounded by a scattering of little shops. Casa Sena opens off the corner of this courtyard, with the cantina next door. We left our names at the restaurant and went over to the cantina to pass the time. Bruce and Lindsay ordered their usual gins and tonic and I had a large, touristy Margarita. I like them touristy: lemonade barely flavored with tequila. Not a macho drinker's choice, I reflected, watching a tourist showing off with straight tequila, salt, and lime at an adjacent table. He was being macho as all hell, repeatedly, until something happened to his insides and he rose bleary-eyed and left in staggering haste.

The cantina waiters sang, as is their wont, not badly, considering. I wondered what the advertisement said. "Waiters wanted, must sing," or "Singers wanted, must wait tables." And did they get paid extra for being ambi-able? Though the restaurant was full when we arrived, the diners thinned out fairly rapidly, and it wasn't long until we were summoned. I had chicken in a piñon nut coating with a hot sweet sauce, thinking of Grace betimes. She'd have eaten two dinners plus all that was going to be left of mine. Lindsay noted my bemused expression.

"What?" she asked alertly.

"Just wishing Grace were here," I murmured.

"Grace?" eyebrows raised, head cocked.

"His significant other," mumbled Bruce, around a mouthful of enchilada. "She's a police-person."

"You're kidding? You, Jason? Enamored of a police-person? I had you down as . . ." Her voice trailed away. Perhaps she'd been going to say something about my wife, Agatha. She had met Agatha long ago. At our wedding, as a matter of fact.

"Grace is very sexy," said Bruce. "Blond. Tiny. Lots of energy."

"She couldn't get away just now," I said, forestalling Lindsay's question.

"Are there plans?" she asked archly.

I gave in to the inevitable. If I didn't tell her, she'd keep digging until she found out. "I have asked Grace to marry me. I have asked Grace more than once to marry me. Grace is somewhat younger than I, however, and on occasion she finds me stodgy."

"I don't find you at all stodgy," Lindsay said in a surprised voice, slightly pink around the cheekbones. "I never have."

Her husband snorted, giving her a look of fond surprise. I had the feeling the two of them had discussed me, probably recently.

"Thank you," I said solemnly. The interchange had elements of farce. How nice that my best friend's wife could assure me I wasn't stodgy. She sounded certain about it, which restored my battered self-esteem, if only temporarily.

"I, on the other hand, think he is stodgy," said Bruce, ruining the whole effect. "Even when we were in college together, he was always quoting chapter and verse. Refusing to get kicked out of school through indulgence in boyish pranks. . . ."

"I simply felt stopping up the plumbing in one of the women's residence halls was neither mature nor amusing," I objected.

"It was pretty expensive," he admitted.

"I never heard about this," said Lindsay.

"Now see what you've done!" he growled at me.

He spent the rest of the meal trying to make the escapade sound anything but what it had been, juvenile and pointless as well as costly. Bruce and his cohorts had been caught red-handed and required to pay the damages.

"What are we going to do tomorrow?" Lindsay asked, when she'd tired of chivvying him.

"I'm going to talk to a man named Xavier Fortunato," I said without thought. Evidently I'd decided this without realizing it. "He's the man who owns the garage where Margaret is working. He's the 'man-friend' Grandma Quivada says Margaret shouldn't have, and the gallery owner who's giving her a show."

"What do you want us to do?"

"See if you can find the Bobbisons. Ask around at the other shelters. We'll meet back at the ranch, then we'll all go to the shopping center near Ernie's church and ask the people there for any information about Ernie or the church."

"Who do you mean? What people there?" Lindsay asked.

"I mean the store managers or clerks. There's a grocery, and a hardware store, and some other shops and offices. From what I've picked up today, I'm guessing most of them will be Hispanic. Native Americans have no mercantile tradition; Hispanics and Anglos do. Of the two, however, the Hispanics have been closer to the pueblo people over time, so I'm betting when the pueblo rented its shopping center spaces, they rented mostly to Hispanics."

This agenda satisfied both Lindsay and Bruce. It gave them something to plan on for the next day, something to tell Bruce's mother they were doing. I had the feeling if it weren't for Phyllis Norman, both Bruce and Lindsay would have gone on home when they heard the news about Margaret's show. In fact, it might be better if they did. I could offer to stay on. Maybe Grace could join me for a few days.

The thought hung there, unresolved. Maybe. Perhaps. Perhaps not. For some reason, I leaned toward not. Let it go until morning.

At nine o'clock Saturday morning, after a sumptuous and too lavish breakfast cooked up by Lindsay, we went our separate ways. I drove directly to the garage I'd spotted the day before, on the theory that though Xavier Fortunato might be absent during the week, he would probably be at home on a weekend. The garage door was closed and locked, as was the gate in the compound wall behind it, its small grilled window also closed. Beside it hung a bell rope with a fancy wrought-iron handle, and when I tugged it, a silvery clang sounded somewhere inside. Eventually came the shuffle of footsteps, the grilled window in the gate slid open, and a broad female face stared out at me, expressionlessly.

"¿Que?"

"Señor Fortunato?"

A flood of Spanish.

"I wish to speak to him," I said. "Is he at home?"

"I tell'm, okay?" said the face, sliding the window shut once more. Shuffling sounds receded to be replaced by silence. No wind today. No rustle in the cottonwood boughs. No bird song or chicken cackle. Everything very quiet. After a time I became conscious of a sound I had not noticed before: the almost subliminal splash of water. Somewhere a fountain. In that quiet, that warmth, the sound was magical, evocative of Eden.

Footsteps again. The grill slid open. This time I was looking at a white mustache and goatee, white hair combed straight back, dark eyes under unwrinkled lids. An old man, but handsomely aged; not at all withered.

"Señor Fortunato?"

"Xavier Fortunato, yes."

"My name is Jason Lynx. I'm a friend of the Quivada family, of Ernie's brother and mother, of Margaret too. We're trying to find out what happened to her husband. I wondered if you'd mind talking with me for a few moments?"

A long, weighing look. The grill slid shut, the larger gate swung open, sagging and creaking slightly as it did so. An old gate. An old house. An old, though not diminished, tenant. He bowed me in.

We stood on a flagstone walk that circled a courtyard surrounded by flower beds, at one end a tiered fountain burbling and dripping as the water flowed down into a reflecting pool. Beside the pool sat a bulky form, shapeless, hulking, a man of forty or so, face without expression, staring into the water, where gold and silver fish glittered momentarily beneath wide lily pads. He did not look up.

The elderly man gestured with his cane and led me, limping slightly, toward a grouping of chairs in the shade of a portal. The adobe walls of the house reached for us like arms, drawing us in. He sat, gesturing toward another chair. I sat as well.

"Your home is very beautiful," I said.

"It is very old," he replied.

"I can see that." The weathering on the beams over the windows spoke of age, as did the splintery ends of the protruding vigas. The walls had settled a little and now seemed to lean on their elbows, listening to what we had to say.

"You are here because I have lent Margaret a place to do her painting," he said.

I nodded. "Partly. Mostly it's because there are things I can't figure out. So far as I can tell, she has a remarkable talent, but Ernie's grandparents, and Ernie himself seemingly, objected to her painting." I gestured, indicating bewilderment. "In my book, they're all peculiar, but still, I'd like to understand what they're objecting to."

He nodded. "Peculiar indeed." He stared angrily at his fountain, soothing himself with the sound of the water while his forehead smoothed, his mouth lost its irritated line. "A few days ago, they came here." He sighed. "They stood outside in the road and accused me of being a *diavolo,* a devil!" After a long pause his lips turned up slightly at the edges. "At my age. I should be flattered."

His voice was quiet. He spoke with only a hint of accent and in formal rhythms.

"How did it come about?" I asked him. "Your knowing Margaret?"

"She has not said?"

"It didn't come up. I only met her yesterday."

"I do not understand. You said you were a friend."

"An old friend of Ernie's mother and his half brother, Bruce. Bruce Norman and I knew one another in school, years ago. I knew Ernie then, too. I will act as Margaret's friend, for their sake, but it was Bruce who asked me to come here, to help determine what happened to Ernie."

His brows were still raised in polite interrogation.

"It's Bruce's mother, Ernie's mother," I confessed. "I know her. She was kind to me when I was a boy. She's elderly, and not well. Ernie's death weighs upon her." I heard in my voice an echo of the man beside me, formal and quiet—a mockingbird, mimicking my surroundings.

"Ah." He turned his cane in the dirt, making a series of small circles, evenly spaced, a design. "I understand. Who cannot understand a mother's grief."

He leaned back, folding his hands on top of his cane. Across the courtyard, the heavy man got up from beside the pool and ambled away through a heavy plank door that closed behind him with a solid thud.

"I have a gallery," Fortunato said. "It is called Millagros, a sort of pun, a thousand miracles. Fine small paintings. Small sculptures. Some gold jewelry, some precious stones. My name is well known in the area. I have been here for a long time. She came here one day, Margaret, bringing with her three paintings. She held them up to the *mirilla,* the peephole. I saw. I opened the gate. She came in to ask me, was she any good." He shook his head, that almost secretive smile showing at the corners of his mouth. "She asked me this in a tone of great innocence, like a child who asks, 'Have I been good.'"

"You told her she is very good," I said. "You told her she is a little miracle herself."

My words surprised both of us.

"Yes," he admitted. "I said that. How did you know?"

"I saw one of her paintings. A Madonna and child."

"The one she painted for him, the husband."

"Yes."

"I saw it when she painted it. As you say, a miracle. I was not the only one who thought so. I have a couple, Ricardo and Lourdes Lalumia. They, too, saw the painting. That was their son, by the pool. He is . . ." He moved his hand at the side of his head. "As you saw him, quiet, sometimes, but more often wild and irrational. Often he is in hospital. Schizophrenic, they say. When Margaret took the painting away from here, Lourdes asked her where it would be. Lourdes told me they were going there, where the painting was hung, to light candles, to pray. And then, this very morning, Lourdes said to me her son is quieter, as though God had touched him. Perhaps it is only their perception, though you saw him for yourself. Quiet, watching the fish, not shouting or threatening. Perhaps it is only superstition. And yet . . . I understand why they went there."

One little mystery solved. "I have the painting," I said. "We hesitated to leave it there, because the building was not locked."

"No one would have injured it," he said simply. "They would have watched over it, like a shepherd his flock."

"It's in the back of my car. I'll leave it here. Margaret can tell me later what she wants done with it." I nodded, sorry to have said it. I didn't want to part with it. "How was it she started painting out there?" I gestured toward the garage.

"She came here first a little over two years ago, as I said, bringing paintings to show me. I said she was very good but as yet lacked discipline. I told her where her paintings went astray, how she sometimes went on with them when she should have stopped. I told her to bring others to me, as she finished them. Shortly thereafter, she came, very distressed, saying there was no longer anyplace she could paint at home. I told her not to worry, to paint here, in my garage, which was otherwise useless to me. It was built so long ago, it does not fit modern cars. It is too short for my own car, it is too low for the truck, so it has filled up, as such places do, with *desperdicios de casa.*" He smiled his private smile. "Rubbish. All those things we do not need and cannot use but will not throw away." He shook his head, perhaps remembering what things he would not throw away.

He went on. "Ricardo and Lourdes cleaned it out. It had a skylight already, and they scrubbed it clean to make a painterly light. Margaret began coming here, almost every day. Some days she shows me things. Other days she comes and goes without my seeing her, silent as a ghost."

"And not long ago, you agreed to give her a show? At your gallery?"

He nodded, pursing his lips. "I knew earlier this spring she was almost ready, but I did not say yes, now, until I saw the Madonna. I knew then her recent things were no accidental creations, no—what is the phrase?—flash in the pan. I knew then she would make me proud of her. It is my conceit, you see. Nothing is shown at Millagros unless it is indeed a . . . a revelation."

"She's excited about it. She couldn't wait to tell her daughter. She said she was going to devote all her attention to her painting for a while."

"I know. She told me on Sunday. She came here directly from church. She had a job, you know, at a greenhouse. It was part-time but it helped them with their needs. She told me when her father died last year, he left her a little money she had hidden away. She was guilty about this, telling me shamefaced she had hidden this money because she thought the time might come when she would need it. As though it had been wrong of her to do so. So, she said, this little money was enough to pay some expense she had. Enough to pay this expense for some months, she said. She was going to leave her job and do nothing but paint for a while. She also said the leeches were very angry with her."

"The leeches?"

"*Las sanguijuelas.* What would you call them? Those people who live in her house, eat her food, expect her to clean for them and wash their dirty clothes? For two years now. What do they do but suck the living blood of her art?"

I shrugged. Leeches was as good a word as any. "Did she call them that?"

"Never!" He moved his head, a fraction of an inch, as though forbidding himself any greater negation. "No, she called them the . . . unfortunates, *los pobres.* This is what her husband called them when he brought them into their home. The poor. Whom we have always with us."

I said, "Nonetheless, on Saturday she told her daughter they were going to have to do for themselves and I believe she told the Bobbisons as well."

He sat a long moment, very still, finally nodding slowly. "For her painting, she would do that. Only for that. For nothing else. She would not do it for her daughter, or for herself. Only for her painting." He got up, leaning on his stick. "Come. You should see."

We went along the walk and through a tall door into a cool, high-ceilinged room, virtually unlighted except by a few small, high windows. Great squared beams supported the ceiling, their ends resting on ornately carved corbels. He flicked a switch and track lights came on, throwing bright cones of light from behind the beams. Each light rested upon a painting, a dozen of them along one wall.

I walked down the line of them, amazed. Landscapes, figures, still lifes. A woman holding a rabbit. Another woman, seated on stone flags, knees drawn up beneath her skirt, a basket of oranges beside her, several rolled away, and each orange a sun, blazing in an infinity of space.

A vase of peonies. A child, bottle-feeding a lamb. The flowers were alive, and the child, and the lamb. Life breathed from her canvases. Each creature, each person, was about to look up and speak.

The limb of a tree or shrub, with insects upon it, and a bird, half-hidden behind a leaf. An adobe church seen from a distance, with people in the middle distance walking to or from it.

"Everything interests her, doesn't it?" I asked in a hushed voice.

"Everything alive," he said, pointing to a corner of a canvas where a tiny plant emerged from between two paving stones, each leaf as moist and vital as if it had grown there. He straightened. "There are more paintings to be hung. Ricardo will bring them in this afternoon. She works like one possessed."

"When is the show to be?"

"Next month. July."

"That's very soon."

"I thought better soon. If it was far away, there would be enough time for distraction. If it is soon, she must work hard."

"You think she'll be ready?"

He nodded. "If she can keep her health. Her eye. If she doesn't wear herself out."

"Is there a danger of that?"

"Not if the leeches stay away. Not if she has time for herself."

"Her daughter's thinking of returning home."

"That would be good, I think. Margaret misses her child. 'My Felicia,' she says. 'I miss my Felicia.' "

Reluctantly, I pulled my eyes from the paintings and thanked him. We went back into the courtyard, to the gentle splash of water and the fragrance of blooms as he escorted me to the gate, where I fetched the painting from the car.

"Do what you can to help her," he said, tenderly taking the Madonna from me. "Do not let them suck her dry!"

I turned, trying to think of a reply to this, but he had shut the gate behind me. The peephole stood open, and through the rusty grill I could hear his feet moving arrythmically as he limped away. Xavier Fortunato. Xavier the lucky. He had been lucky for Margaret, at least.

Back at Los Vientos, I let the animals out of the run, poured them and me a cool drink, then sat down in the breeze-cooled portal to consider what we'd learned thus far. I'd added a number of names to those on my original list: Xavier Fortunato; Ricardo and Lourdes Lalumia; their son; Dwight, Vera, and Bobbi Kay Bobbison.

I sipped and stretched, considering throat slitting.

It would take considerable strength to slit a man's throat if one were holding on to him at the time. If one lashed out with a sword or axe, however, it could happen in a moment, needing no particular strength. The whole thing depended on the weapon. I tried scenarios. Ernie, gone back to the church to do what? Shut the windows, perhaps. Lock the door. Get the painting, which he had decided wouldn't do. But inside he finds the Lalumias, perhaps with their afflicted son, kneeling in prayer before the lighted candles. Ernie couldn't pass up a chance like that. He would what? Pray, loudly. Accuse them of idolatry. Threaten to remove the painting, or actually start to do it. But the Lalumias, who think their son is being helped by the Madonna, can't allow that, so they slit his throat.

With what? They hadn't come to the church with throat slitting in mind. What might they be carrying that would serve as a weapon? Did Ricardo usually carry a knife?

Or perhaps the Bobbisons followed Ernie to the church to tell him Margaret was about to relinquish her role as chief Bobbison tender. Perhaps they found the church empty, Ernie gone over to the shopping center to pray over the shoppers. They decide to steal the painting, Ernie comes in and catches them, so they kill him.

Again, with what? Was Dwight the knife-carrying type? Did Vera hold Ernie while Dwight did him in?

Or Xavier Fortunato comes to the church, hoping to catch Ernie alone, to talk with him about his wife's great talent, to encourage him to treat her with more respect. And Ernie says something quintessentially Ernie-like that deeply offends Xavier's honor, and Fortunato slashes him one with his sword cane. If he has a sword cane.

Or Felicia, for reasons of her own. Or anybody from the shopping center.

I gave it up. Still not enough information. Maybe never enough information. I put my head back and dozed, hearing the sound of leaf and wind and water.

"Lazy sot," said a voice. Lindsay, peering down at me. "How long have you been here?"

I cleared my throat, dazzled by the sun behind her. "Not long," I croaked. "Guess I fell asleep."

"Lucky if your eyebrows aren't roasted," she muttered. "Lying there with your face in the sun. Haven't you ever heard of skin cancer?"

"I haven't had enough exposure to acquire cancer," I said,

looking at my watch. "I was in the shade twenty minutes ago. Where's Bruce?"

"Inside. We brought burritos from the Burrito Company."

I heaved myself up and we went in together, to find Bruce feeding Schnitz and Bela the food intended for us.

"There's plenty," he defended himself, when Lindsay waved a kitchen ladle at him. "We all eat too much anyhow. I'm still full from breakfast!"

While we shared the remaining burritos among ourselves and animals, I filled them in on Señor Fortunato.

"Did you get the feeling there was any . . ." Lindsay waved a limp hand back and forth.

"Hanky-panky?" I asked.

"You know," she said meaningfully.

"I *don't* know, but that's all right. No, I got no feeling there was any hanky-panky. I think he's just what he looks like, an elderly gentleman who happens to be an art lover. He thinks of Margaret as an artist first and a woman second, or third, or tenth, or not at all."

I chewed another bite of burrito. "What did you guys accomplish?"

Bruce filled me in on their morning, going from shelter to shelter, where everyone had seen the Bobbisons but nobody knew where they were now.

"They were seen how recently?" I asked.

"Last night," said Bruce with gloomy satisfaction. "They were at the Salvation Army office, but Vera was complaining loudly of stomach cramps, so the man there sent the whole family to the hospital to have Vera checked out. That's the last he saw of them."

"Are we getting closer?" I asked with a yawn.

"Not noticeably," said Lindsay. "How about an hour's nap before we start the afternoon schedule?"

I'd already had a nap, but I agreed. Bruce fell limply onto the living room couch; Lindsay went to the bedroom; I moved the portal chaise out of the sun and lay back down on it, thinking what questions I wanted to ask of the merchants at the shopping center and formulating strategy for catching up, somehow, somewhere, sometime with the Bobbisons. Somewhere in there, my mind went adrift and I found myself thinking of Margaret. Her bemused expression as she stared after me the day before. The line of her arms as she faced her canvas. The tone of Xavier Fortunato's voice when he spoke her name. . . .

The tone of my voice, which Mark had commented on.

Something going on here, I told myself sternly. Definitely, something going on here.

Three

I DOZED OFF, not for long, and when I woke, Lindsay and Bruce were deep into siesta, Bruce snoring mightily on the couch, Lindsay making small-dog snurffles in the bedroom. Since we had two cars, there was no reason I shouldn't go over to the shopping center and see what I could accomplish by myself. I left a note, telling them where I'd gone and that I'd be back at the ranch around five. The sky was clear, the day was hot, so Bela and Schnitz went back into the run along with a big bowl of cool water.

I started out for the shopping center. I really intended to go to the shopping center. But somehow, I turned off to the east before I got there, and before I admitted it even to myself, there I was, pulling up outside Señor Fortunato's garage. The wide door was cracked open a bit, enough that I could see Margaret working away inside. She stood as before, with her back to me, concentrating upon the canvas.

I knocked lightly then twice more before she turned, her brow furrowed.

"Oh," she said. "You." She stared over my shoulder for a minute. "Come on in," and she turned back to the canvas.

I recognized the scene, a sloping road disappearing around a rocky corner, a haze of dust hanging at the turning to let the viewer know something had just gone that way. It was the road leading from her house, Ernie's house, down and around the corner toward the Quivada place. Or down and around the corner toward somewhere else, out, away. Here, perhaps. Or anywhere else she wanted to go.

"It's the road from your house," I said, merely to let her know I was present.

"Of course," she said flatly, not bothering to look at me. "This morning, I noticed how the dust hangs in that light, how it makes that kind of fiery little cloud. . . ."

"Out at the church, I saw a bush that gave that same effect in the evening light," I said. "As though it were burning, you know. . . ."

She nodded, so slightly I barely saw it. Her hands moved delicately. Her head craned forward, then to the side, then back again. She stood away, looked, stood close, her hand reaching out to add a touch with the palette knife here, a touch there. She scraped the knife across the palette, made two quick swipes at the canvas, then thrust the knife into the little front pocket of her jeans, like a watch pocket, ragged and pierced from being repeatedly used in that fashion. She took up a brush to soften an area of harsh color. One touch, then another. Her neck was bare. The blouse she wore was one of those Carmen-type things, loose and cool-looking, almost dropping from her shoulders. She gave an exasperated little hitch to one arm, shifting the fabric back where it belonged.

"It's finished," I said softly.

"Yes," she said, standing away, putting the brush down, wiping her hands down her denimed thighs before running her fingers through her hair. "Yes, it is. Xavier says I must quit once I get there, not go on fooling with it. I guess I remembered it right."

Which explained that look she had sometimes of seeing beyond what anyone else was seeing. She was remembering the vision, knowing it wouldn't last long enough to paint on the spot, knowing she would have to do it from memory. And that also explained the immediacy I had noticed in all the paintings Fortunato had shown me, the spontaneity of them, the look of an instant preserved without being at all photographic. She was able to distill the essence of a moment and then transfer that distillation to canvas.

She said something under her breath, dropped the brush in a jar, sloshed solvent over it, and set it aside.

"That's all today," she said. "I have to go pick up Felicia."

"Felicia's coming home?"

"She said she would. If the Bobbisons were really gone. I called Xavier a couple of hours ago, and he sent Ricardo and his son over to help me move the extra furniture out, so even if they come back, they can't stay. I got rid of their beds. I put Felicia's bed back in her room and the other single bed in my room. Ricardo took the cribs away too." She smiled fiercely, a carnivore's smile, as exciting as it was surprising. The wolverine had driven the invaders from her lair. No, wolverine was wrong. Mink, maybe. Sleek and shiny. Or otter. I longed to pet her, stroke her. . . .

"Will you paint in your own house now?" I asked.

She shook her head, almost violently. "This is so much better! Xavier says I can go on here." She gestured at her surroundings. "It's the light. And I can leave things lying around. The room at home is so tiny. I can't stand back and look at anything. I thought of the chapel, but there's no light in there either."

"Can I drive you to get Felicia?"

"Would you? That would be nice. The police let me take Ernie's car from where it was, at the church, so I have that now, but I'm never sure about it. Sometimes it gets halfway and stops. I hate that."

"I would too," I said, gesturing toward the Mercedes. "This one almost always gets where it's going."

"Do I need to clean up?" she asked, peering down at herself, holding out her arms. "Did I get paint all over me? I can change. I keep a set of clean clothes here, and I don't want to mess up your car!"

Except for smears of paint around the pocket where she'd thrust the palette knife, she was almost clean. I lifted the knife out and presented it to her, trying so hard to be graceful about it that I ended up nicking myself. Around the finger in my mouth, I mumbled, "There's a little bit on the front of your jeans, not enough to mess up anything. Besides, in Santa Fe, painty jeans are acceptable anywhere, aren't they?"

"Right," she mused as we went out and she locked the door firmly behind us. As we got into the front seat, she said, "Clean shirt and painty jeans." The thought meant something to her, the composition of a self-portrait, perhaps. "Do you know where Felicia's staying?"

"Bruce and Lindsay and I talked to her there," I said. "I think I can find it again."

I did find it, down its twisty side street, after an almost silent drive. Margaret was totally relaxed beside me, a little half smile on her face, looking at this, looking at that, her head turning to keep certain things in view as we went past. I found myself anticipating what she'd look at next, giving myself a gold star when I guessed right. As we went down the last narrow street, she pointed out the window.

"That thick ropy vine, against that wall! It's wisteria. I did a painting of it a few weeks ago. Great clusters, like grapes, hanging against the pink wall. I want to do a whole series on Santa Fe flowers. Forsythia against the adobe. Hollyhocks. Great swatches of yarrow, that unbelievable yellow. The pink yarrows are no good. Muddy. Now I'm looking for zinnias, big ones. Xavier has a pewter pitcher I can put them in."

I parked where I'd parked before, in the alley, trying to see what she was seeing in her head, handicapped by having no notion what yarrow looked like, or zinnias.

"Do you want me to come with you?" I asked.

"You can wait if you'd rather," she said. "Felicia said she'd be ready."

She was out of the car and around the corner of the wall before I could decide either way, so I rolled down the window and waited, feeling the heat pour in and beads of moisture emerge on my arm, around the back of my neck. The heat was a visible force reflected from the house wall; the air was thick with the smell of dust and of flowers. Tar, too. Possibly a roof being repaired nearby.

A skinny black dog sniffed his way up out of the arroyo at the end of the alley and came toward me, detouring around the car while watching me out of the corner of his eyes. Not a stray, for he wore a studded VID (very important dog) collar. Five minutes later he was back again, escorting an equally skinny seven- or eight-year-old boy down the alley and into the arroyo. The boy had an air of exaggerated patience, as though the trip wasn't his idea. I could imagine Mama, somewhere, saying to the dog, "Go fetch Marcos. Go get him!"

And then around the corner behind me came Margaret and Felicia lugging a bulging backpack between them. Felicia put it in the backseat and climbed in after it.

"Hey," she remarked. "Nice car."

"I like it," I murmured. "Do you have everything?"

"Everything I'm taking home," she said, grinning at the back of her mother's head.

"She left her boyfriend behind," Margaret explained.

"Did I meet him the other day?" I asked.

"Prob'ly," said Felicia. "Hector's appointed himself doorman. That's because one of the girls, her father tried to break in and get at her."

"Get at her?" I asked weakly.

"You know," the girl said, making a graphic gesture. "He'd been getting at her since she was ten. That's why she lives here now. So when her father got drunk and tried to get in, Hector bashed him."

I swallowed, wanting to ask several questions at once, stopped by the vivid verb she had used, the picture of Ernie all too clear in my mind.

"With his fist," she continued, narrowing her eyes at me. "It broke Hector's finger, but he stopped the guy." She fumbled in the pocket of her jeans for a stick of chewing gum, tore it in half, unwrapped the half, folded it once, and tucked it between her teeth. "I'll miss seeing him all the time, but I'm glad I'm going home."

"So's your mom," I said, glancing sidewise at Margaret. She wore a contented smile; her hands lay quiet in her lap.

We made the trip in about twenty minutes. When I rounded the corner below the house, we saw there were visitors.

"Oh, no," breathed Margaret.

"Shit," said Felicia under her breath. "There they are."

An ancient mud-tan VW van was parked in the driveway. Its rear doors were tied together with a length of frayed rope, and a large chunk of left rear fender had rusted away in scallops, as though something large and determined had taken a bite out of it. The window was missing on the same side.

I glanced at Margaret, seeing dismay and horror on her face, a kind of cringing.

"Do you want me to take care of it?" I asked.

"Could you just . . . help?" She looked up at me with a pleading expression, which held more than a little fear. "They . . . they're hard to . . ."

"Mom means they're impossible to move," said Felicia in a tone of cold anger. "It'll take all three of us."

"Would they have gone inside?" I asked.

"That's where they'll be," said Felicia. "Even if Mom remembered to lock the door, they wouldn't let that stop them."

"I didn't," murmured Margaret. "I didn't remember. There's nothing left to steal. It was unlocked."

"The extra furniture's gone, right?" I asked. "Ricardo and his son took it away."

Margaret nodded, very pale, her mouth set.

"All right then," said I, putting the car in reverse to get us back around the corner. The road had a shelf leading off from it, like a bypass, and I drove up onto it, about two feet above the road. "So we don't block the way out," I explained. "We'll tackle them together. Come on."

I closed the car doors and made sure they were locked, then took Margaret firmly by one arm and Felicia by the other and we walked up the road toward the rickety van. When we had almost reached it, the screen door slammed open and a girl-child came out as though shot from a cannon. What with the padded bra, the frizzed hair, and the stud earrings, it had to be Bobbi Kay.

"Bobbi Kay Bobbison?" I asked in my most studiedly neutral tone. "Are your parents inside?"

She gaped at me, mouth open. "Yeah," she managed after lengthy thought. "Somebody stole our beds."

"No," I said in sudden inspiration. "Someone stole Margaret's television. And her jewelry. We've come to wait for the sheriff."

Margaret threw me a glance, at first puzzled, but then amused, a quick glint of laughter moving behind her gaze, like those silver fish in Fortunato's pool.

The door banged again as Bobbi Kay fled before us into the echo chamber of the chapel. We followed her inside, moving toward the living room, where Vera and Dwight presumably were. I slowed our pace, letting Bobbi Kay get far enough ahead to share the news before we arrived.

That it was being shared was evident, for I heard "that worthless ole TV" and "sheriff" spoken at sufficient volume to override the sound of screaming children. I could feel Margaret trembling as we came to the door.

When we entered the living room, Vera was facing us, squatted like a large toad in the room's only comfortable chair, her head armored in precise rows of pink plastic curlers. Dwight, bald head gleaming with sweat, was snatching at the two little boys, who were caroming wildly from wall to wall, both red in the face and yelling at the top of their lungs.

I decided the best defense was an offense. "Shut up," I shouted in a voice I hadn't used in years.

Silence. The little boys looked at me wide-eyed, noses dripping, mouths open. "You take those two kids outside," I said to Bobbi Kay. "Or else."

She opened her mouth, but Vera, giving me a snake's eye glare, closed it for her. "Take 'em," she said. "Bobbi Kay, you take 'em."

As the girl departed, Vera darted her head forward, toward me, toward Margaret, demanding, "Who stole our beds?"

I squeezed Margaret's hand to keep her from answering.

"Glad you folks dropped by," I said. "We've been looking for you! Nobody knew where you were."

I went into the kitchen, pulled out chairs for Margaret and Felicia, then turned a third one around in front of them, making a barrier between them and the Bobbisons. I straddled the chair and folded my arms on its back.

"What were your family's movements last Sunday."

Dwight stared uncertainly at Vera. "Movements?"

"You were in Ernie's car after services," I said firmly. "Then what did you do, where did you go?"

"Didn't go nowhere," said Vera. "Stayed right here. Waitin for somethin to eat! We was countin on Sunday dinner, but she" —she tilted her chin toward Margaret, sneering—"she says she's not cookin until nighttime. I ask you, who's gonna go all day without somethin to eat?"

"So, you went somewhere to get something to eat," I said in an uninterested voice.

"Lotaburger . . ." said Dwight.

"You shut up," said Vera.

"Well, we did!"

"Nobody's binness what we ate," shouted Vera.

"The sheriff will want to know," I said. "Exactly where you were, and when."

"So we went to the Lotaburger, so what?" cried Vera. "So we had a hamburger an some fries, so what?"

"When did you get back here?"

"Who cares," she snarled. "Anybody's got eyes can see we ain't got watches. We come back here along about suppertime." She gave me her mean look.

I put on my own mean look and snarled right back at her. "It didn't take five or six hours for you to eat a burger and fries. Where were you the rest of the time?"

Vera pinched her mouth shut and stared out the window. Dwight shuffled from foot to foot.

"Drivin aroun," he said at last. "Jus drivin aroun."

"Did you go out to the church?"

"Don' remember," he said sulkily.

"Don't remember?" I asked. "Come on, Dwight! Don't sound like a blasted idiot. You think the police are going to believe that! Did you go to the church?"

"He don' remember," Very announced. "An I don' remember either. We went ridin aroun, and that's all we got to say about that."

"You were back here when Margaret got here."

"Yeah. We was here."

"When did Ernie leave you?"

"We lef him, he . . ." Dwight began.

"You shut up," yelled Vera. "You butthead. Ernie lef us here. He never even come in when he lef us off. He never."

"He dropped you off, and then he left, is that it?"

"Said he was goin to his folks," said Vera. "That ole bitch. What I wanna know is, where's our beds?"

I was about to reply when Margaret spoke firmly from behind me. "The beds weren't yours," she said. "They belonged to me, and I've sold them. Now that Ernie's gone, I won't . . . I'm afraid you'll have to find somewhere else to live."

"Ernie said . . ." squeaked Dwight.

"He tole us . . ." started Vera.

I glanced sideways, catching a horrified, open-mouthed expression on Felicia's face, which she wiped away, gritting her teeth. What was that all about?

"It might be a good idea to leave now," I said hastily, staring them down. "When the sheriff's men get here, we're going to be talking to them about the things that were stolen when you left before. Margaret's brother-in-law, Bruce Norman, is going to insist we report the jewelry stolen."

Vera, "What's he got to do with—"

I held up my hand.

"Some of that jewelry belonged to Ernie's mother, and Ernie's brother is very angry about the theft. I can't guarantee what he'll do if you're still around when he gets here."

Margaret said, with surprising firmness, "I don't like the idea of people being arrested, but there may not be anything I can do about it. Jason's right. It would probably be a good idea for you to leave and plan to stay away from here. There's no place for you here."

Vera screamed. Dwight waved his fist. I rose from the chair and went into the kitchen, loudly asking Margaret where the phone book was because I wanted to see what was keeping the deputies. I got the dispatcher almost immediately. The yelling stopped. They listened, only for a moment, then Vera heaved herself out of the chair and waddled toward the door, giving me the finger as she passed.

As long as I had the sheriff's office on the line, I went ahead and reported the theft, then hung up and went outside, where I stood on the doorstep while the elder Bobbisons collected Bobbi Kay and the little boys and loaded themselves into the van. Looking through the windshield, I could see it had only one seat. The back had a mattress in it, however, and the kids threw themselves on that with well-practiced abandon. Eventually the engine kicked over and they backed down the driveway, turning right at the road, toward where I'd left my car.

Too tempting for them to pass up, I thought, strolling down the driveway after them and arriving at its foot just in time to see Dwight and Bobbi Kay climbing the bank toward the Mercedes, Dwight bearing a tire iron in one hand.

"That's my car," I said. "And it's locked."

He scuttled back down the embankment, got in the van, and they all sputtered off in a great cloud of black smoke.

No point in leaving the Mercedes where it was, so I drove it up to the house. Margaret was standing outside the door, tears streaking her face.

"Hey," I said, offering her my handkerchief. "It's okay. They've gone."

Felicia came out of the house, shaking her head. "I don't think they took anything else. Not that there was much left to take! I'm surprised they didn't burn the place down."

"Burn it down?" I asked, putting my arm around Margaret, and pulling her close. It was like embracing a sapling, slender but whip strong, yielding and resistant at once. She sighed and relaxed against my chest. I rubbed her shoulders.

Felicia gave me an odd look. I flushed and released her mother.

"They threatened to before," said Felicia, still giving me a *what the hell is going on* look. "Two or three times, when Mom tried to get them to do for themselves, you know. Might as well burn the place down, they said. If they couldn't get meals on time, couldn't get a little laundry done, might as well burn the place down."

"Didn't your father do anything about them?" I asked angrily. "Didn't he at least expect them to clean up after themselves?"

Felicia gave me a quick, secretive look, a shake of the head, saying more clearly than words, some other time, when Mom's not here.

Margaret straightened herself and took a couple of deep breaths. "Thank you, Jason. I couldn't have. At least, I don't think I could have, not alone. That woman scares me so much. . . ."

"Vera hit Mom once," said Felicia. "I told her, she ever did it again, I'd call the police and swear out the complaint myself. She tried it on me once. I was ironing, and I got her a pretty good one with the hot iron. She never tried it again."

"When was this?" I asked, feeling myself getting even angrier.

"Right when they first came. Kind of like they were finding out what they could get away with."

"She never hit you again?" I asked Margaret.

She shook her head. No. No. "She never hit me again," she said. The words were clear, but the tone meant something else. She never hit me, but she did other things.

"Well, when the deputies arrive, I suggest you and Felicia make a complete report. Don't leave anything out."

"You really did call them?" cried Felicia.

"Once I'd met your former tenants, I thought it was a good idea," I said. "They're sending men out to take a report. Whether they can do anything or not, it needs to be on the record.

Felicia took her mother's hand. "Come on, Mom. He's right. You should have reported the stuff stolen when they first left. And we should tell about them hitting you, and about them threatening to burn the place down. Just in case. . . ."

"In case?" Margaret asked, troubled.

"In case something actually happens," Felicia mumbled. "You know. We've got to remember somebody killed Dad. You heard old Dwight in there. He couldn't keep from saying it. They left Dad somewhere, and they were all iffy and nudgy about whether they went to the church. Well, that tells me they did go to the church that afternoon. Probably to complain about you. And they left Dad there." She gave her mother a bleak look. "The question is how they left him."

"You don't think they . . . Dwight . . . Vera . . . she's so clumsy. I can't see either of them . . ."

"I can," I said, giving Margaret a little shake as I recalled Dwight's white-knuckled grip on the tire iron. "It doesn't take a lot of strength to kill someone the way Ernie was killed. All it takes is the right weapon. Come on. Enough talk about the Bobbisons! Somebody offer me a cup of tea or something."

I herded them before me into the house, where Felicia went about, opening all the windows.

"They smell," she said.

Now that she mentioned it, I detected the smell. Faint, but unmistakable. Dirty diapers and what?

"Dwight chews tobacco," Felicia said. "And Vera sweats like a horse."

"Very organic," murmured Margaret from the kitchen, where she was putting the kettle on. "I used to tell myself that. The whole family smelled very organic."

"Yeah," Felicia snarled. "Organic like a zoo! Or like an outhouse." She went into the kitchen and set out three mugs. "I tried to tell Daddy how they smelled, but he said he didn't smell them. He had some kind of disease when he was younger, and he could barely smell anything. I think that's why he didn't care what he ate. Except sugary stuff. Sugar tastes good even if you can't smell it."

The water boiled. The tea was made. We had drunk about half of it when the sheriff's deputies arrived, two of them, one Anglo, one Hispanic. I took my tea into the living room and stood looking out the window while Margaret and Felicia—mostly Felicia—made their report. They told about the disappearance of the TV and the jewelry. Together they remembered and described each piece of jewelry. They reported that Vera had struck them, that she had talked of burning the house down.

"Sound like crazy people to me," said the Hispanic deputy, busily filling out his report form. "Trouble is, we can't lock 'em up unless they're dangerous, and you never know they are until it's too late."

Which echoed my sentiments exactly.

"You better change your locks," said the Anglo deputy, shaking his head. "I would, if I was you."

Margaret and Vera had left something out. I went to the kitchen door and reminded them. "There's reason to think Vera and Dwight were at the church Sunday afternoon. When Ernie was killed."

At the word "killed," two heads came up, like pointer dogs sighting game.

"I'm talking about the murder of Ernie Quivada," I said. "I think it's being handled by the pueblo police. Don't they handle crimes on the reservation?"

"Depends," the Anglo replied. "If it's two guys getting in a fight, sure. But if it was like somebody driving through, not a member of the tribe, could be FBI responsibility."

"Well, Ernie wasn't a member of the tribe," I said. I hadn't considered the possible role of the FBI, but obviously someone would have to take over investigations that extended beyond the jurisdiction of the tribal police.

"When was this?" the hispanic asked.

"Sunday," said Felicia.

"And these Bobbison people were there, at the church, on Sunday?"

Margaret nodded. "Yes. They gave us the distinct impression they were there the afternoon my husband was killed."

"Your husband?" the Anglo asked. "I thought *he* was your husband." He pointed at me.

I could feel myself flushing. "I'm just a friend of the family," I said, wondering why I was embarrassed.

"Well, whoever's investigating the murder, you should tell them about it," said the Hispanic. "I guess we could find out. You haven't talked to any feds?"

Margaret shook her head. "Just the local police. From the office out at the pueblo."

They left muttering to one another.

"He was right," I said. "You should change the locks."

Margaret laughed, though not with any real amusement, shaking her head and shrugging helplessly.

Felicia said, "Half the windows in the house don't lock. Some of them don't even shut. You could get in here with a beer can opener if you wanted."

I looked around me at the little cracker-box house. Felicia was right. Even I could see half a dozen ways to get in, and I wasn't an experienced housebreaker. If it did burn down, it would be no loss. Except—if Felicia and her mother were in it at the time.

The idea brought a surging anger in its wake. Damn people! Vera and Dwight no doubt got through life on a steady flow of begging and threats and whines and whatever abuse they could get away with. No doubt they'd had deprived and abused childhoods and it was the only way of life they knew. As it would be for Bobbi Kay and the two little boys in their turn. But why in the name of heaven had Ernie Quivada brought a family like that into his own home? It was like willingly exposing his own family to a deadly virus!

"I'll walk out to your car with you," said Felicia. I looked up to meet her eyes, narrowed, significant. She wanted to talk to me alone.

"Right," I mumbled. "Bruce and Lindsay may be looking for me over at the shopping center. Meantime, I'll try to think of something to make this place . . . safer."

"We'll be all right," said Margaret. "Really."

"She won't be all right," Felicia told me when we got out to the car. "I mean, she will, so long as she's painting and nobody drives her crazy. But if they come back, she won't be all right."

"Why do you think they'll be back?"

"Because there's this other thing I didn't remember until just a while ago. It was when Vera and Dwight started to tell what Dad said to them about living here. I don't know if Mom even knew about it, but the way they went out of here, I'd bet they remember. I can just tell the shit's going to hit it. It really is."

She'd lost me. "What are you talking about, Felicia?"

"Mom doesn't really own this house."

"What?" I shouted in disbelief.

She cast a look over her shoulder, to be sure we weren't observed or overheard. "Well, like Dad bought it, but he did it in the name of the church, the congregation. Who owns it is the Church of Jesus Triumphant."

"The congregation," I said stupidly.

"The people who went to church. The members. The people who went there all the time were Grandma and Grandpa and Vera and Dwight. And Mom. But there's four of them and only one of her."

I slumped against the car, trying to make sense of it. "Where did he get the money to buy the house?"

"Something he got from his father. There were some bonds his father left him, I don't know exactly what. Anyhow, Dad didn't get them until they matured, and one did, just before we moved here. See, Mom starting painting when we were in Texas. But then Dad moved us to Oklahoma. Then when we were in Oklahoma, there was this woman there that Mom got friendly with, and the woman was an artist and she gave Mom lessons. So then Dad moved us here. And when Mom started painting again, Daddy went out and got the Bobbisons and brought them home. . . ."

"You're saying your father did this purposely? These moves, and this family, to inhibit your mother's painting?"

"He didn't like it one bit because it gave her something . . . you know, something of her own. She was supposed to be totally dedicated to God, and that meant being totally dedicated to Dad. He didn't mind her working for money, because we needed money, but he didn't like her doing stuff she really cared about. . . ."

"The Bobbisons," I reminded her.

"Right. I came over to visit Mom one Sunday afternoon, and I heard Dad talking to Vera and Dwight. This was, oh, a month ago or more. They were complaining about Mom not wanting them here, and he was saying so long as they went to church every Sunday, they had every right to live in the house, it was as much theirs as it was his and Mom's because it belonged to the congregation."

"He bought the place outright? It's all paid for?"

She nodded. "There was some money left over, but he used that to build on the chapel. Mom wanted him to keep some in the bank, because it was costing so much to feed the Bobbisons, she didn't always have enough to pay the gas bill and the electric.

They're two months behind now. Dad wouldn't save any, though. He said the Lord would provide."

"I can't believe it," I said hollowly. "So you think the Bobbisons will remember what your dad said."

"They probably never forgot. They just don't want any sheriff trouble, so they'll back off for a day or so, maybe. But they'll come back. They get real cosy with Grandma, on and off, and they're probably over there right now, talking about it. See, Grandma and Grandpa are part of the congregation, too. So they own the house just as much as the Bobbisons. I think it was Grandma's idea for Daddy to do it that way, I really do."

She rubbed her forehead with the back of one hand, a gesture I had seen her mother make. "I've got to get Mom out of here, Jason. She'll just fall apart if they come back, and I'll bet you anything they'll be back by tomorrow morning. Maybe even this afternoon."

The look she was giving me was questioning, demanding, pleading, all at once. It said, "I know you'll do something, Jason, I'm laying it on you. Help get her out of here."

And she was right, of course. I did feel I had to do something about Margaret. Talent like hers is in short supply. So I told myself, sternly putting down the thought of that sapling slenderness against my chest, that sweet mouth breathing on my shoulder.

I flushed.

"You like her," said Felicia, her eyes lighting up. "You're not married or anything, are you."

"No," I said. "Yes." Then, seeing her confusion. "No, I'm not married. Yes, I do like her. Because she's a fine artist, and I know a bit about art. It's what I do, in a sense."

"I thought you were a private eye," she said in a disappointed voice. "An investigator."

I laughed, glad there was something to laugh at. "I'm an antique dealer." Then I laughed again at the expression on her face, like someone who had just bitten into something sour. "You don't like antique dealers?"

"Every other person in Santa Fe is one of those," she said. "I was hoping . . . maybe you could help."

I was stung. "Just because I'm not a private eye doesn't mean I can't help. Give me a little time." I gave her a pat. "Keep an eye on her. I'll see what I can do."

I drove about half a mile and then stopped by the side of the road to think things over. What could I do? What could Bruce do?

Then I had an inspiration. I drove directly to Xavier Fortunato's place, leaned on the gate, and yanked persistently on the bell rope until the gentleman himself opened the peephole and peered through all drowsy-eyed. I'd interrupted his siesta. When he saw who it was, he frowned slightly, opened the gate, and let me in.

"Trouble?" he asked me. "You're upset about something."

I told him what something, everything, threats and violence and hints of arson and the fact that Margaret didn't own the house she lived in.

"I thought of you," I said weakly, when it was all said. "I thought of you."

"Of course you did," he said in a firm voice. "And you were right to do so." He went across the enclosed patio as though to the beat of a drum, pausing under one corner of the portal at an inconspicuously mounted intercom grill where he pushed a button and spoke briefly. He beckoned to me, and we went through the portal into the dim coolness of his living room: leather furniture, Oriental rugs, huge trastero, and various tables in the Spanish colonial style, but brilliantly constructed and carved in oak and pine, with none of the crudity of early Southwestern carpentry. Custom done, without a doubt, and by an artist in wood. The only windows were to the west, looking out across a desert slope, past the edge of the wide arroyo to the eroded opposite wall and, in the distance, the mountains. It was precisely the environment I would have chosen for him if I'd had to design one.

We sat in two massive chairs near the fireplace. In a few moments, a woman came in carrying a tray. A teapot, porcelain cups, silver spoons, a collector's item majolica plate covered with lemon cookies thin as shavings. A man came in behind the woman, and Fortunato spoke to them both in rapid Spanish. The woman shook her head, as though to say, "Who would believe it?" answering quickly, asking questions.

Then they departed purposefully, still shaking their heads at one another.

"I have a guest house." Xavier Fortunato took an absent-minded bite of lemon cookie. "A large bedroom with two beds, a sitting room, a little kitchen, a bath. It has its own little patio, quite private, quite separate." He nodded to himself, assuring himself. "Quite proper. I think Margaret and her daughter will be safe and comfortable there. It is not being used. It is no trouble for me. Ricardo and Lourdes think highly of Margaret, because of her painting, and they are happy to help. You must convince Margaret of this. Of the propriety, of the fact it makes no inconvenience."

"I must?"

"Yes, you must, for she will refuse. She wants to be no burden to anyone. You must convince her it is proper. Lourdes will be here. She will be . . . duenna. Chaperone? At my age, it should make no talk, but then, people will talk no matter."

"How old are you, señor?"

He drew himself up proudly. "I am ninety-one next month."

I had the courtesy not to smile. If people would talk, more power to him. "When may they come?"

"Lourdes is making the rooms ready now. Ricardo will go with you in the truck. I think they must not leave behind anything they do not wish to lose, you understand?"

I gave a sigh of relief, even while wondering momentarily if both Xavier and I weren't overreacting. Then I remembered Felicia's story, the venom in Vera's eyes, the tire iron in Dwight's hand, and decided better safe than sorry.

Before leaving, I called the ranch. Bruce answered.

"Where the hell have you been?" he asked. "We spent half an hour looking for you at the shopping center."

"I got sidetracked," I admitted. "Good thing, too. The Bobbisons tried to move back in on Margaret."

Confusion, muttered explanations, outright consternation when I explained about the congregation owning the house and the probable implications of that. We ended the conversation when Bruce and Lindsay told me they'd meet me at Margaret's. I hung up, thanked Señor Fortunato, and bowed myself out.

Ricardo was waiting for me outside the gate, the pickup grumbling gently to itself beside the road, his son a bulky and silent presence in the passenger seat. We made a caravan of two back to Margaret's place. I knocked on the door and was greeted by one tearstained face and one angrily red one, Margaret and Felicia, respectively.

"Those . . . those bastards went right down to Grandma and Grandpa's, and they all decided they had a right to live here, and they're coming back, they said. . . ."

"Whoa, Felicia," I said. "Slow down."

She took a deep breath. "Vera and Dwight went to Grandma's house. And Grandma agreed with them they owned the house as much as Mom does, and they could live here if they wanted to. Grandma called here and said so. Mom didn't even know about it until then, like I told you she probably didn't. Anyhow, they're going to go buy some stuff they need, and then they're coming back and Grandma's coming with them."

"I can't," cried Margaret. "God, Jason, I just can't!"

"You don't have to," I said gently, reaching for both of them. "Hey. Calm down. When I left here, I went down to the Fortunato place. I told Señor Fortunato what was happening. He has a guest house he wants you to use, just for the time being, until you decide what you want to do or until Bruce and Lindsay and I can help you come up with something. Ricardo and his son are outside in the truck. So you can take anything you want to save. So it won't get—"

"Trashed," cried Felicia gladly, taking her mother in her arms. "So it won't get trashed, Mom! Come on! I'll take my rocking chair. Grandma Norman gave me that chair on my twelfth birthday. And my bed she gave me!"

I stepped outside and waved. Ricardo nodded and came purposefully toward the house, his son trailing behind.

"Oh, no, no," cried Margaret. "I can't. It would be an imposition."

I took her by the shoulders and shook her just enough to get her attention. "Señor Fortunato is ninety-one next month," I said. "He's a very old gentleman, Margaret. It would be wrong to cause him concern and unnecessary worry. After all, he's put a lot of time and thought into this show he's promised you. He's depending on you, and it would be wrong to disappoint him."

Felicia grinned at me over her mother's shoulder, then dashed into the house after the two men.

Margaret said in a troubled voice, "Do you think so? Would it make him worry?"

"Very definitely. He was extremely upset. The only thing that made him feel better was when he thought of your using his guest house. It's as much for his sake as yours. The house is vacant. It's not as though you were causing any trouble. It's got its own kitchen and everything; you can cook for yourself and clean it up when you leave. It's the sensible thing to do."

I heard a car coming up the drive, so I left her with a pat and intercepted Bruce and Lindsay, to fill them in on the situation.

"Is this Fortunato man all right?" Lindsay asked doubtfully. "We could have her stay with us. Or rent her a place."

"Think of the picture the words 'courtly gentleman' bring to mind," I said. "Think of laudatory things like honor and honesty and all that good stuff. That's Xavier Fortunato. Besides, he's ninety-one next month. I think Margaret and Felicia will be as safe as in church."

"I know at least one church that wasn't exactly safe," muttered Bruce. "But I take your point. Do you need help, convincing Margaret?"

"I think I've convinced her that she shouldn't cause Señor Fortunato any further worry," I said, giving them a significant look. "Because he has an investment in her future."

"Good thought," said Bruce. "I'll back you up."

Backing up was scarcely needed. Felicia emerged from the house, her arms full of clothing, with Ricardo right behind her carrying the rocking chair, and then his son, carrying two small tables. Lindsay chivied Margaret into the house, and a few moments later I saw them packing Margaret's clothes. From a lean-to behind the house, Felicia brought in a stack of boxes, pausing to mutter into my ear:

"Mom's name is on the gas and electric, and the phone. We better get her off that, don't you think?"

I pulled Bruce to one side and suggested he take care of those matters while I went to take Felicia's bed apart. If there's anything I'm good at, it's taking furniture apart. Or putting it back together. Next time I went by the kitchen Bruce was sitting at the table, phone propped on one shoulder, busily making notes. Felicia was behind him, emptying the contents of the cupboards into cardboard boxes.

"Is there somewhere to store this stuff?" I asked Ricardo, as we passed in the hallway.

"Señor Fortunato has a barn," he said with a lopsided grin. "Is not quite full. His other barn, it is full."

Less than an hour after we'd arrived, Ricardo and son departed in the truck. Shortly thereafter, Lindsay, Felicia, and Margaret left in Lindsay's car. Lindsay intended to see Mr. Fortunato for herself, so she said, and I told her to be nice. Once they were out of the way, I heaved a sigh of relief. Now, no matter what happened, there'd be no more battering of either mother or daughter.

Bruce had stayed behind with me, and we made a last, slow circuit of the house. There had been precious little to move. Everything Margaret had in the way of personal possessions or clothing, including her winter coat, had fit into two modest-sized suitcases. Felicia's worldly goods were still in the bulging backpack. The few small pieces of furniture—gifts, Bruce said, from him or his mother to Margaret or Felicia on various birthdays—hadn't taken much truck space. Even the contents of the kitchen had been sparse. A set of gay cannisters—a Mother's Day gift from her, said Felicia—a handful of utensils, a few cans and boxes of this and that. The noisy old refrigerator had been almost empty. Neither Felicia nor Margaret had thought the mismatched dishes and glasses or the battered pans worth packing. The appliances, Felicia said, had been in the house when it was bought, and none of them really worked except the stove.

"The washing machine pooped out months ago, and Mom's been doing the washing by hand," she'd confessed sotto voce.

"Except for the sheets and towels. She's been taking those down to the laundromat."

When everything else was packed, Felicia had systematically stripped the beds, folded the sheets and blankets, taken the towels from the bathroom, and piled everything into a large cardboard box, which was now in the back of Ricardo's truck, on its way to Señor Fortunato's barn.

I went through the kitchen, closing cupboard doors, then into the bedrooms, shutting windows, looking onto closet shelves. In the bedroom Ernie and Margaret had used, there was an old, dark varnished table with one drawer. I pulled the drawer out to see if it had been emptied, and it came out all the way, falling loose in my hand. Papers that had been caught behind the drawer skittered to the floor. I put the drawer back and stuffed the papers into the side pocket of my jacket to give to Margaret when I saw her next.

The bathroom cabinet held nothing but an empty aspirin bottle. The shower wept persistent tears, adding endless tiny increments to the elliptical iron stain beside the drain. I couldn't shut it off. The bathroom window fought me when I tried to close it. At some time or other it had been racked in its frame.

Back in the living room, Bruce and I gave one another a long, dispirited look.

"Shoddy," said Bruce. "Why do people build things like this! It's sure not much to show for a lifetime. Not much for a marriage."

"There's Felicia," I reminded him.

"Right. One hell of a good kid."

"Shall we?" I bowed toward the door.

"After you, Alphonse."

We went through the amateurishly built annex and out into the air with a feeling of relief. I was glad to see it was evening, glad to think the day was over. The next one would be better, for Margaret at least.

"Is this place worth anything?" Bruce asked.

"It's probably worth whatever Ernie paid for it," I replied. "What was this business Felicia mentioned about his getting bonds at intervals from his dad."

"Annuities. There were several of them, I think," Bruce mused, staring down the road where a coyote loped past the drive, paying us no attention at all. "His father's will provided that when each one matured it would be worth fifty thousand and Ernie would get the money. Is that what he used to buy this place?"

"According to Felicia."

"The place isn't worth fifty thousand!"

"The house isn't and never was," I said. "I'd run a bulldozer through it. But the land is worth close to that. I've been noticing land prices in the real estate ads. They're higher than you'd imagine."

"Then it's maybe worth enough for us to see if we can get title cleared for Margaret and Felicia."

"If you think you can get it away from the so-called congregation. I've no idea what a congregation amounts to. Are there papers, do you suppose?"

"Like what? Articles of Incorporation?"

I shrugged. "Churches own property all the time, so I suppose there has to be some kind of legal entity. A nonprofit corporation or something."

"Something," he agreed broodingly. "Can you imagine Ernie doing that? Telling those people they had as much right to live in the house as his family did? You know, I was a little pissed at Felicia, to tell you the truth. I kind of felt she ran out on her mother. But maybe her being gone was the best thing. That way, at least Margaret didn't have to worry about her."

I'd had the same thought. "If Felicia had been here, Vera could have held her hostage, forcing Margaret's compliance. With Felicia gone, there was only so much damage the Bobbisons could do."

"They did enough," he said bitterly.

"I think the thing that bothered Margaret most was the ugliness, but when she was painting, she probably didn't even think of that."

"What bothers *me* most—there was a kind of meanness to it, wasn't there? As though Ernie had it in for Margaret."

I considered this, agreeing, but unable to make sense of it. "I got the same idea from Felicia, but why? She stuck by him. She moved with him, every time he moved. No one's said a word against her except the Bobbisons. I mean, there's no indication of . . . what? An affair? Arguments? Why would he have it in for her?" The thing Felicia had said about his resenting her painting stuck in my craw. I mentioned it to Bruce, doubtfully.

He shook his head. "It sounds farfetched, but I have to admit he was weird. He got ideas in his head sometimes. . . . I used to think he wasn't very bright, but that really wasn't it. He was smart enough when he needed to be. It's as though . . . he *decided* not to use his head. I just can't explain him, Jason."

We mused over this in silence until I asked, "Did you get the gas and electric shut off?"

"Jemez Mountain Electric will be out this afternoon. Gas company man first thing in the morning. Phone's already disconnected. They do that at the exchange, wherever that is."

As though to punctuate his statement, a shiny new Jemez Mountain truck pulled up behind my car, the driver got out, waved at us cheerily, and started around back.

"That was quick," I called to him.

"I was just down the road on another job," he called in return. "They told me on the radio. Did you give the office an address for the bill?"

Bruce went over and handed him a card. Seeing the truck had given me an idea. I went inside to the bathroom. When I came out some considerable time later, the truck had gone and Bruce was standing beside the Mercedes, impatiently drumming on the hood.

"Come on," he yelled. "What were you doing in there? Painting a mural?"

I strolled toward him, turning to look once more at the structure behind me. Already it looked abandoned, and in my opinion it made a more attractive ruin than it did a dwelling.

We got into the car and backed slowly down the drive, turning toward the Fortunato place.

"We'll see if Lindsay's still there," I said. "If she is, we'll park one car somewhere and go out to dinner. Maybe Felicia and Margaret can come along."

"You kind of like her, don't you?" said Bruce.

"She's a good kid," I said.

"I didn't mean Felicia."

"Margaret?" I asked hollowly. "Sure. She's a very talented, very lovely woman."

"Yeah," he said drily. "She sure is. She was nice-looking when Ernie married her, but she got beautiful somewhere along the line."

We came to a four-way stop, where the gravel road joined a paved stretch. I checked left, then right, my eyes coming to rest on a mud-colored van, broken window, rust-eaten fender and all. I grunted and pointed unobtrusively, drawing Bruce's attention to it.

"My God," he said. "It's Evangeline and old man Quivada. Are those the Bobbisons?"

Those were indeed the Bobbisons; at least Dwight was behind the wheel. As the van made a left turn toward us, we saw through the missing window that Vera and the rest of the brood were on the mattress in the back. Their progress was slow enough that we could hear Vera's loudly voiced opinions of us, of our parentage and affinities. We watched, open-mouthed, as the cumbersome vehicle clattered on toward the house we had just left, farting a cloud of black smoke.

"The back was full of grocery sacks," Bruce commented. "But they won't have any electricity to cook with tonight, will they?"

"It's a gas stove," I said. "As are the furnace and water heater. But there won't be lights or refrigeration. And of course, the house doesn't have city water. It's on a well."

He gave me a puzzled look.

I said, "Well, after all, Bruce, I had to use the bathroom. I had to flush the toilet—several times, as I recall. And I had to wash my hands, of course, because they were filthy from all that packing. I never stopped to think about the water being pumped by electricity until it stopped coming out of the faucets. I must have emptied both the water heater and the pressure tank."

"There's no water at the house." He grinned to himself.

"It was thoughtless of me," I confessed.

"Sure it was," he said with great satisfaction. "Sure it was."

When it came to having no utilities, no furniture, and no maid service, Vera and Grandma Quivada did not take the matter lying down. The rickety van showed up outside Xavier Fortunato's house, where Bobbisons and Quivadas found the garage shut and barred and the gate in the high wall firmly closed. Vera and Grandma stood outside, demanding to know where Margaret was, screaming threats and imprecations until a sheriff's car with flashing lights arrived to advise them they could either leave and not come back or they could all go to county jail, as it were, en famille.

At least, so we heard when we returned from dinner at Angelina's in Española. A Denver friend had told me about the place, blessing it both for the good food and the almost complete absence of tourists because, so my friend said, Angelina's had no glitz, only good traditional New Mexican food. Margaret and Felicia had turned down our invitation to dinner, saying they wanted to get settled in, but the moment we got back, the phone rang. It was Felicia with an account of the newest Bobbison atrocity.

Lindsay talked to her, repeating what she heard for our benefit, concluding with, "She says Señor Fortunato has let the dogs loose behind the wall."

I hadn't seen any dogs, which meant they probably weren't pets so much as guard dogs. If they were guard dogs, I was glad they were loose. I kept remembering the purposeful hunch to Dwight's shoulders as he and Bobbi Kay slogged up that slope toward my car. I didn't think a little housebreaking or wall climbing would be beyond them. Quite frankly, a little murder wouldn't be beyond them either, but I couldn't come up with a motive for them to have killed Ernie. He was their meal ticket. Why do him in? Unless it had something to do with the house.

Bela stuck his nose in my ear and rumbled. He wanted to go for a walk. I rumpled his ears and told him in a minute. He subsided with a sigh. Schnitz was asleep on the back of the couch. He didn't care.

"Tomorrow's Sunday," said Lindsay when she'd hung up after a lengthy series of can-you-believe-its and really-they're-impossibles with both Felicia and Margaret. She glared at her husband. "We can't stay here forever, Bruce."

He grumped at her from where he was slumped on the couch. "I know."

"Have we accomplished anything at all?" she asked me snappishly. This latest phone call seemed to have been the straw on Lindsay's camel.

"We know a number of things we didn't know before," I said in my mildest tone. "Not least of which is this strange business of who owns Ernie's house. Perhaps Vera thought if Ernie were dead, the 'congregation' could sell the house and split the money. Assuming five members of the congregation, that would mean about twenty thou for her and Dwight. A not inconsiderable sum. They could buy a new van and a year's supply of curlers and chewing tobacco."

They stared at me in disbelief.

"That is," I continued, "if they could get Grandma and Grandpa Quivada to go along, which they probably would, so long as Ernie's grandparents didn't suspect the Bobbisons of killing him.

"Or there's the couple that works for Xavier Fortunato, Ricardo and Lourdes. If they were in the church praying for help for their unfortunate son, and Ernie interrupted them or even, with his usual lack of tact, forbade them, maybe one of them slashed him. Ricardo might carry a sharp knife as a tool.

"Or we still have the entire shopping center full of merchants to interrogate. . . ."

"Lord," said Bruce. "And you do this for fun?"

I furrowed my brow, thinking about it. Did I? I suppose I did. Do. Which was no reason they should.

"If you guys want to go back to Washington, you can tell your mother I'm going on with it. I'm sure she won't hold it against you that you have to get on with your lives."

"Maybe a couple more days," said Bruce plaintively. "We can talk to the shopping center people tomorrow."

"Only the ones that are open on Sunday," I told him. "Some of them won't be."

Lindsay flounced, then apologized for flouncing, confessing

frustration, which we all shared. She went off to wash her hair and finish a novel she'd brought with her. Bruce settled down before the TV to watch an old Robert Redford spy movie, something about condors. I heeded Bela's needs and took both him and Schnitz for a moonlight walk, after which we sat in the portal until the mosquitoes drove us in. In our room Bela turned around and around on his blanket, unable to get himself settled. Both the animals were schizoid. Schnitz kept raising his head and swiveling his ears, as though he heard something.

I found myself being thankful Vera and Grandma didn't know where we were!

As it turned out, the Bobbisons and Quivadas hadn't needed to know where we were so long as they knew where Margaret's paintings supposedly were. During the night there was a highly suspicious fire at Fortunato's garage. Our peripatetic reporter, Felicia, told us about it at dawn, or nearly then. An hour or so later, when we'd dazedly got ourselves together, we drove over to take her and her mother out for breakfast.

"How many paintings?" I demanded of Margaret the moment she got into the car.

"Only two," she said. Her voice was tight, betraying strain. "Neither of them were finished. Xavier's been hanging the finished ones in the house, and Ricardo took four new ones in yesterday. But all my paints were burned. All my canvases. I don't have money enough to—"

"There are more paints at the market," I said sternly. "Bruce will lend you enough to restock. If he won't, I will. Was Xavier insured?"

Margaret gave me a small, hurt look, evidently at my tone, which brooked no self-pity. Felicia, on the other hand, laughed out loud.

"Mr. Fortunato says he's insured. And he says this time he'll build a garage big enough to put a car in."

"I'm glad you reported the arson threats to the deputies yesterday," Lindsay said.

"It won't do any good," said Margaret. "Dwight and Vera will swear they were together, somewhere else, and Grandma will probably swear she was with them. Bearing false witness doesn't mean a thing when you're fighting Satan." It was the first time I'd heard any bitterness in her voice. "I knew we shouldn't have gone there. I knew there would be trouble."

"What trouble?" I said with determined cheeriness. "Xavier had a garage that was too small to be any good to him; now he'll build one big enough. You're still able to paint, and you're still having your own show. Nobody was hurt. The only people in trouble are the people who did this!"

She looked away from me. I knew she thought it was her fault somehow, and this troubled me. Why her fault? She should have been angry, seething, but she wasn't.

From Xavier's place, the closest restaurant was the one at the Pojoaque Pueblo, where we ordered breakfast without real interest, paid too little attention to the quite acceptable food, and lingered too long over coffee, still trying to assuage Margaret's feelings of guilt and distress. Lindsay and Felicia were making most of the effort.

"This show is important to you," Lindsay said. "It's important to Felicia. If you're going to make a living, if Felicia's going to go on with her education, you need to use your talents, and the show will help you do that! Don't you for one moment take on any guilt because of something those people did. You are not responsible for them."

"Ernie would say none of this would have happened if I'd done my duty. Ernie would say I am my brother's keeper."

Felicia threw up her hands in frustration. "Come off it, Mom. Listen to Aunt Lindsay!"

"It's just . . . everything I do . . . and Ernie was always so—"

"You don't need to tell us what he was like, Margaret," Bruce broke in. "Believe me, we all know what he was like. What we are saying is that Ernie was simply unreasonably wrong about a lot of things. He always had been! I can't figure why you married him in the first place!"

Margaret flushed, turning to her daughter.

Felicia herself turned slightly pink, though she tried to appear blase. "Mom was pregnant with me. Daddy was older, and he sort of seduced her."

"Ernie?" squeaked Bruce, incredulous, his mouth gaping. "Ernie?"

"I was only seventeen," said Margaret. "I got . . . I got sort of trapped. Of course, Ernie said it was God's will that I got pregnant. It was God's way of telling me I was supposed to marry him."

"I see," said Bruce, shutting his mouth.

Felicia said, "Mom told me about it when I moved out, because she wanted me to be careful, not to get caught. Hector calls it the nature trap. He says nature keeps pushing you, but your family traps you too. They don't tell you how not to, and that's the nurture trap. He says between the nature trap and the nurture trap, most of us get caught. Both his sisters did."

"But not you," said Bruce carefully.

"Not yet," she said with cheerful insouciance. "Hector says it's smarter to wait. He's into being smart."

"How interesting," said Lindsay. "Boys rarely said that in my day."

"Well, you know," Felicia replied. "In your day they didn't have AIDS and all that. And a few years back, it wasn't so hard to get by as it is now. Hector says when times are hard, you've got to be really smart about how you live, or else you don't live."

I remarked, "Hector says that? What is he, seventeen going on seventy?"

"I think he's quoting his grandfather a lot. He really likes his grandfather. That's his dad's dad."

"Why does he live in the group home?" I asked.

"His father died and his mother went kind of crazy. And then his sisters got pregnant, one right after the other. Alicia got married and Julia didn't, but they both moved out. Hector says a lot of Hispanics, they think it's macho to get a woman pregnant. The guy that got his sister Julia pregnant is into that stuff. I got this one pregnant, I got that one pregnant, like any jackrabbit can't do that! Anyhow, when his sisters moved out, Hector's mother got kind of focused on him, like he was the only one left, and it got to be too much. It was kind of like he was supposed to take his dad's place, and he says it felt like he was smothering."

"I can imagine," said Lindsay.

"So the school counselor referred him, and he ended up at Los Niños. He would have moved in with his granddad, except he has this tiny little house, about big enough for a dog house. He works and pays his way like I do, partly at least, and he gives his mom money too, and she's getting help and getting better. She's got a job, even. Without him there, she's learning to do other things again."

"Hector is a good boy," said Margaret. "You can see it in his face."

"He really is," agreed Felicia. "If we both don't change a lot, I might end up married to Hector."

"People do change a lot in their late teens and early twenties," said Bruce, sounding deadly avuncular.

Felicia regarded him with fond forbearance. "That's what Hector says."

"Hector sounds like a goddam paragon," said Bruce after we had dropped Margaret and Felicia back at Fortunato's. "He must be gay."

"He couldn't just be mature and thoughtful beyond his years?" I asked innocently. "He couldn't really care for Felicia and be concerned for her welfare?"

"Damned unlikely," snorted Bruce. "More likely he doesn't take the whole thing seriously. I don't."

"Actually, hearing about him reminds me of you," said Lindsay, her lips quirking a little. "At that age."

"You didn't know me at that age!" he spluttered.

"I know a lot about you. You were full of energy. Your mother says it was sometimes 'misdirected,' but she also says you were never intentionally cruel or hateful. I know you and Jason probably want to remember yourselves as Don Juans, but I remember you as more like Hector."

I grinned at Bruce's obvious embarrassment. We'd shared the late sixties and early seventies, a turbulent time when sexual responsibility and sexual indulgence had changed places, the one to be kept secret, the other to be trumpeted. Both of us had been raised to consider responsibility first. After rooming together for a while, we knew this about one another and we each developed a way to deal with it. My way was to smile enigmatically and let my peer group think what it liked. Bruce's way was to stir things up, inventing stories of prowess and mayhem, playing at being one of the boys.

He wasn't alone. Lots of the boys played at being one of the boys. You either strutted like a cock or got pecked like a chicken, or so one of the more homely phrases went. Hector wasn't as unusual as Bruce made him out to be. He could well be sincere in his affection for Felicia, and if Ernie had come all over heavy father with her, Hector might have had grounds for serious objection. Though with certain mental reservations, I added him to my suspect list.

Four

WE SPENT the rest of Sunday morning talking to whomever we could find in the shopping center. Lindsay was better at it than Bruce. He seemed determined to announce that Ernie had been his brother, which effectively shut off all further communication. Lindsay was willing to say she was working for Ernie's invalid mother, which allowed the informant to say what he or she would, expecting Lindsay to filter out the more scurrilous comments. Of which, not surprisingly, both she and I heard more than a few.

The most usual comment was something on the order of, "I'd have killed that holier-than-thou bastard myself if I'd thought I could get away with it." Several of the merchants went into laborious detail about Ernie's effect on business, none of it beneficial.

"They didn't like him," Lindsay said impatiently as we sat with Bruce in the little coffee and doughnut shop beside the police station. "But we already *knew* that."

"One guy told me if God talked through people like Ernie, He wasn't the kind of God people should pay attention to," said Bruce. "It reminded me of that Groucho Marx line, that he wouldn't belong to a club that would have someone like him for a member."

I stretched, feeling a certain frustration, partly at our lack of progress but partly at their attitude toward the process. What did they expect? Instant revelation?

I said, "There was a good deal of animosity, true, but I didn't pick up on any hostility of the wipe-the-guy-out variety. Did you?"

They shook their heads. They hadn't. Of course, a number of the small shops weren't open and we hadn't spoken to anyone at the pueblo tourist office yet. I'd been putting that particular interview off. I hadn't been uncomfortable speaking with the mostly Hispanic merchant types. They had reason for anger, but they'd taken united action by serving Ernie with a court order to stay out of their shops. The pueblo people, on the other hand, had tried to break their lease and couldn't, which might have led to an explosive sort of fury. If so, better Bruce and Lindsay not be involved.

"Would you two like to wait here while I ask one more set of questions?" I asked them.

They nodded, almost in unison, looking depressed. They wanted to forget the whole business and go home. Neither of them shared my sense of . . . curiosity, I suppose it is. Whatever it is that keeps the small muddy dog digging madly in the muck when all the big dogs have given it up as a bad job and gone home to bask by the fire.

The pueblo tourist office was small, featuring a display of rather utilitarian-looking micaceous pottery; a large rack of booklets and brochures; and a pleasant-looking young woman addressing envelopes behind a desk.

"May I help you?" she asked.

I introduced myself, gave her my card, the plain one with just my name, address, and phone number on it, and told her I was working for Ernie Quivadas' mother. Her eyes narrowed.

"I know Ernie was a strange and difficult man," I said, trying to sound relaxed about it. "His mother, however, is a lovely woman, generous and kind. I've known her for over twenty years. She's grieving over him, so we're trying to find out what happened, just to put her mind at rest."

Her eyes became a bit softer as she said, "It is hard for a mother to hear her child was not a good person."

I'd heard a lot of epithets that morning, but no other judgement so simple or uncompromising. I nodded, agreeing with her. "I think he really tried to be. It's just . . . he had it all wrong."

"That may be so." She gave me a level, weighing look. "Most

of us are Catholics. We have our old religion, too, but we are also Catholics since, oh, a long time."

"Since the Spanish came," I said. "I know."

"It makes us angry to hear our religion insulted. Also, many of us are related to people outside the pueblo. We have Hispanic relatives."

I said I knew that, too.

"My sister's husband's aunt is Lourdes Lalumia," she said.

"Who works for Señor Fortunato."

"Lourdes and Ricardo came to pray at the picture of the Mother. There at the church."

"What happened?" I asked.

"It was on Sunday," she said. "They thought no one would be there in the afternoon. But he was there."

"Ernie?"

"Yes. They were praying for their son. He came in. He insulted them. He yelled at them. He called them idolators, bowing before mere paint."

"He really called them idolators?"

"Yes. He called them other names as well. He said it was a sin to worship this idol. And Ricardo asked why it was in a church, then. And he, the man, told them to go." She took a deep breath, regarding me with level brown eyes. "He was not a good man. Ricardo and Lourdes grieve for their son. They are good people, sincere in their religion."

"So they went away."

"They started to go, but other people came in, a woman, a man, and these people also used loud voices, saying bad things."

I thought about this. "A very old man and woman?"

"No. A very fat woman, with"—she made a hair-rolling motion—"And a little man with a nose like a coyote. Lourdes told her nephew, my sister's husband, and my sister told me."

"Ah."

"You know the people who came in?"

"I know who they are, yes. Did Ricardo and Lourdes leave then?"

"Lourdes was frightened, so she ran out, then Ricardo went. And later, Ricardo said it was God Himself who struck the man down, for saying such evil things, for did not God himself command us not to tell lies about others!"

"Ricardo is religious?"

"Since the doctors said they could do nothing for his son. So Ricardo says now it is in God's hands." She smiled, hiding her mouth with one hand. "Maybe, when he was younger, he was not so religious."

"Ricardo and his wife came back later, didn't they? We saw there were candles in the church."

"Not just Lourdes and Ricardo. I went, too, and my mother, and some others. It was after the man was dead. Later, others wanted to see it, but the painting was gone."

"I took the painting because I thought it might come to harm there, in that wind and dirt. I gave it back to Ernie's wife. She painted it, you know."

"Yes, we know that. Ricardo told us, and he said God guided her hands."

I rubbed my chin, thinking. She'd placed Vera and Dwight at the church on Sunday afternoon. As, no doubt, Ricardo would have done if I'd asked him. I would ask him if he'd seen anyone else thereabouts. Of course, anyone could have parked in the shopping center on a Sunday without being noticed. There were a good many cars besides mine around the coffee shop, around the police station, around the grocery store. Someone walking toward or away from the church might have been noticed, but probably not someone who'd merely parked nearby.

"He was bad to so many people," she said in a troubled voice. "He hated people."

I said yes, it was true. Bruce had explained Ernie's mania in pop-psych terms, lack of self-esteem because he had no father of his own, Ernie feeling left out, Ernie feeling like a second fiddle, feelings which Grandma and Grandpa had no doubt exploited. So, Bruce had postulated, if Ernie couldn't be important on his own, he'd take on the mantle of God.

Unfortunately, lack of charisma was lack of charisma, a fact the mantle of God hadn't hidden.

"Did he ever come in here?" I asked.

"One time last summer," she said. "He asked me to come to

his church. I told him I had my own church. He prayed, like he was telling God what to do. I went out back and shut the door. Later, the tenants committee got the restraining order for the whole plaza, everything except the parking lot."

"Except for the parking lot?"

"Yes. So he prayed in the parking lot, standing in the middle of where people drive, and one person drove right at him, and he jumped just in time. After that, he didn't pray there anymore."

"One person drove at him?"

She shrugged. "They said it was a white man."

"They?"

"The people who saw it. The people at the hardware store."

I made a mental note.

"What will happen to the building now?" I wondered out loud, looking out the window at the rickety little church, sitting forlornly upon the pale desert soil amid the chamisa.

"They're going to tear it down," she whispered, as though telling me a secret. "There has been a meeting already to decide. Evil has happened there. It is not worth cleansing, so we will tear it down and burn it."

A spark went off in my head. "He had a lease with the pueblo. Do you know, was it in his name?"

She nodded her head at me. "That is why they can tear it down. It was with him, his name, no one else."

"Not in the name of the church."

She shook her head. "My father is on the council of the pueblo. They would not make a lease except with him. It is the same with all the tenants. Because we wish to work with people we know, people who are friendly and respectful. So, if one of our friends dies, someone else cannot take his place without our approval."

"When will they tear the building down?"

"When the police are finished with it. Soon."

I thanked her and turned to go. She stopped me.

"Maybe the people from Oklahoma killed him."

I turned in amazement. "What people from Oklahoma?"

"They came in a pickup. It had Oklahoma plates on it."

"You noticed the license plates?"

She shrugged expressively, becoming in that instant the quintessence of all teenaged kids who were assigned some tiresome but necessary duty.

"Sometimes there is no work to do, no visitors come, but someone must be here just in case." She shrugged again. "It gets boring. Sometimes I read. Sometimes I paint the pots my mother makes. Sometimes I just look at the people. So I saw this truck back in, and it had an Oklahoma plate. Two fat big men . . ." She made a belly stroke motion with both hands, way out, fat men. "They asked me where he was."

"What did you tell them?"

"I said at the church sometimes. They said he wasn't there. They asked where he lived, and I said I didn't know."

"When? When was this?"

She frowned thoughtfully, counting up. "Two weeks?" she said doubtfully. "It was before Sunday, because it was in the morning. If it had been Sunday, they would have found him at the church. So it was before Sunday."

"So it was at least a week ago yesterday, Saturday?" I pursued.

"Not Saturday," she said, getting into the spirit of the thing. "Not Friday either. I don't work on those days."

I grinned at her. "So it was at least a week ago last Thursday?"

She said yes, that would be about right. Wednesday, maybe, or Thursday. I thanked her, bought some booklets, admired the display of pots, and departed.

Bruce and Lindsay were standing outside the coffee shop in the shade of a totally unnecessary buttress. The building was obviously built of stucco over concrete block and it needed a buttress like I need an additional nostril. The adobe churches this building was patterned on, now, *they* needed buttresses. All those tons and tons of mud, stacked up into great six-foot-thick, thirty-foot-high walls, sometimes getting heavier with rain, only kept from slumping by the equal mass of mud in the buttress. But concrete block or not, buttresses were "Santa Fe Style," and buttresses we had.

I was considering architecture as I approached, but Bruce derailed me:

"If we can get reservations, we're going home tomorrow."

Lindsay looked at her feet, her cheeks an embarrassed red.

It took me a moment to switch gears. "For the love of God, Lindsay," I chided her. "That's all right. You're not running out on me."

"I thought . . . after your coming all this way . . ."

"I come this way every now and then. I like it down here. It's interesting. And without you two stumbling around, feeling diffident, I'll be able to concentrate better on what I'm doing."

"Thanks a lot," said Bruce.

"Well, you are diffident. And uncomfortable. It shows."

"You're right, we do," said Lindsay. "I feel like a real . . . I don't know. Even doing it for Mother Norman, I just don't like it."

I gave her a hug and suggested we go back to the ranch and see what kind of flight reservations they could get. I didn't mention the "white man" who'd almost run Ernie down with his car. I didn't mention the two fat men from Oklahoma. They were long shots, at best; better followed up by me alone, without distractions.

Lindsay sighed with relief. "Thank you, Jason. You really are a dear. I want to check with Margaret or Felicia to see if anything else terrible has happened, and I do hope not, because I'd like to have one nice relaxed afternoon at the ranch before we leave!"

Lindsay called Felicia, who reported that nothing else horrible had happened. Ricardo and his son and a crew of several friends or relatives were knocking down what was left of the adobe garage. Margaret had gone to buy painting supplies and was now preparing canvasses, fiercely determined to reconstruct the two works that had perished in the fire while she still remembered them. Felicia herself was watching a favorite movie on TV and enjoying the fact—that Bobbi Kay wasn't there to switch channels or play her radio at top volume. I suggested that Lindsay invite Margaret and Felicia to join us for dinner whenever Margaret finished her work, and we agreed to call back around five o'clock.

As soon as Lindsay hung up, Bruce got on the phone, eventually putting together a flight plan that would get them back to Washington if they left at four in the morning, went only a few hundred miles out of the way, and added two extra stops. I considered it a measure of their frustration and discomfort that they both agreed to this without a second thought.

Then, while Bruce was conferring with Lindsay about packing and scheduling and rental cars, I called Grace and told her I'd been abandoned.

"I'd really love to come down," she cried over the phone. "But I can't. I'm on double shifts!"

I grumped and snarled unattractively. She said a few sweet things, patting my bruised ego, then asked whether we'd made any progress. I told her little enough so far, giving her as many details as I could.

Long silence. "What does Margaret look like?" she asked in a studied casual voice.

"She's about your age," I said. "Taller. Brown hair. She's no centerfold."

"No, but," she said. "Watch it, Jason. Be careful."

"Of what?" I cried. "You sound like Mark!"

"I don't like the sound of those people," she said soberly. "Those Bobbisons. I don't like the sound of these mysterious men from Oklahoma. The whole thing is creepy."

"What makes it creepy?" I demanded. "You investigate murders all the time."

"Not murders in churches, I don't. Not murders in front of mysterious paintings. . . ."

"What was mysterious about it?"

"The fact that his wife painted it, that strangers were praying in front of it, Jason. For heaven's sake, you know it's creepy!"

I sighed, much put upon. "I probably made it sound more . . . ah, exotic than it actually is."

"There was something of tom-toms in the background and feathered warriors just over the ridge," she said.

"There's none of that. And if anybody's feathered, it's for a dance, not a war party."

"I've been down there with you," she said. "I know what Santa Fe is like. It's all touristy on the surface, glitz and glamour, but underneath it's like digging down to find prehistoric bones. And I still say, be careful."

When Bruce came out, I asked him if he considered Ernie's murder creepy. He said he didn't, but Lindsay did. Which is one reason she wanted to go home.

"Why creepy?" I demanded of her, when she emerged from the bedroom.

She thought about it. "Well, creepy isn't exactly the word. But you've got to admit it's not your garden-variety mugging. The place is . . . what it is. The culture, the cast of characters. I told Bruce last night, I feel like a little boat on top of the water. There are all these things going on down under, and all we can see are the ripples. Nessie may be down there, for all I know."

So both she and Grace thought there was something going on beneath the surface. And possibly they were right.

I said, "It may turn out, however, that Ernie was slashed because he got involved with some man's wife or girlfriend down in Oklahoma. Attempted a conversion, or made a pass . . ."

"You make it sound like football!" Bruce guffawed.

". . . or had an affair," I concluded. "Maybe her husband happened to be an Anglo ex–Green Beret."

Lindsay said soberly, "I'd have thought that unlikely until Felicia's revelation over breakfast this morning."

"I still consider it unlikely," I said. "What I'm trying to get at: Though the setting is rather purposefully exotic, the murder may have been nothing more than garden-variety violence motivated by plain old garden-variety lust or anger."

Lindsay patted me on the cheek, said I was probably right, and what was I going to do next? I was going to get some information from Margaret, I replied, such as where had they lived in Oklahoma.

"You're going to follow up on that?"

"I'm going to follow up on everything."

Famous last words.

That night we went to El Nido, near Tesuque, because Felicia said she hadn't had a real steak since her birthday two years ago. Felicia was looking happier than she had earlier, more relaxed, as though the quiet and space at Fortunato's had allowed her to blossom. Margaret, on the other hand, was quiet, remote, almost indifferent, wearing a closed and unrevealing face. Though I had thought her strangely beautiful the first time I'd met her, tonight she was plain. No spark. No life. Not ugly, just ordinary.

I told her I needed addresses for home and church in Oklahoma, and she gave me three separate home addresses.

"We'd run out of money, and we got evicted a couple of times before I managed to find a steady job," she said. "We only lived at those first two addresses a few months."

"Where was Ernie's church?"

"There wasn't any one church. In Oklahoma, Ernie mostly filled in for pastors who were on vacation."

"Was that true in Texas, too?"

She nodded. "Partly. He had a church for a little while in Texas, that's why we went there, but it voted to merge with another congregation, and they already had a pastor."

The words just slipped out, before I thought. "It seems impossible to me! How have you managed?"

She looked me solidly in the eye, thought a minute, as though deciding whether to tell me it was none of my business. I started to apologize, and she shook her head at me.

"It's all right," she said matter-of-factly. "There's no secret about it. Until we moved to Texas, Ernie had a full-time job, and once Felicia was old enough to go to preschool, so did I. Then, ten years ago, when Felicia was about six, Ernie got the first annuity his father left him, and that's when he decided he could quit working full-time and move to Texas to take the church there. He heard about it through the Bible college he'd been attending. We were there five years, then when he got another annuity, we moved to Oklahoma. Each time we made the money stretch for at least five years. I could have made it last longer, but Ernie kept using it for stuff like Bible study leaflets and ads in the newspaper. Of course, he always had at least a part-time job. He drove ambulances and delivery trucks, and I worked half-time or better."

"What did you do?"

"When I was growing up, my dad ran a greenhouse and I helped him. I had typing in high school. I've usually been able to find part-time work in an office or a nursery, or I can be a receptionist or sell movie tickets. Stuff like that. And even in Texas, before my paintings were any good, I sold a few little ones. And I have a job here. I didn't work last week, but I will this week, if they need me. . . ."

Her voice ran off into thoughtful silence. After a pause, she began again.

"Ernie wasn't happy with things in Oklahoma. He had a car accident that upset him, and when he got his last annuity, he decided to move here. He came up to look around, and he bought that house while he was here. I didn't even see it before he bought it, and it took all the annuity. We could still have made out all right. If you don't care much about clothes or furniture or things, it doesn't cost all that much to live."

It came out without emotion. Like a knife blade, level and flat, yet razor sharp. If one doesn't care . . . If things don't matter . . . Why then, it isn't hard to live. If one can call that living. What she meant was, it wasn't hard to survive, if one didn't care how. Or perhaps if one had given up caring how.

"We could have managed," she repeated, nodding to herself. "We really could. If it just hadn't been for the Bobbisons."

"It must have cost quite a bit to feed that family," I said.

"It wasn't just feeding them," she went on. "After they came, it took two thirds of what I earned to keep Felicia in Los Niños."

"You paid for that?"

Margaret's lips narrowed, her eyes grew hard. "She couldn't stay in the house with that family. Her grades were going down. Her teacher said she was falling asleep in class. She was getting . . . surly. And Los Niños has to get money from somewhere. When the courts send children there, the county pays. But if it's someone like Felicia . . . someone has to pay something."

I breathed deeply, exorcising the despair I felt on her behalf. That was past, I assured myself. Over. Things would be better for her now.

"Why did you want to know where we lived in Oklahoma?" she asked.

I told her about the two men. She seemed puzzled. "I can't imagine who would be looking for Ernie from Oklahoma," she said. "We hardly knew . . ." Her voice faded.

She'd thought of someone. I could see her considering it.

"We hardly knew anyone there," she said firmly. "Except the people I worked for and the people Ernie worked for."

She wasn't going to tell me willingly, and this wasn't the place to get into an interrogation.

I said, "None of this may have any bearing, but it helps me understand. Did you know about Ernie almost being run down at the shopping center?"

"Ernie told me about it," she said dispiritedly. "He knew who it was. William Reiserling. His daughter, Helen, is my friend. Was."

"Was?"

"Her wedding . . . Ernie . . ." She shook her head, tears in the corners of her eyes.

"Oh, right. I heard about Ernie praying out loud during the ceremony. What was Mr. Reiserling doing at the pueblo shopping center?"

"They live in the hills near there, a big, elegant house. When I got to know Helen, I didn't know she was rich. She was working in the gallery that bought some of my paintings. She's a . . . she's a lovely person. She's . . . helpful. It was nice having a friend. . . ."

She seemed further depressed by this memory, so I quit pushing her for information, put my mental notebook away, and concentrated on distracting her, though without much success. Later, when Lindsay and Margaret and Bruce took themselves off to the rest rooms, I asked Felicia if she thought her mother was all right.

Felicia gave me a look, one that said a great deal about why she thought I was asking. "She will be. She gets down sometimes, for a day or two. That business about the garage fire really upset her. When it happened, she just went on and on about not being what Dad wanted. She said if she'd just been able to make herself into what Dad wanted, none of it would have happened."

"None of what?"

"The Bobbisons. If she'd been what Dad wanted, he wouldn't have brought in the Bobbisons."

"What need did your father have that the Bobbisons fulfilled?" I spluttered.

Felicia made a face. "They took up Mom's time. Feeding them. Doing their laundry."

"And that's what he wanted your mother to do?"

She shrugged. "It sounds bad when you put it into words, but that was about it. It wasn't what he wanted from them so much as that he wanted Mom to do what he wanted her to do, and the rest of the time he didn't want to have to think about her at all."

I suppose I looked blank, because she got two deep vertical creases between her eyebrows as she tried to explain.

"Dad didn't think about other people, you know? He wanted them to do what he wanted, be what he wanted, but he didn't think about what *they* wanted. Not ever. I used to try to get him to see my point of view, you know? Hopeless. I was his daughter, and his daughter fit into this little box in his head, and that was all there was to it. It's like when Mom was taking art lessons in Oklahoma. This really nice woman, Joy Shepherd, was teaching her, free, it didn't cost anything, but Dad had a fit because it didn't fit in with what Mom was supposed to do. I think that's one reason we moved, just to get Mom away from Joy. Maybe he thought if he got her away from Joy, she'd stop painting, but she didn't. So then, I guess he thought if the Bobbisons were there, she'd be so busy looking after them, she couldn't do anything else, and he wouldn't need to think about her."

"Jealousy?" I asked, still trying to understand what she was saying.

"Like, you mean, other men?" Felicia shook her head violently. "No way. No, it was more like it actually hurt him to try and see Mom as a person. That's what Hector and I figured out. Dad never thought of Mom as a separate person. She was just wife, like I was just daughter. And he felt—it was all feelings with Dad, not anything thought out—he felt it was dangerous for her to have any separate life at all." She rubbed her forehead, thinking. "Sinful maybe? Hector said that, when we talked about it. . . ."

She thought a moment more. "I know," she said suddenly. "There's this book written by this Egyptian. Mafouz? Is that it? He won a Nobel prize for literature, our social studies teacher said. Anyhow, he wrote about this man in Cairo, and he has a wife, and she lives in a three-story house and she's not allowed to go out. She has chickens up on the roof, and she has a kitchen down in the courtyard, and she has a balcony with screens all around so nobody can see in, and that's where she's supposed to be. See?"

I said I saw.

"So, her husband goes away on a business trip, and her kids encourage her to go to the . . . mosque, is that it? She's always wanted to see this mosque, always wanted to go there and pray. So she does, and she gets hurt in traffic, and so when her husband comes home, he finds out she went, and as soon as she's able to move, he sends her home to her mother, away from her children, see. He punishes her. Not for doing anything evil, it wasn't evil to go to the mosque, but for doing something that made him think about her. She was part of that house, and the house was just there. Like . . . when the roof leaks, you get really annoyed, because you have to think about it. You want your house just to be there. And I thought, that's like Dad wanting Mom just to be there like the house was, without any thoughts or feelings of its own. You see?"

I saw. I didn't like what I saw. And for the first time, reluctantly, I understood what Lindsay and Grace seemingly felt. There was something definitely creepy about the whole thing.

Mr. William R. Reiserling had an office a block and a half from the Santa Fe Plaza, in a low, rambling complex centered on a paved court landscaped with low evergreens. ATTORNEY AT LAW, his door said. I straightened my tie and tried to look Monday-ish. It was a little late in the morning to hope to find him available, but I'd been wakened at 2 A.M. by the Normans' flurry of departure: Bruce had some instructions for me that wouldn't wait until morning. I hadn't gotten back to sleep until about five. Then there'd been breakfast for self and animals, a run down in the river valley for self and animals, a long shower with no one else needing hot water to worry about. And now, at almost eleven, William R. Reiserling.

I caught him in his shirtsleeves, bald head shining, as he leaned on the desk in the outer office talking to his gray-haired secretary. I told him who I was and why I was there.

"Is his family wanting vengeance?" he asked me. "Is that why they've hired an investigator?"

"I'm not a licensed investigator," I said mildly. "I'm a friend of Ernie's mother. I have no official standing whatsoever, I'm just trying to find out what happened, and your name came up as a man with a legitimate grievance."

He beckoned me to follow him into his office, a rather fusty office, one that had accumulated comfortably over the years rather than being designed. He lowered himself into his worn leather chair, time-sculpted into a reverse image of his sizable butt, a valley beneath each thigh. He made a tent of his fingers and stared at me over it, taking a few moments to sort out his thoughts before saying:

"My wife, Michelle, would very much have liked to kill that man. She spent six months and I don't know how many thousand dollars—the bills aren't all in yet—planning that wedding. Helen is our only child. Twenty-six years old. Michelle thought she never would get married. Never seemed that interested, didn't want a wedding at all but finally agreed, and here it was, finally, Mother's big day. . . ." He shook his head, as though unable to find words.

"I understand Ernie prayed."

"During the vows. Three of the ushers removed him. The minister called for a moment of silence, then he started over. I paid him extra for sang froid."

"And then you tried to run Ernie down."

He looked thoughtful. "I'm not sure," he said at last. "I like to think if he hadn't jumped, I'd have swerved. There was plenty of room to swerve. I'd never had a chance to cuss him out, you see. . . ."

"And you hadn't thought it out."

"I really hadn't. He was just there, and I felt this flash of pure . . . energy."

"It's called homicidal mania," I said drily. "Or vehicular homicide. But I know how you feel. I can recall the same impulse where Ernie was concerned."

"It's how I felt. When I read about his being killed, I actually felt sorry for Margaret. Helen cares a lot for Margaret."

"It might help if Helen called Margaret and told her that," I said. "Margaret's feeling . . ." I stopped, unable to go on. How was Margaret feeling? "Depressed," I finished lamely.

"The Hawaiian honeymoon's still got a week to run," he said. "I'm sure Helen will call her when she gets back. Meantime, I've got an early afternoon appointment, so I have to lunch early today. Why don't you come along?"

Surprising myself, I said yes, I'd be glad to, and we went down the street to the Palace, arriving just as the doors opened and before the crowds descended. It turned out he knew Mike Wilson and knew of Cecily Stephens and Habitación, so my bona fides were established.

"Who do you think killed him?" he asked.

"There were some men from Oklahoma looking for him."

"He came from there?"

"He was there, before he came to Santa Fe. None of the usual kinds of things come to mind where Ernie's concerned. He wasn't a womanizer, not that I know of. He wasn't a gambler. He didn't take drugs."

"No, and if he knew somebody who did, he'd be on 'em like a rattler on a mouse," Reiserling said emphatically, surprising me considerably. "The man was rabid about sin. If he caught a sinner, he'd never let him go. He'd follow the sinner around like a two-wheel trailer, right on his bumpers. And he'd pray right out loud, where anybody could hear him. Oh, dear God, smite down these men runnin' whores, goin' to prostitutes, bein' perverts, writin' porn. Whatever."

I hadn't thought of that. What might one call it? Spiritual blackmail?

"You're offering this as a possible motive for the men from Oklahoma? But he'd been here for almost three years. Why would they come looking for him after all that time."

He thought about this. "Guys get sent to jail. They blame some other guy for sending them to jail. Sometimes they can't follow up on a grievance right away. Sometimes they save it up."

He said it comfortably, just reciting a truth. And I, if anyone, knew how grievances could be saved up! For generations!

"It's an idea," I admitted. "If there had been anything like that, I'd have thought Margaret would have mentioned it, but it's possible she didn't know. I've got the addresses where she and Ernie lived in a town near Tulsa, a suburb, maybe? I thought I might fly over there, spend a day or two."

"Tulsa. Well, now. I've got an associate down there," he said. "My son, in fact. From my first marriage. Why don't you let me see what I can find out."

I leaned back, considering the offer.

He shook his head, grinning at me. "Look, Jason, if I help you find out who did it, you'll know I didn't. Doesn't do a lawyer any good to get suspected of killing somebody. Simple. Besides, Willy Junior is on the police commission. He's got what you might call an in."

"All entirely too fortuitous," I commented.

"Yeah, well, sometimes God quits teasing and settles down to work," he said. "My daddy used to say that."

"Another lawyer?"

"Ended up a Superior Court judge."

Who was I to argue with a Superior Court judge? Our lunches arrived and we talked of other things: the art scene (he owned part interest in the gallery where Helen worked), the opera (Michelle was on a committee), the separation of society in Santa Fe, and where it touched tangentially (over Indian crafts and ceremonials, at Hispanic festivals, and in Anglo-owned galleries).

"Not that there's anything wrong with that. Some of my best friends are gallery owners," he said with a straight face.

"Ernie stepped on a lot of Hispanic and Indian toes," I told him. "He didn't respect the sincerity of their beliefs any more than he did the solemnity of your daughter's wedding."

"You may find that's the answer," he said gravely, taking the check from our waitress and waving away my offer to either pay it or split it. "Quite frankly, I hope Willy Junior comes up with something in Oklahoma. I'd rather see someone there answer for it than someone here. Anyone here."

I walked him back to his office, telling him about Bruce's

instructions to me early that morning. Find an attorney to represent Margaret in clearing title to the house. Bruce would pay for it. I mentioned the fact the lease on the church had been in Ernie's name, not in the name of a congregation.

Reiserling said he'd be happy to take care of it, have Margaret call him with the details.

I stopped at the nearest market for some groceries, odds and ends including several pounds of bargain hamburger to give the animals a treat. They liked it fried with a little garlic powder. Reiserling's offer of a contact in Tulsa had been too good to pass up, but it did leave me with a large hole in my plans for the next day or so. I'd planned to hire Mike's caretaker to look after Bela and Schnitz while I flew to Tulsa, but since I wouldn't have to go after all—at least for the time being—I needed something else to occupy my time.

I talked it over with Bela and Schnitz when I got back to Los Vientos.

Bela didn't think Tulsa would come to anything. Probably lots of fat guys there, he said, and no way to know which fat guys had been looking for Ernie.

Schnitz agreed. He thought it would be a good idea to forget the whole thing and go back to Denver, where he had a whole house to prowl, with a big basement to hunt mice in.

I took their comments under advisement while I had a swim in Mike's pool and then lay in the sun for half an hour, considering matters. I still had to talk to Ricardo. When I talked to Ricardo, maybe I could tell Margaret about Reiserling representing her on the house matter, and also I could ask her again about Oklahoma. She might be ready to tell me about it now.

She'd be working in the afternoon. I didn't want to disturb her. I'd call her later. Which gave me time to make up for the sleep Bruce had deprived me of.

I called Señor Fortunato's around four-thirty and was told to come on over. When I arrived outside the gate, I saw several members of a concrete contractor's crew just leaving. Footings for two sides of a new garage had been neatly dug out behind them. Ricardo and another man were loading mud chunks into a truck while Ricardo's son chopped at the last of the charred vigas with a machete, hacking it into manageable pieces. They had not torn down the rear garage wall, which was continuous with the courtyard wall, but they had installed a heavy plank door where the old door from the courtyard had been. From the way they were moving, it looked like the last load of the day, and I decided not to bother Ricardo until he'd finished and had a chance to relax.

Margaret and Felicia were in the courtyard with Xavier, all three of them gilded by the mellow glow of the late afternoon sun. I collapsed in the nearest chair, noting an extra wineglass on a cocktail table next to an open bottle of Pedro Domeq fino sherry. Felicia and Xavier were themselves, but Margaret looked far better than she had the night before. It was almost as though her beauty were a separate creature, one that came and went on its own schedule and for its own reasons. Today it was present.

"Your work must have gone well today," I commented.

Without actually saying anything, she indicated it had through a combination of a smile and a stretch and a nod. She rose, filled the empty glass, and handed it to me.

I sipped, my eyebrows rising involuntarily. Um. "I see footing trenches out there," I said to Xavier, nodding toward the wall. "You're going to make the new one bigger."

Xavier said yes, considerably bigger. "Two cars, at least. And space for the winter tires, as well. And perhaps the wheelbarrow and the lawnmower." He did not seem at all unhappy about this.

"I talked to William Reiserling this morning," I told Margaret and Felicia. "He'd be happy to represent you in clearing title to the house, if it can be done. He needs you to give him the details."

"What details?" asked Felicia as Margaret frowned silently into her glass.

"I imagine he needs to know when it was bought, and from whom. And who has the deed. Things like that."

"I don't know any of that," said Margaret. "Ernie bought it before we moved here. I've never seen any papers on it at all."

"Taxes?" Xavier asked. "Who paid the property taxes?"

"It might be in Ernie's checkbook," she said. "I do have his checkbook. Who would it be made out to?"

"Manager of revenue," I said. "Santa Fe County. Something like that."

"I'll get it, Mom," said Felicia. "I know where it is."

She was back in five minutes, leafing through the checkbook. "Here's one," she said, handing it to me.

The lined check register listed a check for several hundred odd dollars drawn in April of the previous year and made out to the Taxation and Revenue Department.

"You've got the canceled checks?" I asked.

Margaret nodded. "They're in a box with his other checks, years of them."

"Well, dig out this one, and the one for the year before that if there was one. That'll give Will Reiserling a starting point. The sale had to have been recorded, or Ernie would never have received the tax bill.

"I looked through it backwards, but there isn't one for this year," Felicia said in a worried voice. "If you don't pay, they can take it away, can't they?"

Xavier soothed her. "He may have paid in cash. Even if he didn't, they can't take property without notice. There is a considerable redemption time."

"I found out Ricardo saw Ernie on the day Ernie died." I tried to make the words bland and unthreatening. "Out at the church. When Ricardo and Lourdes left, the Bobbisons were there. I need to ask Ricardo or Lourdes if they saw anyone else that afternoon."

"Lourdes would be in the kitchen," said Xavier. "Felicia can show you where."

I set my glass down and went with Felicia, through the living room I had seen before, through a dining room with an old trestle table that would easily seat sixteen, and into a large, shining kitchen full of Mexican tile and polished copper pots. Lourdes was taking a pan of charred chiles from the oven.

"Momento," she said, dumping the chiles into a bag and twisting it shut. "To make the skins come off," she explained.

"Lourdes showed me how," said Felicia. "You really burn the

chiles under the broiler, turning them so they get black all over, then you put them in a bag for about fifteen minutes, and when you take them out, the skins rub right off. Then you take out the insides. But I put my fingers in my mouth." She made a face.

"I tol' you," said Lourdes, waving her finger at the girl. "I said, you wash your hans firs or you burn youself."

I seated myself on the banco that ran along one wall, under the window. "Señora Lalumia, when you and Ricardo were out at the church the day Felicia's father was killed, did you see anyone besides the fat lady and the little man?"

"The Bobbisons," said Felicia. "You told me you saw them, Lourdes."

"Anybody else?" Lourdes asked. "At the church?"

"Around there? Walking nearby?"

She shook her head slowly. "I ask Ricardo, but I don' think so. Jus those people an the little ones."

"Bobbi Kay. And the little boys," offered Felicia.

"Jus the little boys," corrected Lourdes. "Two little boys."

"Do you know what time you were there?"

"Aroun t'ree o'clock," she said.

"You know that for sure?"

"My nephew, he had a birt'day. We had cabrito. I made tamales. All the family was there. Ricardo and me and our boy, we went in the car from the church, an we got there aroun t'ree-t'irty."

"Please ask Ricardo if he saw anyone else," I said, getting up. "Thank you, Señora Lalumia."

We left. On the way, I asked Felicia, "Does the Lalumia son have a name? Every time I hear him mentioned, he's just, the boy, the son."

"His name is Eusequio Manuel. His mother calls him Sequito. It sounds Japanese, doesn't it."

"Does he live here?"

"When he's not in the hospital. Mr. Fortunato says he goes in and out. Lourdes and Ricardo have a kind of separate house inside this house. It has a door between, and it faces out back, toward the arroyo. Ricardo has a little garden out there where he grows vegetables, and there's an apricot tree and an apple tree and some kind of berries."

I stopped just inside the living room door, and she paused beside me.

"You've learned quite a bit about them," I said.

"They're nice. I thought, you know, they'd be mad at me and Mom because of the way Dad was, but they've been really nice. Lourdes is teaching me to cook New Mexican."

"And your mother's feeling better."

"Because two nice things happened. The first thing was, Helen Reiserling called her. Helen somebody else now, I forget her husband's name. Anyhow, she called this morning."

"I thought Helen was still on her honeymoon."

"Well, she is. She called from Hawaii."

My Lord, I thought. It would have been the middle of the night in Hawaii. Or the crack of dawn.

"How did she know where you were staying?"

"She didn't. She just knew Mom painted here. She tried the other number, and it was disconnected, so she called here. I'm glad she did. It made Mom feel better. She felt so bad, you know, about the wedding."

I did indeed know. "You said two nice things happened."

"Mom got another call, from her painting teacher in Oklahoma."

"Her teacher?"

"The woman I told you about, the one who taught her painting. Mom had called her to tell her about the show, but Joy's husband got on the phone. He's a real . . . Well, anyway, Joy couldn't talk then, so this morning she called to tell Mom how happy she was for her."

"She needs to know she has friends," I said firmly. "I thought I might make that point by asking her out to dinner."

Felicia fidgeted. "Tonight? She sort of told Mr. Fortunato she'd have dinner with him."

"Well, then. I'll make it another time. Xavier certainly has a prior claim."

"Maybe they'll invite you to stay," she said. "If I ask them."

She sounded quite worried, as though she might have overstepped her daughtering license.

"You don't need to do that, Felicia. I'll manage."

"Oh, pooh," she said. "We're having Lourdes' Azteca Budim. I helped make the chile strips. You'd be crazy to turn it down."

I would, indeed, have been crazy to turn it down. We had a pleasant, totally unstressful dinner, not in the large dining room but in the kitchen, where Lourdes put everything on the table and then went away to her own family, saying she'd be back to straighten up later.

"Felicia and I will straighten up," said Margaret, firmly. "If we don't know where things go, we will at least wash them."

I helped with the washing up and didn't get home until nine. The animals were hungry. I left Schnitz in the house while Bela and I went for our evening run, walk, stroll. I thought the afternoon's nap might have ruined my night's sleep, but it didn't. I collapsed into bed and didn't even roll over until well after dawn Tuesday morning.

First thing Tuesday, I called the Pueblo Police and told them the Bobbisons had been placed at the church on the afternoon Ernie died. They wanted to know by whom, and I told them. The fact they knew who I was talking about was encouraging. At the very least, they might go find Dwight and Vera and rake them over the coals.

As for me, Reiserling's offer had created a hiatus in the inquiries, so I thought I'd take care of my client's desire to upgrade his office decor. Mark's memo arrived in the morning mail, brought to me by Mike's caretaker, and I spread the contents out on the kitchen table where Bela, Schnitz, and I were having late breakfast. Mark had enclosed the original floor plan as well as the carpet sample, fabric swatches, and paint chips, all of which I regarded with some annoyance. Green carpet. Green turquoise and copper-striped fabric for the drapes. They were not colors that would be improved by proximity with what my client probably thought of us traditional "Indian rugs," in itself a misnomer.

Before the Spanish conquest, Southwestern Indians made garments and blankets from tanned hides and furs, and from woven cotton and woven strips of fur, like rabbit fur. They didn't use "rugs." Once they'd obtained sheep from the Spanish, weavings were done in natural wool colors: black, white, and brown, with various intermediate shades achieved by carding these colors together. When the Spanish imported *bayeta*, "baize," a coarsely woven wool fabric which was often dyed red, the Indian weavers unraveled the cloth and combined the bright threads with the natural wool colors to produce the familiar black, white, brown, and red scheme many people think of as characteristic of "Navajo rugs."

After the American conquest of the area, commercial dyes became available, and there was a period during which so-called "eye dazzler" weavings were done, brilliant geometrics and stripes with strikingly vivid colors. The workmanship was coarse, however, and it became coarser because Eastern merchants were paying by the pound, which made it profitable to leave the wool as greasy and full of weighty grit as possible. The results were too heavy to wear and too stiff to be anything but "rugs."

Eventually, buyers began to discriminate, and over the ensuing decades higher prices were paid to weavers who produced finer and finer fabrics. When I was in Santa Fe during Indian Market Week a few years ago, I saw tapestry-quality "rugs" selling for tens of thousands of dollars. Native jewelry and pottery have changed in much the same way, with greater artistic quality and finer workmanship resulting in ever higher prices. Prices, by the way, that are still far less than the weavers and potters deserve. Even at current prices, too many of them are still making under minimum wage while having to compete with misleadingly labeled machine-made and imported copies.

My client's budget for upgrade was adequate but not generous. It certainly wouldn't buy him the finest quality available. I'd have to avoid the extremes while finding him some authentic pots and weaving of reasonable quality in colors that would work with his existing carpet and drapes. A not unpleasant way to spend a day. I always enjoy spending other people's money!

The Wheelwright Museum in Santa Fe has a shop for Indian crafts. I started there, on the theory that since I'd pay a sizable mark-up no matter what, I preferred the museum to have the advantage of it. I took notes. My client could not afford and would not know what to do with a prehistoric piece. Instead, I'd give him something current, but marvelous. The heavily carved Santa Clara black and red pots have a sculptural quality I knew he'd find appealing. They look "important," which is no doubt why they sell so well. The San Ildefonso matte-black on polished black or red on red ditto are less massive, more subtle. In addition, there are the many dramatic black on white, red and black on white, black on red, all in varying traditional patterns from all the pueblos, all the way west to the Hopi and Zuni towns in Arizona. To say nothing of the pots that are polished like gems, inset with turquoise and coral and decorated with parrot feathers!

I set my mind on a couple of things that would do, then drove into Santa Fe and left the car in the parking garage. Among downtown shops, I've always enjoyed Packards, I suppose because I'd bought things there that I've treasured, either as possessions or as gifts, or perhaps because the salespeople seem well informed without being pushy. I spent two hours browsing through the rug collection before settling on a four by six Burnt Water that cost only about two hundred fifty a square foot. The Burnt Water style, a fairly recent departure, is traditional in pattern but not in color. The colors are, or seem to be, vegetal, soft and organic-looking, but used in profusion so the result rather resembles a flat-weave Kilim. The one I'd picked had the green, turquoise, and copper of my client's drapes, but also ochre, burnt orange, grayed-violet, and coral pink. If he went for pots in the natural orange-red clay, there'd be no need to change the carpet or drapery fabric he already had.

That decided, it was time to think of furniture. Furniture actually dating from the colonial period would be crude, for it was made in soft wood by native carpenters using inadequate tools and copying the style of pieces brought from Spain. Turned spindles, for example: the native workmen had no lathes, so they improvised crude imitation spindles by making a shallow saw-cut all the way around square sticks of wood, then chiseling and sanding a convex curve on both sides of the cut. The finished piece resembles a string of rather clumsy beads with none of the graceful concave curves that make lathe-turned spindles so attractive. Today there are factories in Mexico turning out endless wormy pine copies of colonial furniture. Every piece looks three hundred years old, at least, and has all the inconveniences one would expect.

Such furnishings, somewhat modified for usefulness, were what my client had now. I would "upgrade" him by buying one or two small authentic antiques as focal points, and for the rest we would use modern interpretations of the colonial style, immaculately made in fine woods. Just the kind of thing, in short, I had seen in Xavier Fortunato's living room.

When I called, the courtly gentleman was happy to offer advice on local craftsmen. His list, though brief, was comprehensive and enlightening, which is why it took only an hour to complete my order with the man at the top of his list.

The "genuine article" shopping took a bit longer. I found a little chest I liked, a small thing, only about two feet long, dating from the early 1700s. It stood upon low, "false spindle" legs, and sported a curlicue apron, panel sides and front, and meticulous dove-tailing at the corners. It had a round iron lockplate, ornamented by a band of triangular perforations around the edge, and a hasp in the shape of a lizard. It had been painted a deep turquoise at one time; but the paint had faded everywhere and had worn off at the corners and at the edge of the top where the mellow wood showed through. It would make a perfect foil for a deeply carved Indian pot.

Another thing that caught my eye was an *alabrija,* a papier-mâché demon, a "lizard witch." Back in Spain, during the Inquisition, heretics were presumed to be possessed by demons, and both heretic and possessor were burned at the stake on the Saturday before Easter. When the Inquisition was halted, the Andalusians continued burning demons, but only brightly painted ones made of papier-mâché. The custom was eagerly taken up by the natives of Mexico, and the horrible-marvelous little creatures are still made, though they are far less often burned than formerly. One such capering monster had such an expression of gleeful anticipation that I coveted him badly, even while doubting my client would share my enthusiasm. I wondered if Margaret would like the beasty, then realized such a gift would merely add to the creepiness of recent events. There were enough devils floating about without my adding to them. Reluctantly, I left it where it was.

By midafternoon, I was at the Collected Works bookstore, where I picked up half a dozen things I'd been promising myself I'd read, or people had said I ought to read. Then I went back to the ranch, changed into trunks, and took the animals out to the pool where, against all the rules, Bela joined me in a swim. I did penance for this dereliction by cleaning the pool filters myself before we adjourned to the house for a snack.

Bruce called to say they'd been stuck for six hours in Atlanta between planes. Mark called to ask whether I'd received the stuff he'd sent. I gave him a progress report, the phone propped on one shoulder while I made myself a plate of cheese and cold cuts, with extras for the animals. After our snack, the three of us went to Bandelier and spent a pleasant evening wandering there, Schnitz at the end of his leash or lying across my shoulder. It felt vacationlike. Open ended. A bit like a flag flapping in the breeze, only very loosely tied to anything at all.

We did Bela's favorite thing and shared Kentucky Fried Chicken on the way home. When he was a puppy, he would go frantic at the smell of Kentucky Fried Chicken. Now, if allowed, he could swallow a bucketful in thirty seconds. He wasn't allowed. I carefully pulled the meat from the bones and let him have a scrap at a time. Cooked chicken bones are not good news for dogs. He had learned to be patient.

Night is time for cogitation. Bela asleep on the rug, Schnitz curled into a furry ball at the couch arm, the end of his tail twitching slowly, rhythmically, as though to fur-dream music, drums and flutes, feline-fugue, cat-counterpoint. Outside the wind had come up, gusting gently, recurrently, making a rhythm of its own. Push and then pause, then push again, rustling the leaves, thrusting the branches, a ballet of advance and retreat. And me, sitting on the couch in the lamplight, notebook on knee, pretending to think, pretending to note what I thought, while the wind pushed and pushed, me floating on it, as on surf, slowly being washed ashore, perhaps, or what was more likely, farther out to sea.

Margaret. Felicia. Xavier Fortunato.

I wished Grace could break loose and come down to Santa Fe, be here beside me now.

Ricardo. Lourdes. Eusequio Manuel.

I wished for her in the lamplight as I'd seen her last at her place, Critter, her thirty-pound Maine coon cat, sprawling over her lap like a fur rug. Like many fathers and sons, Critter and Schnitz did not get on. Of course Critter was a *tom* and Schnitz was an *it.* Critter no doubt despised him for being uncatly. That old machismo intolerance.

Vera. Dwight. Bobbi Kay and the tots.

I needed Grace. As a defense against the devils. As an anchor to windward. To save me from myself.

Evangeline and the old man. Whatever his name was, I'd forgotten. Oh, yes. Eduardo.

No discernible pattern, only this swirl of dark and light, God and Satan, devils and angels, and Ernie with his throat cut lying there in his rickety little church, a house of God, with no God in it but the painting on the wall, and Ernie hadn't known who that was.

William Reiserling, mad enough to kill, or perhaps only mad enough to make the gesture, not intending anything, really. Michelle, his wife, with her lovely, lovely wedding all ruined, because it was obviously her wedding, not her daughter Helen's wedding, her daughter didn't want a wedding. I hadn't met Michelle, but she didn't sound like the throat-cutting type.

And I hadn't met the gentlemen from Oklahoma.

There wasn't anyone else. Except them, they, the amorphous, anonymous people from the pueblo, people from the shopping center. Angry people, annoyed people, but no one who had seemed murderous. What had Grace said? The sound of tom-toms and feathered warriors?

What had Ernie thought about the day he died? What had he wanted? To keep his wife at home, being his wife, helpmeet, a thinking animal to do the cooking and the wash. She did the cooking and the wash, but was not busy enough with the cooking and the wash to keep her from slipping away, into this other world where he could not follow. Or would not. Paints. How had she gotten started on painting? No matter to Ernie, who would have thought to recall her to her duties by multiplying those duties: more cooking, more washing, if not for him, if not for Felicia (who had also slipped away), then for the poor.

Unfortunately, not poor for whom one could feel pity, sympathy, empathy. These poor were poor by choice, because theft and grievance and whining were easier than work. Or because they had no knowledge or habit of work but only this habit they had been shown, learned from parents, perhaps, or from unseemly guardians, or from their inadequate peers in whatever slum they had inhabited or created around themselves. Pigs, so it is said, would not choose a sty of their own accord. Pigs, so it is said, would rather root in the clean earth beneath a tree with shiny leaves, would rather smell truffles than pig shit, would not choose to be swinish if not constrained to be so.

I had known people who were unconstrained to be anything and were still swinish.

What would Dwight choose to be? Or Vera?

And could they kill? Would they kill?

Oh, in a moment, I said to myself. In a moment, never meaning to, just lashing out to protect themselves; but what did they have to protect against Ernie? Nothing, nothing at all.

And not Ricardo because I didn't want it to be Ricardo. Though perhaps his son, who could not be greatly harmed even if he had harmed someone else, because of insanity. Did he go anywhere alone? If he went alone, did he carry the lethal machete I'd seen him working with on the burned garage vigas? Had anyone noticed that machete but me? Would he have lashed out with his parents present? Would they have sneaked him away, quietly, to protect him? *Oh, see what Sequito has done! He has killed the bad man. Come, Sequito, let us go away quietly and pretend we were not here at all.*

Possible.

Because, except for the phantoms from Oklahoma, there was no one else. No one at all. . . .

Except, perhaps, Felicia's friend, Hector? Who had bashed another father, so Felicia said. Of course, that father had well deserved bashing. Felicia's father had not abused her, he had merely made her life untenable. Do we kill others because they make our lives untenable? Because they make the lives of those we love untenable? Perhaps.

The phone rang three times before I really heard it. It rang three times more before I struggled to my feet and answered it. William Reiserling, wouldn't you know?

"Jason?"

So, we were on a first-name basis now.

"Yes. Sorry, I think I'd dozed off on the couch. I didn't hear the phone at first."

"Does the name 'Joy Shepherd' mean anything to you?"

I stood there stupidly, wondering where I'd heard it.

"Art teacher," I said at last. "In Oklahoma. Taught Margaret painting."

"She's got a brother-in-law and a husband, the Shepherd brothers, Buster and Boomer-Bob."

"You're joking."

"Would I take up my own time and yours just foolin' around, Jason? Come on now, snap to. Boomer-Bob and Buster Shepherd, citizens of the great state of Oklahoma, and they were arrested around two and a half years back for assaulting a preacher. Guess who?"

"Ernie?" My voice squeaked. I lowered it. "Ernie?"

"No motive for the assault given on the arrest sheet, except that said preacher was alleged to have insulted Joy Shepherd, who is wife to Robert P. Shepherd, otherwise known as Boomer-Bob, because, so I am reliably informed, he used to fly navy fighters and enjoyed booming his girlfriend's house—not Joy's, some other girl's—in Wherever, California. Of course that was before his discharge from the Navy under, so son William says, difficult circumstances. Then, as now, the Navy would ignore an assault on a woman—just boys being boys, right?—but not an assault on a superior officer over a woman."

"Ah."

"According to the descriptions my son William abstracted from certain police documents, both men are in their late forties, balding, six foot and six one, and have given up on military fitness to acquire an ominous quantity of belt overhang. Which, according to Willy Jr., hasn't interfered with their brawling, which they do a lot of. Five or six arrests, I think he said, resulting in dropped charges or probation. They have a tolerant judiciary down there. Besides, these two are well-known guides for those officials of the court who want to do a little hunting, in or out of season."

"I'm going to have to go down there, aren't I?" I asked plaintively. "No way around it."

"If you want to know what it was about, I'd guess so. I'd also suggest talking to her, not to them."

"I'd already figured that out," I commented around a yawn. Lord, I was sleepy. Bela nudged me with his head, then walked over to stand before the door, yawning.

"Let me know what you find out," he said after he'd given me Joy Shepherd's address and phone number.

I told him I would. Taking Bela out woke me up enough to call the airlines and get a reservation from Albuquerque to Tulsa early the following morning. Mike's caretaker would look after Bela and Schnitz. I didn't even have that as an excuse for not going.

Five

MY WIFE, YES. MY DOG, MAYBE. MY GUN, NEVER, said the bumper sticker on the back of the pickup in front of me when I left the Tulsa airport. The pickup driver pulled over and got out to check his tires, and I saw that a similar sentiment embellished his sweatshirt. Something about taking his gun over his cold dead body. Needless to say, there was a gunrack in the pickup. Maybe his opinion was common in Oklahoma. Maybe he, along with Boomer and Buster, were dedicated members of the well-regulated militia envisioned by the framers of our constitution. A chilling thought.

It was Wednesday, midmorning. The map unfolded on the rental car seat beside me was full of names like Catoosa and Owasso and Skiatook. Different from but no more exotic than Pojoaque and Tesuque and Nambe. I wondered if Oklahoma had managed to become more genuinely intercultural than New Mexico was. Indian stuff was big bucks in both places, only here it was powwows and rodeos rather than art. Maybe it was easier to be bicultural than tricultural, though from the English-only signs it was apparent the bi didn't extend to language. Of course, Native Americans hadn't had a written language, as such. Their genetic stock had been isolated from that wide pool of Mediterranean/European/Asian cultural cross-fertilization that had come up with hundreds of written languages.

The idea didn't occupy me for long. It was a strange town with unfamiliar landmarks, and the address I had was a suburb where the streets drifted aimlessly away from the main thoroughfare only to curve back in two or three blocks under a different name, an area of houses that had probably been built in the fifties or sixties, many of them under centuries-old trees since augmented by others that had had time to grow. Altogether, a woodsy area. I'm no horticulturist, but oaks and maples I know. When I finally found my way onto Oak Crescent, the numbers I was looking for were tacked to a tree beside the curb in front of a solidly midwestern story-and-a-half ranch with an oversize two-car garage and an RV parked in the driveway. Ah, the good life!

I am not into macho confrontation. On occasion I have accused myself of being a profound coward. Grace says I show good sense. Whether cowardly or sensible, if either Boomer-Bob or Buster was present, I didn't want to go near the place, so I backtracked a few blocks to a business strip, found a public phone outside a motel, and called the house. A woman answered. I told her who I was and what I was doing. After a long, doubtful silence, she said she was Joy, and I could come to the house just for a minute. Something in her voice raised the hairs on the back of my neck.

When I met her at her front door, I knew why. She was too thin, too gray, too tired, a woman who wore fear as she did the old blue bathrobe she had on, pulling it around her, sheltering in its familiar folds. Something besides years had changed her, taking the color from her hair and skin. Bruises that had faded to chartreuse shadows surrounded one eye, and she stood like a person who hurts, one arm curled protectively forward and around her. I guessed a cracked or broken rib. Maybe a collarbone.

"I can't ask you in," she whispered. "Not when I'm here alone. Could you pretend to be a salesman or something?"

I fished my notebook out of my pocket and readied a pen, making quite a production of it. "I'm selling subscriptions to a magazine for RV owners," I said. "How will that be."

She said that would be fine. She didn't smile.

"As I said on the phone, I'm inquiring into Ernie Quivada's death," I said softly. "Two men from Oklahoma were looking for him ten days or so before he died. Could that have been your husband and his brother?"

She nodded, an absolute minimum nod. "I suppose," she said. "They were gone from Wednesday through that weekend."

"Did they say why?" I asked.

"I can't talk here," she whispered. "The neighbors watch. Somebody'll say something to Boomer."

"Is there somewhere else we can talk," I asked her. "I'll meet you anyplace you say."

"Our washer's broken." She clutched the robe more tightly. "I have to take the laundry to the laundromat. It's the one down there, in the shopping center." She ducked her head slightly leftward, east. "Launder-Ama," she said. "I go after lunch, about two."

I nodded, wrote busily in my book, nodded again, turned, and left, waving as I did so. The perfect picture of a convivial salesman type. Lord, what was happening here? If I'd been playing the part to perfection, I'd have stopped at a few other houses. Maybe I should have, but I didn't know that then.

I went east, the way she'd indicated, found the shopping center and the laundromat, then stopped at a department store to buy a couple of cheap sheets, some towels, and a laundry bag. I took these back to the motel I'd phoned from, where I took a room just to have a place to unpack. The new sheets together with a few things from my suitcase made a convincing enough laundry load, once I'd remembered to take the tags off the new things. The lightweight jacket I'd been wearing that morning went into the closet along with my tie. I rolled my shirtsleeves halfway to the elbows and dug out my dark glasses. A veritable master of disguise. I couldn't do anything about my reddish hair, but the gray would show up more inside.

After a hasty and unsatisfactory lunch at the fast-food place nearest the laundry, I got the bag from the car, went into the laundromat, and loaded a machine. The washers were on one side, the driers on the other, chairs set back to back in short groups down the middle, separated by the spaces around three folding tables, one at the front, one in the middle, and one way at the back, where two women were huddled with their heads together in front of some larger machines. I picked up an abandoned copy of *U.S.A. Today* from one of the chairs and sat down, trying not to fidget. About fifteen minutes later, just when I was about to give her up, Joy Shepherd came in carrying a basket. Neatly dressed in a crisp white blouse and khaki skirt, with her hair combed and makeup on, she looked like a different woman, not striking, perhaps, but with a definite style. Also, as though in response to being in public, she wore dark glasses and she didn't cringe. It made a difference.

She loaded her own laundry into three separate machines, whites, colors, and towels, added soap, inserted quarters, and finally sat down a couple of chairs away from me to open a magazine she'd brought with her. Except for the two women at the back, we were the only people in the place.

I'd written the name and phone number of the motel on the back of one of my cards, and I passed this to her across the intervening plastic seat. "Just in case you want to get in touch with me later," I murmured.

She slipped it into the pocket of the skirt she was wearing, never taking her eyes from her magazine.

"So, how did you get to know Margaret?" I asked.

"I was teaching at the community college." She paused, seeming to gather herself for the effort of speaking, as though speaking had become something less than habitual. As perhaps it had.

"Margaret took my class, and we . . . we got to be friends. Sometimes when Boomer was gone, she'd come over to the house. Sometimes she'd bring Felicia. Or I'd go to her house. Then one time her husband. . . ." She stalled, unable to go on.

After a long pause, I said, "Let me guess. He came over and tried to convert you."

She threw me a tiny glance of surprise and . . . was it relief?

"Actually, he tried to convert all of us, Boomer too," she said, turning the pages of her magazine.

"And of course that made Boomer mad."

She flushed and bit her lip. After a little, she nodded hesitantly, again that minuscule nod. "That's right. He . . . he told me if I ever had anything to do with either of them again, he'd . . . he'd hurt me."

"How long after that did Ernie and Margaret leave Oklahoma."

"Almost right away. I think Boomer scared him off. Boomer was arrested for something about that time. I never found out exactly, but I wondered if maybe he and Buster beat up on Ernie. They do that. Beat up on people."

Including me, her sudden sagging posture said.

"There are laws against wife battering," I said softly. "It's illegal."

"I know," she whispered. "I do know. It's just . . ."

I knew all about what it was just. Grace had told me about it, one of her major frustrations. Even though most states now have laws that allow abusers to be arrested by the police without a complaint, cases are better prosecuted if wives cooperate. Too often, they don't, engaging instead in an endless series of excuses and delays. He really loves me. He doesn't mean to. I deserved it. I provoked him. He said he'd never do it again. Or, and not without reason, he'll hurt me. He'll kill me. He'll do something worse than he's doing already.

Of course, by the time Grace got into the case, he had done something worse and the wife was dead. Or in a few cases of the worm turning, the husband was.

"So, what set him off this time?" I asked.

"Margaret knows she's not supposed to call me, but she was so excited she just wasn't thinking. I guess she thought he wouldn't be home that time of day, but Boomer answered the phone. He recognized her voice right away. He got angry. He wouldn't let her talk to me." She twisted one hand in her skirt. "I always call her, from a pay phone, while I'm here or while I'm shopping. She wasn't supposed to call me at home. I guess she was just too excited to wait until I called her next."

"What was she excited about?"

"The show. Her show. It wasn't certain yet, but she thought this gallery owner was going to give her a show."

"When did she call?"

She made a gesture, a what-good-will-this-do kind of shrug. "It was . . . oh, a couple of weeks before her husband died."

"So she called you, and your husband answered. And then he beat up on you because she'd called you." She nodded, but her eyes didn't meet mine. There was something else. Something she didn't want to talk about. "So how did you find out what she was calling about?"

"Because I called her from here, just a few days ago." She nodded toward the pay phone next to the toilets, hidden from the parking lot by the bulk of a big drier. "I hadn't talked to her in almost a month. She was really worried about me, but I told her I was all right. . . ."

She was anything but all right.

"She called, your husband wouldn't let you talk to her, and then he went to New Mexico looking for Ernie. Why?"

She was silent for a long time. When she spoke at last, it was in an agonized whisper. "He told Ernie to keep her away from me. He figured it was Ernie's fault. It's always the husband's fault if his wife gets out of line. Like if a hunting dog isn't well trained, it's not the dog's fault. It's the man who owns him."

Oh, right. I felt a cold, hideous fury. My wife, yes; my dog, maybe; my gun, never. Pithecanthropus was alive and well in the American West!

"And where was he the Sunday that Ernie was killed?"

"He and Buster took the RV and were gone all that weekend. Boomer said they went hunting."

The buzzer went off on my laundry. I took it out of the machine and put it in the drier, sat back down, trying to put it all together. Joy was shifting one of her wash loads, and I seemed to have run out of questions. I glanced out the window and saw a pickup pulling into a parking space, two men in it, both of them staring through the windshield into the Launder-Ama. Joy began to fold damp kitchen towels. I buried myself in my paper.

"Don't look out suddenly, but is that your husband watching this place?" I asked.

She raised her head from her laundry basket, her hands busy smoothing and folding the damp fabric. I saw her eyes widen.

"Pretend I'm not even here," I said, the paper masking my mouth. "I'm a stranger. You don't know me. Do whatever you'd do if I weren't here."

I could tell she was thinking it through. Then she went out the door. I got up and inspected my drying wash through the glass window, the laundry bag ostentatiously over my shoulder. I stretched and yawned. Joy was leaning in the truck window. No, she was being held against the truck door by a hand clamped on her shoulder. I ignored it, sagged against the drier, tapped my foot, looked at my watch.

The door behind me opened. I glanced uninterestedly in that direction. Two men and Joy. She was whiter than my sheets. The one glance confirmed the stereotype I'd already imagined. Work shirts with sleeves rolled up onto bulging biceps; shit-kicker caps pushed back off balding foreheads; arms marked by navy tattoos. When I was in the Navy, the officers who had tattoos tended to be guys who drank too much and bragged about it. These two were trying to watch me and Joy at the same time.

Fortuitously, the buzzer went off. I opened the drier, scooped out the laundry, and dumped it on the folding table, where I took my time smoothing the sheets and folding them into meticulous squares before loading them into the laundry sack. When I folded the jockey shorts and T-shirts, they looked at each other, one of them mumbling something. I could just pick up the sense of it. *It's his laundry. The guy's just doin' his laundry.* I studiously ignored them. When I started to leave, Joy was sitting in a chair, staring at her towels going around and around. The two men were bracketing the door, one scowling, one frowning undecidedly at the other.

I reached for the door.

"Hey," said the scowler, putting his hand over mine.

"Yeah," I drawled, frowning at him. "What?"

"You know her?" he asked, indicating Joy.

I looked at her, taking my time. "You tryin' to get her a date?" I asked. "She your sister or something?"

Joy looked both hurt and relieved.

"Smart ass," snarled the other fatman.

One of the two women in the back stood up and turned toward us, attracting the attention of my questioner. He was startled, put a little off stride. He hadn't seen the women until now.

If he planned violence, he wouldn't want witnesses. I took advantage of the distraction.

"Look, buddy, I don't know what the problem is, but leave me out of it."

I hoisted the sack onto my shoulder and strolled slowly across the lot to the rental car, stowed the laundry in back, got into the driver's seat, and drove away. They were still there, the one I guessed was Boomer glowering through the window, more in disappointment than anything else. He wasn't quite sure I was involved; his brother had halfheartedly said I wasn't; but mere suspicion might be enough to provoke an assault. Had someone tipped them off that Joy had had a visitor? Was there a neighborhood spy? Joy had seemed sure there was. Though perhaps Boomer monitored Joy's Launder-Ama visits as a matter of course.

A more difficult question: Had I done anything to endanger her? We'd stopped talking before Boomer's truck arrived. There had been no suspicious moves. He had no reason at all to connect me to his wife, and best we keep it that way, for her sake. Was this a clinical case of paranoia? Or jealousy? And if so, for what? He wanted his wife to stay away from Margaret, because of Margaret's husband? He'd beat up on her, just for talking to Margaret?

It didn't fit. The thing didn't work. The dynamics were all wrong, even given that Boomer wanted to possess his wife in standard good-old-boy fashion: barefoot, beaten, and broke. But Joy wasn't—that is, hadn't been—an ignorant woman without position or friends. She had an income. She taught at the college. Or did she still teach? I hadn't asked. I should have asked. Damn!

I couldn't go back to her now. I didn't kid myself I could get away with questioning Boomer and Buster, certainly not on my own. The police would have to pursue the question of their whereabouts on the weekend Ernie was murdered. Or the FBI. Let them deal with the Shepherd brothers. They were better equipped to do so than I. So, if I wanted to find out whether Joy still taught at the college, I'd have to go to the college and ask.

I spent a few fruitless minutes trying to figure out what I could do for Joy. Report the abuse to the police? I hadn't seen it. I had no idea what the local laws were regarding domestic violence, but whatever they were, someone would have to complain. I doubted very much that on the basis of an anonymous complaint, the police could obtain a warrant, go into the house, look at Joy's face and arms, decide she'd been battered, and pick up Boomer on suspicion. She needed a home for battered women. Perhaps I could get a woman from some such service to go by and visit her.

I located the college on the map. It wasn't far. I parked as close as I could to the administration building and went in to ask where Joy Shepherd taught. Where she *had* taught up until a few months before, said the erect white-haired woman behind the counter. So now I knew.

"She resigned." The clerk tapped a stack of folders together, clipping them neatly at one side.

"Resigned?"

"Health, I think. I know she was hospitalized at the time."

I remembered that curved arm, protecting the body behind it. Broken ribs sometimes took a long time to heal. Particularly if you kept getting hit on them.

The white-haired woman was looking at me sympathetically. "Were you a student of hers? I know her students were very fond of her."

"No." I shook my head. No, I hadn't been a student. "I'm a little old for that."

"Oh, not for us," she said. "We get them all ages. Even old biddies like me."

I thanked her and left, wondering how one might locate Joy's students . . . ex-students. Even though it was summer, there were a lot of people around. I asked the first person I bumped into, and he told me where to find the art department.

Two young women had found a shady spot on the steps outside the art department, where they were sharing a sketch pad and giggling about something. One of them had blond braids twisted into a knot on top of her head; the other wore her dark hair in a flurry of uncombed ringlets that had no doubt taken hours to achieve.

"Excuse me," I begged. "I'm trying to find someone who knew . . . knows Joy Shepherd."

The two heads turned as one.

"What's happened to her?" demanded the blonde. She shared a covert look with her friend, who shook her head slightly.

"Why did you think something had happened to her?" I asked.

The blonde made a face. Again they exchanged glances.

"Because it's only a matter of time until her bastard husband kills her," drawled the brunette in a deep, throaty voice. She sounded careless and uninvolved, merely stating a fact.

"You knew about him?" I asked, astonished. "She told you about him?"

The dark-haired one shook her head, regarding me narrowly. "Why? What difference does it make to you? Has he hired you to follow her or something?"

"I've never met the gentleman," I lied. "I have met Joy. I'm just interested in how you knew."

"For Crissake, you can only fall down stairs so many times," said the blonde, not quite able to match her colleague's offhandedness. Her tone kept slipping into sympathy. "That was her excuse, she fell down stairs. I don't know who she thought she was kidding."

"Classic," said the dark one. "A classic case. Right out of 'Law and Order.' She'd come in wearing dark glasses, but you could see the bruises from the side, and bruises on her arms and wrists where he'd grabbed her. And she'd walk funny, like she hurt. When she ended up in the hospital a few months ago, I told Barb she wouldn't be back. It's obvious he didn't want her to work!"

"Why didn't he want her to work?"

"Because women who work are independent," said the brunette impatiently, as though to a rather stupid child. "Because women who work have money of their own, and friends of their own. People who can testify to what's going on. Maybe she'd even meet another man."

"I don't think she wanted a man," said the blonde.

"Did she say that?"

The blonde shrugged. "No. It's just, you know. She isn't old. Forty-something, I suppose. But she acted like . . . oh, standoffish around men."

"People," corrected the other. "It wasn't just men, Barb, it was people. Most teachers, at least the good ones, they flirt a

little with their students. The men with the girls, the women with
the boys. . . ."

"The men with the boys," said the blonde innocently.

"Right," laughed the brunette. "Well, you know what I mean.
A pat on the arm. A hug, even. Nothing really sexy, just mentor-
ish. But not Joy Shepherd. We had her for composition. She'd
never even lean over your shoulder. Like she was afraid to touch
you."

"For fear her husband would see it and beat up on whoever
she was near," agreed the blonde.

Not for the first time recently, I wished for Grace. She might
understand the situation, but I had to confess I did not. It made
no sense. What they were describing was not simply sexual jealousy, which I could understand. I'd felt that way from time to
time myself. But what Boomer seemed to be up to was patholog-
ical possessiveness. Or some of what Felicia was trying to describe
to me. Putting a woman in a place where one need not think
about her.

"Did her husband hang around here?" I asked. "Keeping an
eye on her?"

They shrugged, both at once. "Who'd know?" asked the
blonde. "I never met him."

"Paula," said the other. "If anyone knew, it would be Paula."

"Paula?"

"Paula French. You remember, Barb! She and Joy were tight. I
used to see them together in the cafeteria all the time. She was
one of the older students, you know the type. Her kids are in
school so she goes back herself. Always wanted to be an artist.
This place is full of middle-aged wannabes." And she gave me a
look that placed me in their company.

Only slightly offended, I took out my notebook and wrote
down the name. "Mrs. Somebody French?" I asked.

They shrugged again. They didn't know. Just Paula.

I thanked them and went back to administration. My white-
haired informant was still there. I asked where I could find Paula
French, and after glancing over her shoulder to see if she was
observed, she looked up the address for me. It was Mrs. Donald
French.

"We're not supposed to do this," she said quietly. "But I can always tell when people are up to no good. You're not one of them."

I didn't ask her how she knew. It's the way lots of women react to me. They seem to trust me, God knows why. They tell me things they don't even tell their female friends. Grace has commented on it more than once—snappishly on occasion—telling me I'd be great at interrogating women. I told her I don't really interrogate women. They just tell me things. Of course, sometimes I lead the conversation a little.

The Frenches' address was an almost downtown apartment house; one with a doorman who called upstairs before reluctantly allowing me access to the elevators. Despite the spare elegance of the lobby, Paula's apartment was cluttered and looked well lived in. The crayon drawings taped to the front of the bookcases testified to there being at least one grade-schooler in residence, and the stereo equipment and scattered CDs indicated an older child as well. So much I could see from the front door, which was as far as she let me get.

She was a fortyish ash blonde, pale skin, eyes so light they looked blind, dressed in a softly faded fabric the color of her own skin and hair. She was the color of weathered wood, silvered by sun and rain, and she leaned in the door like a slender barricade. This far, her body said. And no farther.

"You said you need information about Joy?" she asked, from lips that were barely pink.

I said no, not exactly, and started to tell her what I was there for. The minute I mentioned Ernie's name, her face slammed shut like a prison door, unyielding.

"Pardon me if I'm stepping into something unmentionable," I begged, "but Ernie's dead."

"And about time," she replied without a moment's hesitation.

I didn't know what to say to that. Weakly, I managed, "Did you know Ernie's wife, Margaret?"

"I did not," she snapped. "Is that all?"

"But you do know Joy," I persevered. "Is she a good enough friend that you might . . . help her?"

Her face changed abruptly. "Why? What's happened?"

"I think it's probably more of the same," I said. "She's been hurt. Someone's got to get her away."

"That shithead," she murmured softly. "That unmitigated bastard. The only brains he has are in his fists and between his legs. He's nothing but a talking ape!"

I blinked. "What does he do for a living? He seems to have a lot of free time on his hands."

"He runs an auto-wrecking yard," she laughed. "Wouldn't you know? Can't you just see him pulling the fenders off those poor, innocent cars. Loving it when the metal shrieks for mercy."

Her words were vivid enough that I could hear the metal rending, but it got me nowhere.

I rubbed my forehead with a forefinger, trying to think where to go next. "When I spoke with Joy I didn't ask, but does she have children?"

"A child. A girl. That's the hold he's got on her! I've urged her, begged her to get out of there. I've told her she can come here. There's a shelter that would take her. No, she won't leave because he's got her convinced he'll get custody if she leaves him."

"That's crazy."

"I know it. You know it. She doesn't believe it. She's more scared for Lucy than she is for herself."

In complete frustration, I blurted, "Well, if I can convince the FBI to take a look at Boomer Shepherd and his brother, maybe they'll be so busy they'll leave Joy alone for a while."

"The FBI?"

"For killing Ernie Quivada."

"That's right. You said he's dead." Her face lit up, then closed again. Elation, followed by discretion. Whatever it was, she didn't intend to tell me about it.

"You sound glad," I poked at her.

"He wasn't a nice man," she said. "In fact, he was a vicious little turd. Full of rage and impotent fury."

I blinked again. It was a judgment I would never have made of Ernie. Bumbling, yes. Harmful to those around him, yes. But vicious? Her odd, light eyes regarded me without emotion. Like the eyes of a lizard, I told myself. Quite unblinking.

My lack of comprehension seemed to amuse her, if anything. "Now that he's gone, maybe Joy will have an easier time of it," she said enigmatically.

What Ernie's death had to do with Joy was beyond me. "Would Joy have had any reason to kill him?" I asked.

"Well, of course she had *reasons*," she snapped. "But she couldn't kill a mouse! If *reasons* were enough, she'd have killed that shithead husband of hers. If *reasons* were enough, so would I!"

"You're fond of her."

She regarded me balefully, shaking her head at my stupidity. "Yes," she said at last. "I'm fond of her. She's my dear friend. She's a good artist, she has a wonderful sense of humor, she's intelligent, she's just plain nice! I would give anything to be able to help her. I've tried over and over again. I've even driven her to the safe house, right up to the door, but I can't break her loose from that bastard. She's afraid he'll kill Lucy if she tries to do anything at all to protect herself."

"Wouldn't Lucy have something to say about it? Don't judges give a lot of weight to what children have to say about custody?"

She shook her head. "Lucy . . . Lucy's not normal. She's mentally . . . she's profoundly retarded. Not like the sweetly retarded people you see on TV programs. She's more like a vegetable that very occasionally does something to make Joy hope there's a person there. Like smile. Or make a sound that might be a word. She's institutionalized, a private home. Joy's family paid for it for a while, then Joy took over paying for it, when she worked. Now Boomer's paying for it. But he doesn't have to. He could always take her out."

"So by injuring Joy enough that she couldn't go on working, he increased his control over her."

"Of course he did. Lucy's his hole card. He's her daddy. He pays the bills. He has a right to take her out of that place and bring her home. At which point, Joy will lose her mind—what little she has left. The only way she's kept herself going has been by working to provide for Lucy, but not—mind you—seeing Lucy very often."

It seemed ambiguous. I said so.

She shook her head at me, angrily. "Joy's got this dream Lucy in her mind. The dream Lucy is disabled but is living some inner life of angelic happiness that's invisible from outside. It's total self-delusion; probably it's how she stays sane; I know damn well she couldn't take the everyday reality. I mean, Lucy is just flesh that takes in food at one end and puts out shit at the other. She's flesh that gets sores on her that don't heal. She's flesh that sort of whines, like a hurt animal. There's no mind there. The doctors have told Joy that, over and over, but what can you do? The damn laws! I mean, you can kill a porpoise or a whale or a chimpanzee, any of whom have undeniable intelligence, and nobody says anything. But you let a Lucy die, and it's murder! We have no right keeping babies like that alive! God would let them die!"

It sounded harsh, but I knew from personal experience what she meant.

"I know," I said. "I had . . . a son who was brain dead for a long, long time."

The words loosened something in her. Her belligerence vanished.

"Come on in," she said, suddenly standing back from the door, removing the barrier.

I went in. She gestured toward the couch, where a small shaggy dog was curled up. It lifted its head and gave me a resentful look when I sat down beside it. Paula French spoke chidingly. Its tail thumped the cushion as it curled tighter and went back to sleep.

Paula sat down opposite me. "Look," she said. "I'll explain the situation to you. The thing to keep in mind is that Joy was an absolutely stunning girl when Boomer first saw her. She was beautiful. I mean gorgeous, like a model. Pictures of her taken when she was nineteen or twenty are just unbelievable. That's when Boomer went after her, say seventeen years ago."

"She's only thirty-seven?" I couldn't believe it.

She gave me a look. "Being married to Boomer has aged her fast. Anyhow, he overwhelmed her, swept her off her feet, may have raped her, anyhow got her pregnant before she knew what was happening. He was better-looking then, muscular, with hair, a pilot, an officer and a gentleman! Well, she was pregnant so she had to get married. That may have been the liberated seventies for some people, but not for Joy's mother. Joy had to get married, for her mother's sake.

"Then she had this child, and right away it was apparent Lucy wasn't normal. That broke Joy's heart. And when the doctor told her it could be genetic, she had her tubes tied. She didn't ask anybody, not Mama, not Boomer. Well, Boomer didn't like that one bit. He was counting on ten or twelve little Boomers running around. Enough for a football team.

"So, there she was, barely into her twenties, married, and at loose ends, so her daddy paid for the baby to get private care and for Joy to go on with college. She'd had two years, I think, before she met Boomer."

"I'm surprised Boomer went along with that."

"Boomer didn't have any choice. From what Joy told me about her daddy, otherwise known as Old Man Hartzog, he was not a man you'd cross. There was money there, which was part of Joy's attraction, no doubt, and money means power. Boomer understands power, and violence. It's about all he does understand. Anyhow, Joy went to school and got to be a teaching assistant, and then she got to be a full-time teacher. She loved it. It let her work with all kinds of people, particularly with younger ones. They took the place of the family she didn't really have. And then a few years back, Joy's daddy died."

Full stop. I didn't say anything.

After a moment she went on. "Pity it couldn't have been Mrs. Hartzog. She's the one who thinks divorce is a sin. She's the one who tells Joy to be patient and forgiving and long-suffering. Isn't that a word? Long-suffering? Just how long and how much suffering, I'd like to know!

"Well, as soon as Old Man Hartzog wasn't around to interfere anymore, Boomer started Joy right out on the long-suffering jazz. Oh, she put up a little fight at first. She told him if he didn't like her working, he could divorce her, marry someone else. He said never. She'd never get away from him. She was going to start being the kind of wife she should have been all along. It's like he was getting even with Joy's daddy. The more she wanted to get away, the tighter he held on. It's a contest, a football game.

When he found out he couldn't control her by beating on her, he started threatening the people she cares about. Me. Or Lucy. Or the Quivada woman."

"But you didn't know Margaret Quivada?"

"She left here before I even met Joy, but Joy talks about her all the time. They became friends because they had such similar lives, both of them married young, already pregnant, both of them married to men who were . . . abusive, though in different ways. Joy talks about how beautiful she is, about her talent. Genius, Joy said. A painting genius." The words were flat, holding more than a hint of jealousy. She heard herself and flushed. "Well, damn it, I paint too."

It seemed an appropriate time to pursue the odd connection I'd noted earlier. "Why did you say Ernie's death would make Joy's life easier?"

"Ernie was Boomer's deputy. With Ernie gone, Joy won't need to be so afraid for Margaret."

I didn't get it. I was baffled.

She sighed. "Boomer doesn't just threaten to hurt somebody, he makes a production of it. He tells Joy exactly how he's going to do it, so she can visualize it. The man's a real sadist. He'll get drunk and come home and sit on the couch with his arm around her and tell her how he's going to bring Lucy home, and then smother her so it looks like an accident. He'll say, 'You'll know it wasn't an accident, baby, but you won't be able to prove it.' He'll tell her how he and some of his friends are going to hide in the parking garage downstairs and wait for me to come in at night. 'You'll know who raped her, baby, but nobody'll be able to prove it.' But when he talks about hurting Margaret, he always says he'll have Margaret's husband do it for him."

"How?" I asked, astonished.

"Oh, Joy said Ernie was scared to death of Boomer. All Boomer had to do was threaten to beat him up. That's all it took to make him leave Oklahoma."

It had been more than mere threat, but I didn't go into that.

"Just because Ernie tried to convert him?" I asked incredulously.

She gave me another of those long looks, at first incredulous, then weighing, deciding what to tell me. Finally, she said, "I don't know where you got the idea it had anything to do with religion."

"Joy said it did," I said, then caught myself. "No, I assumed it did, and she confirmed it."

"I can see why, but that's not the way it happened. Quivada couldn't stand it that his wife was beginning to talk about a career in painting. So, he came to their house, Joy's and Boomer's, and accused Joy of corrupting his wife. Joy said he used the word 'perversion.' That's a word that pushed all Boomer's buttons. The word only has one meaning around here. He went up the wall! Somebody accusing his wife of being perverted, right here in the homophobic heartland of America!" She snorted.

"So Boomer . . . ah, threatened Ernie?"

"Right. Stay away from my wife. Keep your wife away from my wife."

"Or else?"

She stood up and went to the tall window, full of late afternoon sun, becoming a sculpture in light and shadow, a talking icon as she intoned: "Keep your woman away from my woman. Beat her if necessary. Kill her if necessary, but keep her away from Joy."

She turned back to me, human again, making a gesture of rejection. "Joy told me about it, to explain Boomer's attitude. Ever since then, he's watched her like a hawk."

"He couldn't watch her in class, of course."

"Which is one reason he wanted to stop her working. And it's a crime! Art means everything to Joy." She laughed harshly. "It meant a lot to me, too, until Joy gave me some of Margaret's paintings to keep for her because she knew Boomer would destroy them if he knew she had them. I look at them and I want to spit, I'm so frustrated. It's enough to make you give up! Talent like that! God. What I wouldn't give . . ."

The door banged open. A boy about nine and a girl barely in her teens came in like a noisy and self-important crowd, full of themselves, sparing only an incurious glance for me as they greeted their mother. All at once she became another person, soft and welcoming and warm.

I rose, wondering if I'd gotten anywhere. Paula introduced her children and goaded them through the obligatory how-do-you-dos before sending them off down the hallway to change their clothes.

She saw me to the door. "Make trouble for them," she whispered, back to her brittle, belligerent self. "Boomer and that brother of his. Make all the trouble you can. Get them off her." Her eyes actually blazed.

"I'll do what I can," I said.

What I did was go back to the motel. It was late, I was tired, I'd left most of my lunch uneaten, so I was hungry.

I called Grace and left a message on her machine. I called Phil Hauptman, the caretaker at the ranch, and inquired after my animals. One dozing at his feet, said Phil, the other exploring his closet for mice.

"You could have left them in the run, Phil. You didn't have to bring them in."

"No trouble," he rumbled at me. "I figure, one or the other of 'em gets this mouse that's been leaving mouse shit all over my kitchen, they'll have earned a night's lodging."

It was too late to catch Mark at the shop. I asked the woman in the motel office where the nearest acceptable restaurant was, and she fished out a dog-eared copy of a restaurant guide. I settled on a nearby steakhouse, where I ate a huge salad and a rare chunk of fairly good prime rib, returning to the motel by nine. I had no sense of travel or exploration. The city was a city like all other American cities, the restaurant had its counterpart in every good-sized town, the motel was a motel. The only useful information I'd gained from the whole day was that Boomer and Buster might have been in New Mexico when Ernie was killed.

The day was not yet over, however.

About one in the morning, came a knock on the door. I'd dozed off with the TV on, so it took a while before I realized it wasn't program noise. When I did, I got up, turned off the television, and padded over to inspect the visitor through the fisheye lens. A uniform. I left the chain on when I opened the door.

"Jason Lynx?"

"Yes."

"I wonder if you'd mind getting dressed and coming on down to the station with me, Mr. Lynx?"

"Why?" I asked. "What's happened?"

"I'm sure they'll tell you down at the station. If you wouldn't mind?"

He wasn't arresting me, or threatening to. I could simply refuse, of course. On the other hand . . . The small muddy dog scented something nasty in the wind. I thumbed through my mental file, looking for the name of Reiserling's son. The Tulsa lawyer. Maybe I'd need him!

"I'll be out in a minute," I told the uniform. Actually, it was closer to ten, but I took time for a quick shower. The cop watched impassively while I locked the door behind me and pocketed the key.

"In town for long, Mr. Lynx."

"One day more at most," I said.

"Here on business?"

"Of a sort," I replied, being laconic.

The ride was not lengthy. When we got where we were going —all police stations are essentially alike, just like most cities—the uniform turned me over to a plain clothes person who introduced himself as Lieutenant Jack Snitel. He led me down a flight of stairs into the bowels of the place, and I suddenly knew what I was there for. He hadn't said homicide, but that's who he worked for.

"Somebody's dead," I said. "Somebody's been killed."

"Yeah, well," he said. "It happens."

From the size of the bulge under the sheet, I knew who it was, and I knew why they'd come for me.

"Joy Shepherd," I said when he lifted the sheet to let me see her face. Beside her, in a plastic bag, were the clothes I'd seen her wearing at the laundromat. White blouse, khaki skirt, underwear, shoes. Her face looked peaceful. Truly at rest. As though it was nice not to have to care anymore. Not about herself, or her daughter, or Margaret.

"Her full name?" he asked.

"Mrs. Robert P. Shepherd," I said, adding the address. "Those bastards."

"What bastards would those be, Mr. Lynx."

"Can we get out of here," I asked roughly. Paula had tried, and I had thought of trying. Neither of us had done anything useful. And now here she was, dead. I wondered if Margaret's elated phone call was the proximate cause. Or whether my visit was. Or whether it would have happened anyhow.

Jack Snitel stopped to pass Joy's name and address on to someone else before we went upstairs to his office. Once there, he gave me a cup of mud-textured stuff he called coffee. I gave him my bona fides and told him all about everything. Ernie's death. Bruce's asking me to inquire. How the trail led to Oklahoma.

"You got a license?"

"I don't need a license to ask questions," I said quietly. "I guess I would need one if I got paid for it, but I don't take pay."

"Outa the goodness of your heart, right?"

I sat back and gave him a long look. There'd been only a little sarcasm in the question. Less than policemen usually use when they think you're poaching on their preserve. "Curiosity," I said at last. "Mostly."

"And you think these bastards who did her in include her husband?"

"Her husband, maybe with or without his brother." I told him about the girls at the college, about Paula French. "I've only been here a day, and everybody I've met knows he beat her to hell whenever he felt like it."

"You haven't asked me what happened to her," he said.

"I figure you'll tell me if you want to," I said. "And if you don't want to, my asking won't do any good."

"Looks like she got hit in the face. There's old bruises, but new ones too. She fell back, and the back of her head hit something else, and that killed her. Depressed fracture and bleeding into the brain, the examiner says. Probably. He guesses sometime yesterday evening. Suppertime, say. He won't say for sure until after the autopsy."

"Where was she?"

"Where she was found wasn't where it happened. Guy found

her beside a road, out east of here. Wouldn't have found her at all if he hadn't had his dog in the car, and the dog started yapping to get out. Dog had to go, you know. So he pulled over and let it out. Dog wandered off, and pretty soon it started yapping again. He had it with him when we questioned him, and it's one of those noisy useless little potlicker dogs. Anyhow, when the guy took his flashlight and went to see what the dog was fussin' over —man said he thought it was a porcupine, so he hurried some— he got down in this gully where there was a pile of branches with the little dog diggin away in there. Dog had uncovered one hand and arm, and the man saw it in the light from the flash.

"I give him credit, he says he got down in there and checked, but she was already cold, so he got back in the car and read the odometer to where he found a phone to call us. You'd think a man's got a dog like that wouldn't have good sense, but he backtracked us right to the spot, couldn't of done better if he'd knowed how."

"She could have been there a long time without being found?"

He nodded thoughtfully. "It's within our jurisdiction, but it's not a built-up area. She was in a gully that collects trash when it rains, but it's downhill of the road, so there'd be no reason to clean it out. Smart place to leave her, actually. She could have stayed there years without bein found. The way it happened, though, she was found when she hadn't been dead more'n a few hours." He grinned mirthlessly. "God bless all stupid little potlicker dogs."

"He probably killed her at home," I said. "Didn't mean to, exactly. Just hit her one too many times. Or maybe it happened at the auto-wrecking yard. Some piece of machinery got in the way. His brother might have been with him. They were together around two-thirty this afternoon." I told him about my conversation with Joy at the Launder-Ama.

"You think these two killed the man up in New Mexico?"

I gave him an open-handed shrug. Who knew? "Slitting his throat doesn't seem their style, somehow," I said. "If Ernie'd been beaten to death, maybe. I understand they've both got records for assault and general mayhem."

"Now, how would you know that?"

I flushed and mumbled something about having my sources.

"You didn't ask how we got on to you."

"I gave Joy a card with the motel name and number on it. She put it in her pocket. I figure it was still there when you found her."

"It was."

I heaved a sigh. If the card had still been in her skirt pocket, it meant Boomer hadn't seen it. I hadn't been the cause of her death, I told myself, hoping it was true.

Snitel excused himself and went outside to talk to someone, returning in a few moments to say, "Mr. Robert P. Shepherd was not at home when we went looking for him just now."

"Robert Shepherd may be hard to find," I said. "A lot of people know about his beating Joy. His wife's friends, her former students. Maybe he's decided to go away for a while, as though they'd gone away together. Maybe he figures if nobody finds the body, he'll come back later and tell people his wife stayed with her relatives in Cleveland."

"She have relatives in Cleveland?"

"God knows. It was a for instance," I said. "A hypothetical example of what he might say."

He grunted at me. "Can we get hold of you here?" He tapped my card on his desk.

"No, I'm staying in New Mexico for a while. I'll probably go back there tomorrow . . . that is, today. I'll give you the address." I wrote it down for him. "I don't know who's handling the case there. Your best bet might be the nearest FBI field office."

"You haven't talked to the police there?" He sounded surprised.

"Bruce did. Ernie's half-brother. He got the feeling they weren't doing much. But if there's a connection with what happened down here, it'll be an FBI matter, won't it? Tribal police don't handle things across state borders, do they?"

He didn't answer. "You goin' back today?"

I told him I was, providing I got enough sleep to go anywhere. When I got back to the motel, however, after divagating around for the better part of an hour, I convinced myself it was my duty to let Paula French know what had happened. She shouldn't be allowed to read about it in the morning papers.

Her number was in the phone book. Her phone rang almost twenty times before she answered. When she finally understood who it was, she said, "What's happened."

"It's Joy," I said. "We were too late, Paula. I was too late."

Long silence.

"Dead?" she asked, knowing but unbelieving. "Dead?"

I told her what I knew. She asked few questions. She knew who had done it, and so did I. When she hung up, I was no longer sleepy. When dawn came, I was still sitting up in bed, thinking, or pretending to.

The Thursday morning flight back to Albuquerque was uneventful. I dozed during most of it. I picked up my car in the lot and got back to Los Vientos around noon. Phil and the animals were there to greet me, Phil with an outstretched hand, the animals with one wagging tail and one lashing one. Schnitz was annoyed about something.

"Did he eat your mouse?" I asked Phil.

"The big guy did," he indicated Bela. "Swallowed it whole."

Bela looked at me shamefaced, knowing we were talking about him, not certain if he'd done something wrong.

I resolutely refused to think about swallowing mice, whole or any other way. Mice are eaten by wolves, why not by Kuvasz dogs. Dog and wolf are about the same size. On the other hand, I hadn't known Bela to be a mouser.

"The cat caught it," Phil clarified for me. "He just didn't know what to do with it. So the big guy took it away from him."

Fine. I had a hundred-twenty-pound mouse hound. And a twenty-pound game-playing cat. Both of whom were ready for a run, and so was I. When I'd changed my clothes, we went down into the bosquet by the river and trotted along the sandy watercourse, tumbled for so many generations it was almost as fine as silt. The tamarisks were beginning to bloom, pink feathers against the sky. I risked letting Schnitz off the leash. He bounded along, darting off to hide along the way, then rejoining us. One of the nicest personality traits of Maine coon cats, at least in my limited experience, is their good sense. The day was still and warm, not yet really hot, though it would get there before night. I had to tell Margaret about Joy. I didn't look forward to it. The run was actually a way of forestalling that duty.

But weariness brought it to an end, and I staggered back home, making the return trip among the trees, where we could stop to observe this bird and that creature. We got back to the ranch around one-thirty. I had a sandwich and gave the animals a drink. I was about to leave when the phone rang.

It was Phyllis Norman.

"Jason," she said. "My dear boy, are we putting you through some great problem?"

She sounded just the same, warm and gentle and as though she really cared.

"Not at all, Phyll. Not at all."

She went on. "I didn't have anyone else, you see. Bruce isn't the type, nor Lindsay, and I did worry so about Margaret and Felicia."

"I know, Phyll." She'd told me to call her Phyll years ago, after I'd politely said Mrs. Norman for about the hundredth time in one afternoon. "And it's not a big problem for me. What made you think it was."

"Bruce feels bad about leaving it all in your hands."

"Tell Bruce he owes me one, that's all."

"I do hope . . . I do hope you can find out who. . . . I need to know who, Jason."

I told her I knew that, that I'd do my best, not to worry, not to be impatient, sometimes these things take a little time. When I hung up, I was worried and impatient. Damn. I'd actually considered letting the thing go, or not go, on its own. Now how could I?

The animals were soundly asleep in the living room when I set out for Xavier Fortunato's to find the foundation forms for the garage had been finished and the slab had been poured, as recently as that morning perhaps. Also, the gate was locked.

I knocked but received no reply. Nobody home.

I'd never seen Señor Fortunato's shop, gallery, whatever. Perhaps now was a good time.

Millagros was up one level from the street in a multileveled, staggered block adobe building not far from the Plaza. It faced on a saltillo-tiled terrace set with huge pots of bright flowers and a few uncomfortable-looking iron chairs. The window held three objects: a glass vase in which a swirl of irridescent colors faded from brilliant at the bulbous bottom to pale at the irregular top; a pair of gold earrings in the shape of crescent moons with diamond stars trembling on hair-thin wires; and a small impressionistic painting of a humming bird hovering over a deep-toned blossom. One of Margaret's.

A bell chimed softly as I went in. The woman who greeted me was an Erté print. Dress, shoes, stockings, brows, and helmet of shining hair were black. Neck, arms, and face were white, except for red, red lips. Paris or New York, not Santa Fe.

"I saw you looking at the earrings," she said. "Let me show you."

She reached into the window and took them out, bending to fasten one of them to her own ear. When she turned toward me, the diamonds thrust glittering through her hair, then vanished again when she turned her head. Stars against the black.

"The concept works best for someone dark," she said matter-of-factly, putting the jewelry back. "Someone who wears her hair down, as I do. The artist's name is Neale. He's made some amethyst hair ornaments in the shape of butterflies. They have little springs in them."

"Which work best for someone active," I said, straight-faced.

"Rather, yes," she agreed, perfectly seriously. "Especially effective when one is dancing. Did you have something specific in mind?"

"Is Xavier Fortunato in?"

"He left about half an hour ago. Is it anything I can help you with?"

"Actually, I'm looking for Margaret Quivada," I said. "I thought Xavier might know where she was."

"I think he was meeting her and her daughter," the woman

said in a distant, none-of-my-business-but voice. "At Suzette's. Something to do with a dress for the opening."

She disapproved of anyone's needing help selecting a dress for any occasion; so much was clear. But considering Margaret's financial situation and Suzette's prices (which Grace had investigated during one of our visits to Santa Fe), it was likely Xavier was providing more than mere advice. A delicate situation, not one I wanted to intrude upon.

So, trusting in providence, I went into La Fonda—Suzette's is off the lobby—for a drink in the bar. Providence came through. Xavier, Felicia, and Margaret came in ten minutes later. I hailed them and they joined me. Not the best occasion for telling Margaret about Joy. I dithered while drinks were ordered and Felicia bubbled about the beautiful dress Mom was going to have. I decided not to say anything just yet, but then Felicia nailed me.

"You went to Tulsa, didn't you? We called the ranch and the man there told us."

Well, I hadn't told him not to. Conversation stopped while drinks were delivered.

Margaret took a sip, then turned to me with a puzzled look. "Why did you go to Oklahoma, Jason?"

"I told you about the two men who were here looking for Ernie," I said. "In a car with Oklahoma plates?"

She nodded. I plowed on. "There's reason to believe it may have been Boomer Shepherd and his brother."

She turned very pale and still. "Joy's husband?"

I nodded.

Felicia said, "What is it, Mom?"

"Why would Joy's husband . . ." she murmured. "I don't understand."

". . . You didn't know that Joy's husband beat up on Ernie, back in Oklahoma?"

Her eyes went wide. "No. Ernie never said . . ."

"So that's what happened," said Felicia, nodding. "The time Daddy said he was in a car accident."

"But it was a car accident," Margaret cried, considerably agitated. "The headlight was all broken, the—"

"Shhh," I calmed them both, with an apologetic glance at

Xavier. "Hush, Margaret. Don't come all unglued. Ernie got into some kind of fracas with Joy's husband, and there was an assault, and Boomer was arrested for it."

"He used to beat Joy," whispered Margaret. "Badly. He broke her arm once."

"You never told me . . ." said Felicia.

"She told me not to tell." Margaret spoke over Felicia's comment, her hands clenched on the table top so tightly the knuckles were white. "She said I should never tell." She seemed almost not to know the rest of us were there.

Xavier leaned forward, pressed Margaret's glass to her lips, and urged her to drink. "Here. Just a little. Calm down, Margaret. Jason didn't realize you didn't know."

Though anyone but an oaf should have realized, his expression said. Which presented me with a nice dilemma. Tell her about Joy's death, or not.

Not, said Xavier's intent face. Not, said Felicia's concerned eyes, looking at me over her mother's bent head.

Margaret wiped at her eyes and excused herself. Felicia went with her to the ladies' room. I leaned forward and told Xavier what had happened in Tulsa.

"Don't tell her here," he said.

"I won't," I said. "I thought she must have known about the assault incident but just didn't want to talk about it."

"Probably, her husband did not tell her," he said. "If it had been me, I would not have told. A wife should admire her husband, if only a little. How can she, if she knows he has been whipped like a dog." His beard bristled with disdain. "You say this Shepherd man was arrested?"

"It was the arrest report that led me to Joy Shepherd, though Felicia had already mentioned her name to me. She'd told me about her mother's art-teacher friend in Oklahoma."

He asked what the cause of the disagreement had been, and I tried to tell him. He knew about possessive men, as what Latino does not, but even he considered the situation I described to be extreme.

"Even in Mexico," he said sadly, "where one is careful what men are invited to one's home, it is not considered proper to forbid a woman her women friends or relatives. If they have not a good husband and have not one another, what do they have?" Which was a damned good question. "I'll invite you to dine with us," he said. "That will give you an opportunity to tell Margaret about this."

When the others got ready to leave, Xavier suggested in a casual voice that I join them for supper, and half an hour later, in the shadowed portal at one side of the courtyard, I told Margaret and Felicia what had happened to Joy.

Felicia cried out, dismayed, but Margaret seemed already drained of emotion, as though intuition had informed her before I had. She merely stared into my face, tearless, as though she sought some intelligence beyond what I had told her, something she had expected but hadn't heard. I thought she might ask, but she did not. Her face changed, dismissively, and she asked something else.

"Will they catch him?"

"Probably," I said. "Sooner or later."

"I hope they kill him. What they do to us. What they do. They don't deserve to live." The words were almost gentle, without emphasis.

She turned and went away. Felicia gave me a horrified glance and ran after her. I hung my head, wondering how I could have told her more gently.

"It is hard," said Xavier from the doorway. "Being the carrier of ill news. Come have some brandy."

We had some brandy. We talked. About life, women, love, families, war, and the cost of civilization. We grew eloquent. He was remarkable: courtly, intelligent. Later, Lourdes brought us a bite of supper and we ate together, alone, without the ladies. Felicia, said Lourdes, had carried plates to the guest house for her mother and herself.

"Margaret cared a great deal for Joy," Xavier said when we parted. "She has spoken of her often to me, of her and of Helen Reiserling." He examined me narrowly, as though expecting some comment.

"Her friends," I murmured.

"Yes. Friends who have helped her bear her struggles. She will have to grieve for a while."

I thought what I had seen in Margaret's face had been anger more than grief, though an anger with banked fires, ash-covered coals, one that gave little evidence of its furious heat. Still, I could believe she would grieve, now or later, as I, on my way home through the dusk, was grieving for her.

"What they do to us," Margaret had said. I sat on the couch with the TV talking to itself, thinking about that. "What they do to us." What they do to women? What men do to women? Or to artists? What certain kinds of men do to female artists, perhaps. Who were *they*? Men like the Shepherds, men like Ernie? And people like the Quivadas?

Perhaps I could talk to Grandma Quivada again. Last time had been no picnic, but now that a little time had gone by, she might be more forthcoming. Meantime, since it wasn't late, I decided to call William Reiserling and tell him what the results of the Tulsa trip had been.

His home number was in the phone book, and he was there, sounding tired and a little frayed. "You feel like a drink?" he asked me. "I can say you're a client."

"I am a client. Sort of."

"Close enough. I need to get out of here."

I looked at my watch. It was only nine, so I said sure, anytime, and we agreed to meet in the bar at the Hilton.

He beat me there by some time. His glass was already almost empty when I got to the table. He shook his head at me wearily. "Women!" he said.

There's no reply to that. Not to "Women," or "Bosses," or "Lawyers!" I squeezed his shoulder, asked what he was drinking, and went over to the bar to get us each one. The bartender said he'd send the drinks over, but the pause had given Bill a chance to marshal his thoughts.

"I don't mean to say they're completely impossible," he greeted me as I sat back down. "They aren't. My wife has a few aberrations, as what wife hasn't, but basically she's a delightful person. My daughter, however . . ."

"Helen?" I asked, knowing full well. "In Hawaii."

"Was in Hawaii," he said. "Is now home."

"But she was on her honeymoon," I gaped.

"Was is the operant word," he sighed. "She and her new husband have had a falling out."

"Don't tell me it resulted from that fracas at the wedding. That would be too much." And it would, for poor Margaret, who was feeling quite guilty and upset enough.

"I have no idea. She's not talking to me. She's not talking to her mother. She just says it was a mistake, she wants to send all the gifts back. Her mother says, after that big wedding, she'll never be able to hold her head up again. To which Helen replies she never wanted a wedding in the first place. Which is true. She didn't."

"What does she want?"

"She wants her own apartment back. She wants her mother to quit urging her to get married and produce grandchildren. She wants a productive career in the art field, gallery or museum. She wants to go back to school. Mostly she wants to lie in her bedroom with the blinds closed, crying."

"Have you talked to her husband?"

"Briefly. He agrees with her. It was a mistake, he says. He's remarkably close-mouthed about the whole thing, but I get the impression he got drunk and committed some basic indecency." He sighed. "Seemed a nice enough fellow."

Our drinks arrived. Bill sank into his like a man who had been lost in the desert and finally found an oasis. He plunged. I sipped. He had the look of a man set for a long evening, and it would be wisest for one of us to stay halfway sober. Particularly considering the steady absorption of brandy Xavier and I had managed that afternoon.

"So what happened in Tulsa?" he asked.

I told him. He reacted—interest, amazement, horror, anger. All the right emotions in the right places. I must have told it well. He even stopped drinking during parts of it.

"My God," he said at last. "That poor woman. I've seen it in court, with kids, you know, the abused ones. Family'll have two or three kids they treat perfectly normally and one they beat on.

One that just starts all their rages going, somehow. And men, they'll get along all right with most people, but they save up all their furies for their wives. You wonder what goes on in their heads."

I said yes, you wonder.

He asked me the same thing Margaret had. "You think they'll catch him?"

"Oh, I think so," I said. "If necessary, they'll put him on 'Unsolved Mysteries,' or 'America's Most Wanted.' Paula will help them put the story together, and he won't be able to hide those tattoos."

"Do you think he killed Margaret's husband?"

I gave him the same answer I'd given Jack Snitel. Maybe. Not his style, but maybe.

He started talking about style, which he called MO, and that led to talking about crooks he'd known, and that led to something else, and it was almost midnight before he decided to let me drop him at his house because he was far too sozzled to drive. Which I did.

The lights were on upstairs.

"Helen's room," he said, pointing waveringly at the light. "She's probably sitting up there crying. What the hell went wrong?"

"She'll probably tell you eventually, or she'll tell her mother and her mother will tell you," I said.

"Yeah," he grunted, unconvinced. "I suppose." He staggered off toward the front door, and I turned the car around and headed back to the ranch.

Why I decided to go by way of Xavier Fortunato's, I don't know. It wasn't far out of the way, but it wasn't the most direct route either. When I came around the curve, my headlights caught two cars parked beside the new slab in front of the wall, and beside them two people sitting side by side. Felicia, and Hector. He had his arm around her shoulders.

I slowed, rolled down the window, and said hi, what's going on.

"Mom's got company." Felicia got up and came over to the car. "Helen came over."

"I thought she was in Hawaii," I remarked, all innocence.

"She was. It got cut short for some reason or other. Something's wrong, I don't know what, and Mom said disappear for a while, so I've disappeared." She made a monkey's face at me. "I called Hector to come keep me company."

"I'm sure Xavier would let you sit in the courtyard," I said.

"Yeah, well, we wanted to talk. Privately, you know."

The gate creaked open. In the light from the suspended lantern, I saw Margaret and another woman, Helen, presumably, quite tear-stained and looking more like fifteen than twenty-six. Without a glance in our direction, she went to her car, backed it, maneuvered around me, and slowly trundled away, in no hurry to get anywhere at all.

Margaret joined the rest of us. She looked calmer than she had when she'd left us earlier. "I didn't thank you for trying to help Joy," she said. "I know you did."

"Not enough. Not soon enough," I said. "Her friends in Tulsa tried to help her, too, but they just couldn't." I risked a question. "I thought Bill Reiserling told me Helen was on her honeymoon in Hawaii?"

She turned away from the car. "She was. I guess they aren't suited to one another. Sometimes that happens. Better she knows now, rather than later." She turned back toward me, her face a remote mask in the lamplight. "Would you like to come in for a drink?"

Her invitation was only conventional courtesy, but before I quite realized it, I'd said yes. I parked the car, got out, and went into the courtyard with her. It was lit by lanterns here and there, under the portal, over the various doors leading to kitchen wing and guest quarters, each throwing a dim pool of yellow light. The cocktail table I'd seen earlier was standing under the portal roof.

"The ice has all melted," she said. "I'll get some."

I put my hand on her arm, feeling her skin quiver at my touch, as I cast a quick glance along the array of bottles. "No. It's all right. Just give me a little port. Not much. I can't stay. It's already been a long evening."

She selected glasses and poured, half a glass for me, a drop for her. I sat down at the table, but she leaned against one of the portal posts, staring out at the shadowy garden.

"Hector seems to be very fond of Felicia," I said.

"I hope she's careful," she said with an intensity that concerned me. "God, I hope she's careful."

"Because you weren't a lot older than she when you were married?" I said. "You feel you were too young?"

"I was, yes. And Joy was. Yes." She laughed at something only she found amusing. "Too young and too hopeful and too foolish."

"I'm so sorry about Joy," I blurted. "I feel responsible somehow."

She turned, came close, leaned down, and kissed me, her lips fluttering against mine. "I know you tried," she whispered. "I know you tried."

The sound of my heart was enough to deafen me. If she hadn't moved away immediately, I would have reached for her. I took a deep breath, astonished at what I was feeling.

"Don't blame yourself," she murmured. "It was Joy's mistake. It was my mistake. It's always our mistake, we women. As you say, too young."

It was a moment before I could speak. "You're still young," I said carefully. "All men aren't like Ernie."

"Too many are. I've met some."

I found words sliding on my tongue and bit them back. "I'm not like that," I'd been going to say. "Margaret, I'm not like that."

What the hell. I was running away with myself!

I drank the port, gulped it, a fate it didn't deserve.

"It's late," I said. "Got to get on back to my animals."

It sounded weak and peevish, the last way I wanted to sound. Nonetheless, I made myself get up, shake her hand without grabbing it, walk to the gate beside her without touching her. When we reached the car, I got in despite wanting to take her in my arms, drag her back from that distance she retreated to, hold her close, and carry her off with me. Young Lochinvar, him and his damned white horse.

Bring her back to safety, my emotions said. Here, with us. But

I didn't know how to reach her, reach for her, without seeming to be like every other man who had reached for her. Besides, what right did I have to do it? What were my intentions?

Too many questions. Too much liquor, too troubling a presence, she. So, I said again, "It's late," as I put the car in gear.

"Goodnight, then," she said.

"Goodnight," echoed Felicia, Hector.

As I turned the corner, I could still see them in the rearview mirror, like a group of statuary, standing frozen in place, staring after me.

It was several miles to the ranch, but all the way there the feel of that feathery kiss remained on my lips.

Six

FRIDAY MORNING AT LAST. All night I'd slept and wakened, slept and wakened, telling myself to stop this nonsense, only to fall asleep and find myself dreaming of Margaret, waking with my blood throbbing and my head splitting. Too stuffy in the small bedroom, I told myself, actually getting up and moving into the larger one, trailing sheets and Bela's blanket and two puzzled animals. I put Bela's blanket in the corner, and after grumbling about the interruption, he settled on it with a sigh. Schnitz jumped up on the bed, washed his face with one paw as though giving me time to be sure I was settled, then curled into a lump at the back of my knees.

How much longer, I asked myself, not coming up with an answer. Why not go home, let the police find Boomer Shepherd, see what he had to say for himself. Chances were, the whole thing would be solved right there.

I didn't believe it, couldn't make myself believe it. I also couldn't make myself believe I was doing much good hanging around in Santa Fe. Exposing myself to temptation. The whole thing was an exercise in futility. Well then, find some other excuse for staying in Santa Fe for another few days.

Why did I want an excuse to stay?

I knew damned well why. Margaret Quivada had kissed me, and I couldn't forget it. Not that it had been passionate, it hadn't. It had, however, been stirring, perhaps more stirring than passion would have been. There had been a strange fragility to it, the lure of the exotic. Perhaps the lure of the forbidden? Which was in itself an odd thought. She was a widow, after all, not a married woman. Where was the taboo? Was there one on my side? Grace had not agreed to marry me. I had taken no oath of fidelity. Besides, she was stuck in Denver.

Despite all this self-serving rationalization, I felt I was behaving very badly. So I told myself while shaving. Then I went in the other room and called Mark.

"What's the matter, do you have time on your hands?" he asked.

I admitted it in a falsely cheerful voice. "I just thought, maybe there's something you'd like me to look for."

"You're not exactly in the wholesale capital of America, Jason. Prices there are higher than they are here."

"I know," I said, so exasperated I blurted the truth before I thought. "I'm looking for an excuse to stick around down here."

"Oh, an excuse. Now why would that be?"

"Because the trail is cold, and I'm not likely to come up with anything, but I need to tell Bruce and his mother I did my best," I snapped. "Why else?"

Long pause. Then, "Well, let me think."

He let me hang for a moment, then came back to say, "Got it. Remember that penthouse atrium job I'm doing for Mother's friends? The Van Zants?"

I said I remembered Zebra (Zeebie) and Wilhelm Van Zant. Where she got her odd name, I do not know. He ran businesses here and there, mostly on the West Coast, and she ran him ragged. He was haughty and she was twinky, but that was neither here nor there. The building that would eventually serve as a pedestal for the penthouse had been built as an office building, had stood mostly vacant for a decade, and was now having its top half remodeled into expensive downtown apartments. Mark had been presented thus far with three consecutive and quite different sets of penthouse plans.

Mark said, "Now she's got it in her head to have a fountain. She wants it not too watery, and not too Spanish. Not a drippy one, either."

"What does she have in mind?"

"Something, she says, trickly. Something that makes a pretty trickling sound. A burbly noise."

"A burbly noise?" I repeated hollowly, the phrase reminding me of Margaret's laughter. I gritted my teeth. "Burbly!"

Muffled explosion at the other end. He'd been trying to stifle laughter and not succeeding. "Well, Jason, you did ask for something to do."

"Anything else?" I demanded stiffly.

"Since you've asked, yes. I need some doors, double doors, carved or spindled or something to let the air through, anything up to six-feet-seven wide for the pair, and they should be at least seven-and-a-half high, on up to nine."

"To go with the burbly fountain?"

"Right. Needless to say the styles should . . . conform. We could design something, or have it designed, but Zeebie prefers something old, so she says. Something with history."

"But not too Spanish."

"Right."

"Do you have a budget?"

"Not really. What I will need is a reason for high prices, however. Willy has a nose for padding."

"Like 'Once owned by the Queen of Castile,' or something."

"Too Spanish, but something like that."

"I've never talked to Zeebie about decor. What kind of thing does she react to?" I asked. It always helps to know what kind of thing a client gravitates toward instinctively. Your client can tell you she wants Art Deco because her friend has Art Deco, but if she instinctively reaches for country fabrics, it's not going to suit no matter what she says.

"Zebra? Oh, hell, Jason, I don't know. One time one thing, another time another. Her vision of this atrium is—and I'm quoting—a green oasis in the heart of the city. A silent place for contemplation of her navel. She finds the word 'navel' hilariously funny. She says it and giggles, like a little kid saying pee-pee. I told her it won't be silent. There'll be some traffic noise, but it will be fairly quiet, since it's on the thirty-fifth floor, and also because of Wilhelm's new idea. The latest set of plans includes a vaulted glass roof."

Mark went on at some length, describing it for me.

"Where do the doors go?" I asked.

"Well, the latest set of plans say they'll stand at the end of the foyer, which is just off the elevator lobby. Living room to the right, atrium dead ahead, dining room to the right of the atrium. The elevator lobby is windowless, so the doors will probably stand open a good deal of the time."

Current thinking on the floor, he said, was marble, extending unbroken from foyer through atrium into dining room. There was to be greenery. Surfaces hadn't been decided. Glass, of course, for the roof.

"I'll see what I can do," I said dispiritedly. The idea of that vaulted glass roof depressed me. In the first set of plans, the roof had been designed with a rank and file of bubble skylights, which made structural sense at least. But Wilhelm had decided that wasn't dramatic enough, so the engineers had come up with a vault, which would reflect sound like the inside of a tympani, or was it tympanum? It would be grungy, most of the time, from exhaust and city grime. It would have to be washed weekly to look like anything at all. And though skylights would have been difficult enough to keep clean, as Mark described the location of this extravagance, there would be no way to get at the glass at all. Two sides of the roof would be at a back corner of the building, so where did the window washers stand? And how did they reach the top of this proposed vault?

Not our problem, I reminded myself sternly. We hadn't designed or recommended the glass roof. With Van Zant's money, he could afford to have a helicopter hover over it and lower window cleaners on ropes.

Nonetheless, the idea of the vaulted glass bothered me. I found myself making sketches on the backs of envelopes. Suppose the thing wasn't vaulted all the way to the edge of the building. Suppose it didn't start over the exterior walls, but two or three feet inside. Then you'd have a walkway around the perimeter of the roof, perhaps with a parapet on the outside. At least it would give cleaners somewhere to stand.

Then, suppose the inside walls of this courtyard were made of stone, with pockets of soil, and suppose you had water trickling . . . *burbling* down that stone into a long trough at the foot, from which it would recirculate and recirculate, *burbling* the whole damn time. Over ferns, and mosses, and whatever other things there were that grew on wet, trickly walls. This was in Denver, after all, where the humidity was generally very low. Many places used humidifiers. Wet walls would be good humidifiers. It would work better if it was more of a seep than a trickle. Maybe you'd have to do the burble at the bottom, an aerator, maybe, making bubbles. Have to experiment to get the right sound.

I called Mark back and explained the whole concept, illustrating with one hand, which he couldn't see, of course.

"You are frustrated, aren't you," he asked, more amused than anything. "You've just described a botanical garden rain forest or a tropical exhibit in a zoo. All it needs is monkeys and parrots. I think what the Van Zants have in mind is an atrium."

"With a damned vaulted glass roof," I snapped. "Which will be covered with snow in winter and smog all year, both making it dark as pitch in there. You'll have to have artificial light anyhow, so why not put halogen lights under this walkway I've proposed and give them a rain forest! It'll sure as hell be an oasis, if that's what Zeebie wants."

"The idea has some merit, Jason," he said, humoring me. "If we tone it down a little. I'll talk to Wilhelm. He has a whole troop of California engineers just panting to do designs for him, so no reason we can't discuss feasibility. Meantime, are you going to look for some doors for me?"

I told him yes, I'd look for some doors.

"By the way," he said. "I thought I was the one into decor, and you were just an antique dealer."

"Sorry," I mumbled. "It was an idea that came to me. I promise never to have another one."

He was laughing when he hung up. I wasn't. It was the first really exciting idea I'd had in a long time. Maybe I needed a commission to do a zoo!

Or something. Thinking of zoos reminded me, however, that on my way downtown I should stop by the Quivadas' place to see how Grandma and Grandpa were making out.

The little trailer house was empty. Vacant. The front door

hung on one hinge, as though willfully damaged, nothing inside but trash. Abandoned.

On a hunch, I went on down the road to Margaret's old place and found it very much occupied. Grandma Quivada was in her rocking chair under a tree. Vera sat nearby in an overstuffed monstrosity that looked as though it had been hauled in from the town dump. From inside the house I heard the skirl and skirmish of children, with the plaintive cry, "Vangy," hovering above the general furor like the cry of a lonely bird. If Dwight was present, he was invisible.

I got out to go pay my respects.

"Thought she was smart, din she?" challenged Vera when I drew near. "Well, Dwight got the power back on. Only takes a pair of little snips to take the seal off. Same with the gas. We gotta right. Don care what she does, we gotta right."

"Sure you do," I soothed. "Of course, the gas company may not see it that way, but they probably won't catch on for a while."

"Still got Ernie's deposit," she said defiantly. "Two hunnert dollars they still got. Got Grandma's deposit, too. Figure we should have a while comin."

Grandma hitched herself forward in her chair. "When's she comin' back?" she demanded. "We got nobody to do for us."

I assumed she meant Margaret. "She's not coming back," I told them firmly. "Not ever."

The result was interesting. Vera turning very red, Grandma very pale, each shouting at the other, "But you said she'd havta stop paintin and do for us." "I never." "You did too."

"What's all this racket?" Dwight, coming out of the house, slowly lifting his suspenders over his bony shoulders. "Oh, you," he said, with an attempt at a snarl. "What're you doin here."

"I came to ask you and Vera to tell me what happened at the church the Sunday afternoon Ernie was killed," I said. "I have a witness who saw you there about two-thirty or three."

"Nothin happened," he cried, giving Vera a shifty-eyed glance. "Nothin happened. Anybody says anythin happened, they're liars."

Grandma turned on Vera. "You tole me you didn't go over there."

"Ernie called and said . . . Well, it was just for a minute, to take Ernie somethin."

"You tole me you didn't go over there!"

"Well, we didn't hardly. Just stopped in for a minute!" Dwight dredged for something to change the subject. His face lighted up. "There was people Ernie was havin' words with."

"Who?" demanded Grandma. "Who was there?"

"Some local people," I said, to put an end to this colloquy. "They came to see the painting."

"Idolators!" she cried. "Them idolators!"

"Oh, I don't think so," I said. "They just thought it was a beautiful painting of the Virgin Mary, and they wanted to say a prayer, that's all."

"Oh, ye who bow down to wood and stone!" she cried. "Woe on ye who bow down."

"What I wanted to know," I continued to Dwight, ignoring Grandma with some difficulty, "was what happened. Did you see anyone around there when you left?"

"Anyone who?" he demanded suspiciously.

"I don't know who! I'm asking you if you saw anyone."

"We just went to see if Ernie was . . . if he was doin anything," Vera shouted. "An he wasn't, so we left."

"You and Dwight and the little boys. Where was Bobbi Kay?"

"She went over to the store to get a popsicle," said Dwight. "For her'n the boys. And we went in and saw Ernie there with these folks, and he was yellin, and they was on their way, and when Bobbi Kay got back, we left too."

"Did some yellin yourself," commented Vera, moving uneasily in her chair. "Yellin and wavin things around."

"You mind yourself," shouted Dwight.

"Got nothin else to mind," she said. "Wisht we had a TV."

"Well, and whose fault is it we don't." He made a face at her and started back to the house.

I'd had enough. I went back to the car, hearing Grandma's voice soaring behind me. "You tell her, you hear. You tell her she's Satan's woman, walkin on Satan's road so her feet offend her, they do."

The sound of her voice was like chalk shrieking on a blackboard, unbearable. I closed the car window and drove on into town, hearing with gratitude only the muted sounds of traffic and the hush of the air conditioner. I've never understood people who have to have noise around them, people who leave a radio playing all the time, people who leave the TV on, day in day out, as though they cannot bear to be quiet. Silence is increasingly rare, and therefore increasingly precious, it seems to me. If I'd had to live within sound of Grandma's voice for more than about an hour, I'd have lost my mind. And Vera was no fount of euphony, either. Or Dwight. How had Margaret stood it?

Earplugs, maybe. Real or psychic. Or a lack of interest so deep and abiding that she truly did not hear them. I found it difficult to hear their words, like deciphering the screeching of parrots. What was it Dwight had said? Ernie had wanted something brought to the church? What was that about?

I put the matter aside and went shopping for doors. There were none at the four antique shops I visited. However, at the last of these, I asked to use the toilet, and on my way out I passed the staff bulletin board, where my attention was caught by a circular touting an auction at a consignment gallery on Cerillos Road, beginning at two o'clock that afternoon. Serendipity. That left me time for lunch. I went to the Coyote Café and spoiled myself with mushroom chilaques, thinking the whole time how Grace would have loved them. By the time I finished my wine and a helping of delectable lemon-flavored bread pudding, a nap seemed a better choice than an auction.

Duty prevailed. It wasn't that I expected to find doors at the auction. What was more likely was that I'd mention what I was looking for to someone else, and that person might mention it to someone else, who, given enough time, might recall where they'd seen something of the sort. The whole process was imprecise enough that I could spend several days at it without feeling either guilty or slothful. So I went to the consignment hall, made the rounds of the stuff piled along the sides, seeing nothing particularly attractive or useful, and took my seat with a feeling of pleasant drowsiness, unstressed by necessity.

Imagine my feelings when the second item up for sale was a screen of four panels, each about six and a half feet tall and about thirty inches wide, the whole considerably dilapidated and with missing parts, while, at the same time, being beautifully carved, and with sufficient redundancy of individual pieces to allow one to take the whole thing apart, condense four panels to two, with or without two narrow framing side pieces. Voilà. A pair of doors.

Eighteenth century, the auctioneer said, which I doubted. Mid-nineteenth was more like it. Originally made for the sala of a townhouse in Morelia, he said, which might well have been. I had no idea where Morelia was. Have to look it up.

They'd brought the screen out of a back room and partly unfolded it, but the area behind it was piled high with sale items. I wished they'd unfolded it against a plain wall, so the pattern would show. This openwork sort of thing is tricky, whether it's done in wood or wrought iron or whatever. It can look charmingly lacelike, or it can look like Grandma's crocheted antimacassar, bunchy and whopper-jawed. Fancy jigsaw work, as on restorations of Victorian houses, for example, is now usually done in plywood, but pieces this age were cut from quite thin planks, which tend to split along the grain as they age and dry. Pieces drop off and are lost, leaving holes in the overall design. In this case the jigsawing was limited to a series of interlocked circles at the top of the panels, and while one of the sections was badly mutilated, three of them were whole. Except for the linked circles and the leaf and flower carvings on the solid panels at the bottom, the rest was a repeated pattern of narrow, wavy-edged ovals made by scalloped horizontal pieces joined vertically by delicate spindles.

The screen had been painted white, but not heavily. The edges showed clean, not mucked up with repeated paint layers. Something like this is very difficult to strip neatly. The labor costs are enormous, so having it relatively clean was important. There seemed to be flecks of gold on the carving, but the light wasn't good enough to be sure. In a Spanish setting, it would look

Spanish. In a Victorian setting, it would look Victorian. What would it look like in an atrium?

Like Nachez, I thought. Or New Orleans. Or possibly something Mediterranean. Pity I couldn't go up and look at it closely without betraying the fact I was interested. I'd simply pay no more for it than I was sure I could get out of it, regardless.

I let the bidding go on without me until it reached nine hundred dollars, then I upped it to nine and a quarter. The other bidder, a youngish fellow in a hat, cast me a puzzled look and upped it to a thousand. I said a thousand fifty, and then a thousand two. At that point, the other bidder shook his head at me and grinned. It was then I first began to wonder how I was going to get my acquisition home, something I'd foolishly overlooked until then.

It cost almost as much for packing and shipping the screen as it had to buy it. I should have tied it to the top of the Mercedes, driven it back to the ranch, taken it apart, and packed the pieces in boxes.

Someone else had another idea. "You should have let me have it," he said from behind me as I was concluding these business arrangements.

I turned to confront the other bidder. He was interestingly fox-faced, a little younger than I, with artfully touseled hair and twinkly hazel eyes, costumed in a leather vest over open shirt, leather-belted trousers with a silver and turquoise buckle, and a concho band on his hat. He was booted in snakeskin, which seemed to fit. He gave me a calculating look as he offered his hand, which stayed rather lingeringly in my own.

"Warren Chamberlain. Chamberlain's Decor. What are you going to do with it?" He gestured at the screen.

"Make a pair of doors," I said.

"Well, if you're going to do *that*," he announced, "you need the transom I've got at the shop to go with them. That's why *I* wanted them, to go with the transom." He offered a card, I gave him one of mine. "Denver," he said. "What on earth are you doing buying down here?"

"Combining business with pleasure. I'm on vacation," I lied. Or maybe not. Maybe that's exactly what I was doing.

"Well, if you're not busy, come have a drink at my place. I'll show you the transom and we'll dicker." He waved his eyelashes at me.

I wasn't intrigued by the dickering he had in mind, but I might be interested in the transom, so we went to his shop, where he poured me an extraordinary combination of fruit juices, brandy, and red wine, his own sangria adaptation, he said, and we looked at the transom, out back in the workshop.

"It does match," I admitted ruefully, carefully sipping the concoction he'd given me. After yesterday, I'd resolved to drink nothing stronger than beer for several days, and certainly not this lethal stuff. The transom had the same motif of linked circles as the screen, the same scalloped edge making a half circle from which a series of spindles radiated inward to a fancifully carved half sun. The spindles were not identical to those in the screen, but the scale was the same. The semicircular piece was over sixty inches across, so it would fit over the doors.

We chatted in desultory fashion: where he'd bought it, how long he'd had it. I called Mark and asked him if there was any way the transom could fit into the job. It would take at least nine and a half feet, and Mark had said nine. He wanted to know some detail or other, and I put Warren on the phone. Inside thirty seconds my host had established who Mark was and where they'd met and the fact they had mutual friends.

Warren was all business when he got off the phone. Evidently Mark had told him I'm invincibly straight.

"He'll let me know tomorrow," said Warren. "You work with Mark McMillan! I think that's extraordinary. By the way, if you don't have dinner plans, *do* join me. I'm taking some clients to Encore Provence for seafood, then they want to go to Chez What for the dancing, which they will do almost entirely with one another, and that will leave me sitting alone for much of the evening, during which I'll drink too much out of sheer boredom. One cannot, in these situations, take a date, and my only dear girl is no longer available."

"Dear girl?" I asked, amused.

"Helen Reiserling," he said, shaking his head. "She's a very pretty, quite amusing, and undemanding woman, but it seems she's gotten herself married."

Something clanged inside my head. Coincidence is suspect, always. I said I knew her father, and yes, I'd love to have dinner with him and his clients.

"Well then," he said, giving me a look that took quick inventory of everything from my hairstyle to my shoes, "Run on home and change. I'm meeting the Humbolts here at six-thirty. And don't worry about the transom. I won't do a thing with it until Mark calls."

I went home and fed the animals, took them for a run, came back, had a shower, and dressed appropriately for dinner out. I called Grace. Guilty conscience. She wasn't home. I left yet another message on her machine. She might have tried to call me today. She might try to call me tonight. I told her I'd be home by midnight—I would be!—and to call me then if she was still up. I needed Grace. Otherwise . . . otherwise something. I refused to admit to myself what that something might be.

I told myself to worry about it later. It was six-ten, and I was going to be late.

Late or not, I made it before the Humbolts did. Warren showed me into his patio-cum-office-cum-parlor, lit from above by natural light. I looked up, saw a shallowly vaulted glass roof, and grinned. It was a day for coincidences. "How did you get away with that here in Santa Fe?" I asked. "Glass roofs are not Santa Fe Style."

"I know people on the zoning board," he said. "Besides, you can't see it from outside. The parapets are very high, and they hide it."

I told him about Mark's atrium job, and my concern about vaulted glass roofs.

"You're so right!" he said. "Not that it snows that often here in Santa Fe, but my dear, when it does! We had two inches in February and it was black as pitch in here. One simply had to wait for it to melt."

"You could heat the glass," I offered. "A blower, maybe?"

"Oh, it heats itself from the warm air in here. Once the sun comes up, it doesn't take long for it all to slide off."

That gave me something to think about. He was talking about two inches of snow, and Denver sometimes had two feet! And when we had two feet, where did it go when it all slid off that roof of the Van Zants? Straight down the face of the building onto whomever was walking along the sidewalk, thirty-five floors below? We'd have to call out the avalanche rescue people! I made a mental note. I bet Wilhelm's California engineers hadn't thought about that one!

Warren's doorbell rang, and he went to greet the Humbolts. We were introduced. She asked me rather remotely if I knew so and so in Denver, and on about the third try, we had a mutual acquaintance. Her formality changed to instant friendship. We knew the same people; therefore I must be all right.

We had drinks. I nursed mine, refusing second and third rounds. We went to dinner. I drank one glass of wine, making it last. We went dancing. I had Perrier and lime. The Humbolts danced, well and tirelessly, with all the spontaneity of little steam engines, never missing a beat.

"They take lessons," said Warren, watching them amusedly. "They say it's marvelous exercise. I think it's taken the place of their sex drive, to tell you the truth."

"Tell me about Helen Reiserling," I said.

"Why?" he asked, not taking his eyes off his guests. "Why are you interested?"

"For no reason detrimental to her," I said. Then honesty compelled me to add, "I don't think."

"You tell me first," he said. "Helen is a dear girl. Sweet-natured. Confused. She told me once she loved going out with me because I didn't paw at her. She had a horror of being pawed at, or so she said."

"She understood the . . . ah, situation, didn't she?"

He shook his head, rather ruefully. "At the time, I'm quite sure she did not. I met her via the art scene, you know, and while she was knowledgeable about that, she was incredibly naive about life. Oh, she knew the *words,* but she didn't know how they applied to people. I don't think she had any idea about me until a couple of years ago when she asked me one night, very seriously and rather pink in the face, if I was gay. When I said I was, she seemed rather surprised. 'But you're a nice person,' she said. I told her many of us are. She seemed surprised by that as well."

"As though being gay were equated with being evil?"

"Well, I got the distinct impression her mother had made that equation. I think Mama had told her she had to quit going out with that fag, or words to that effect. Later Helen asked me when I'd chosen to be gay, repeating Mama again, I should imagine."

"What did you tell her?"

"I told her I'd never chosen it, it had chosen me. I know a few men who say they chose it and quite a few women who say so, but so far as I can tell, those who claim to have chosen it either didn't need it at all, or they'd do it with anything warm."

Mark had made similar remarks about people he knew, men and a very few women who liked anonymous encounters, with anyone, with anything. "Most of them are dead," he'd told me. "Or dying."

"So." Warren gave me a look. "Tell me why you're interested in Helen."

He'd been forthcoming with me, so I told him I was really interested in understanding Margaret Quivada, which meant I was interested in her friends and kinfolk and neighbors and anyone else who could throw light on the situation. Of course, this led to the story of the investigation of Ernie's death. I sat back and swiveled my chair around so I was beside him at the table, where we could talk quietly without appearing conspiratorial. He made interested noises while I told the story, ending with:

"Joy's friend Paula called Ernie vicious, the reason being that he came to the Shepherd house and, in front of Boomer, accused Joy of having an unnatural relationship with Margaret. Knowing Ernie, I'm sure he believed that any relationship was unnatural if it took a woman away from her family or religious duties. In his opinion, Margaret's painting was probably the most unnatural thing about her."

Warren shook his head in amazement. "He said this in front of the woman's husband? He was practically sentencing her to death!"

I agreed. That's how I figured it, too. What Paula had called viciousness hadn't been that. It had been Ernie's usual and customary insensitivity to people and their reactions to the things he did. He could do and say appalling things with no intention to hurt anyone.

"So what happened?" he asked.

"Joy denied any wrongdoing, so Boomer attacked Ernie, saying by God, if there's any perversion going on, it's Margaret who's perverted! Boomer had been married to Joy for fifteen years, and he figured he knew all about her, so this religious nut should get his perverted wife out of town."

"And Ernie did?"

"Well, evidently the suggestion was reinforced by a beating, at least so says the arrest report. Mind you, this is all around two and a half years ago."

Warren mused, "It would explain the custody business you mentioned. A brutal husband really might get custody of a child by charging his wife with some sexual abnormality. That's Bible Belt country down there. A rotten heterosexual is always more acceptable than a good homosexual."

It was true. I wondered what Lieutenant Snitel would say about it when I told him. If I told him.

"So the Quivada family came to New Mexico," Warren went on. "But Margaret missed her friend and missed her painting, so she began to paint again. And she began to sell, and she met and made a friend of Helen in the process. Two lonely, diffident women, one trapped in this strange marriage you describe, and the other one either asexual or constitutionally frigid—at least so I always thought. I believe Helen only got married to please her mother."

"It didn't take," I said. "She cut the honeymoon short and came home. She told her mother she couldn't stay married to him."

"How on earth did you know that?"

"Last night when I came by the place Margaret is staying, Helen was there. Margaret told me."

"Poor Helen," he mused. "She's such a pleasant companion."

The Humbolts came bouncily back to the table, and she asked me to dance with her. I begged off, saying I'd injured my leg, so she dragged Warren onto the dance floor and I spent the next quarter of an hour chatting with Mr. Humbolt, whose world seemed totally devoted to cruises, tours, the pictures he took on these occasions, and the equipment he used to do so. I say chatting, though what actually went on was a lecture on his part and grunted monosyllables on mine.

When Warren returned, I greeted him with some relief. The catalog of lenses had gotten abstruse.

"You said they're clients?" I asked.

"They have a town house here. They're never in it. Every time they go on a cruise or a tour, they redo it. Two years ago we did it Greek. Everything white, with a lot of tile and painted vases. This year we're doing it Cambodian. They give me photographs." He made a face. "Have you ever seen the temple of Ta Prohm in Angkor? Visualize it as a town house! All those elephants! I ask you!"

I shared his amusement while telling him about my rain forest idea.

"Now that sounds Cambodian," he admitted.

"Mark says it sounds like a botanical garden."

"That too," he said.

I yawned and apologized and yawned again.

"Warren, I'm going to get on back to the ranch. I've got animals to take for a walk before I go to bed, and I've had more to drink and eat today than is good for me. Thanks for your ear."

"It was a fascinating story," he said, offering his hand. "I hope you catch the culprit. You and Mark must have interesting times."

"Mark regards my curiosity as an aberration. But he's nice about it."

I stood up, waved at the Humbolts as they executed a clever series of side steps ending in a dip, and went out to find my car. The night had turned chilly, with a cold wind gusting out of gathered cloud in the south. We were in for a thunder storm, perhaps. It hit when I was halfway home, pelting rain, then a flurry of small hailstones that bounced harmlessly in the headlights, then rain again, then as suddenly clear. When I got to the ranch, it was dry. The cloud had missed it completely.

I stopped at the run to get the animals, parked, unlocked the door with Schnitz under my arm, and paused, one foot in midair. There was a sizable fur rug under my foot, one that opened an amber eye and glared at me from an expanse of copper-colored fur.

"Critter?" I asked.

He yawned, showing his back teeth and an expanse of pink throat.

"Grace?" I hollered.

She came trundling out of the master bedroom in a long pink gown and matching peignoir, pale hair loose and flowing. "Hello, stranger," she said in a Garbo voice. "You can put your foot down now."

I looked down, surprised. The foot was still in midair, but Critter had moved.

"That is," she said, "if you're the kind of man who can put his foot down."

I did not, thank God, have time to think about Margaret Quivada for the rest of the night.

Grace said she had managed to get the weekend off by dint of trading shifts and taking on extra duties and one thing and another. She did it, so she said, because my voice on her machine had sounded so forlorn. Besides, she was worried about this Margaret person. I had sounded most taken with this Margaret person.

I refused to talk about Margaret. The recent what-ever-it-had-been was still too freshly in mind. I was afraid I'd betray something I didn't want to betray. What, I wasn't exactly sure. It wasn't lust, not exactly. Temptation, of a sort, but what sort? I set the matter aside and concentrated on the present moment. And the one after that. And the one after that.

In the morning, we took the animals out early before lazing around over breakfast while I told her the entire Quivada saga. By this time, I could include Margaret as part of the general picture without quivering every time I said her name.

"Take me to see the church," Grace demanded when I'd finished. "I want to see it."

"Should we get dressed first? Or go as we are and give the natives something to talk about?"

She blushed all over, pink as the peignoir she did not have on. "Get dressed, idiot!"

The morning was coolish. The thunderheads had massed into a general cloud cover, so we put the animals in the car with us, Schnitz in the carrier so he and Critter wouldn't fight. All thirty pounds of Critter usually stands in the backseat with his front legs on the arm rest, looking out, which is surprising for people who drive up alongside. He has a head the size of a large cantaloupe. With teeth to match, of course.

When we arrived at the church, I parked and went around to help Grace get out without the animals escaping. Hand in hand we went up the rickety steps, she murmuring at each thing she saw, as though making an oral index. *Look at the cactus, there's a chopping block, do they chop wood here? I guess, there's a hatchet, it's all rusty. . . .*

"Whoa," I said.

"Whoa what?"

"The hatchet. I didn't see a hatchet here before."

"There's one here now," she said, continuing her catalog. *Yes, there's the stove, for winter. What a saggy floor. There's a pulpit.*

I wouldn't have called it a pulpit, but she did. A pulpit, to me, was elevated and dignified somehow. This shabby scarred-up thing wasn't.

"What's the reference?" she asked.

"What reference?"

"The text for his last sermon," she said, pointing to the dusty sheet of paper taped to the front of the lectern. The numbers of the hymns they'd sung. The text for the day. Mark 9: verses 43–48.

"Grace, I haven't the foggiest," I said. "My Bible knowledge is limited to whatever Charleton Heston felt the general public should know."

"I'll look it up when I get home," she said. "I've got Grandma's Bible."

She made her way around the room, looking at everything, stopping beside the candle stubs and puddled wax, stopping again at the iron stove and the little cardboard closet at the back. "Wood stove," she said. "Use that in the winter only, I should think. Brush. Dustpan. What he needed was an industrial-sized vacuum cleaner."

"The hymnals are gone," I said. "There were about a dozen hymnals here when I looked at the place last."

"I figured there must have been. Otherwise the hymn numbers made no sense. Who played the piano?"

I turned around. The piano was gone!

"You can see where it was, in the dust," she said. "I guess somebody came and got it?"

"If I know Vera and Dwight, they probably sold it. I don't know who played it."

"It's a minor inconsistency," she said. "When Bruce talked about the murder, he said the congregation amounted to only half a dozen people. Now maybe he meant that as synonymous with 'a few,' but maybe he meant it as an actual count: six. The Bobbisons, the elder Quivadas, and Margaret make five. Was Bobbi Kay along? Was she the sixth? Or was she home babysitting the little boys? Was there a sixth? Who? Who played the piano?"

"We'll ask Margaret." We got back in the car, and I drove to Fortunato's, where we walked around a crew of men who were building cement block walls around the edges of the new slab. Ninety years old or not, Fortunato knew how to get things done!

Felicia let us in the gate and was introduced to Grace. I thought she might know the answer to Grace's question about the piano, so I asked.

She looked at me blankly for a moment. "The piano? For the hymns? I've never met her, but Mom's mentioned her. Her name's Garvey. Melissa or Melinda, I think. Something like that. Daddy told her she could use the piano to practice on if she'd play for services."

"I shouldn't think that was very convenient," said Grace. "Coming all the way to the church to practice."

"No, she lives right there," Felicia answered. "Down behind the church, in the arroyo."

I was puzzled. "There's no road there."

"I know there isn't. By road, it's a long way round. But all she has to do is climb up the arroyo, and it's right there. It's like this place and the church. By road, it's a long way, but the church is right over there." She pointed slightly northwest. "Five minutes walk down into the arroyo, across the arroyo, and up the other side," she said. "Santa Fe's funny that way. You can yell to somebody across an arroyo, but then it'll take ten minutes driving to get to them."

"I wanted to introduce Grace to your mother," I said.

"Not home," she replied. "She's having a fitting at Suzette's. And when she's through there, she's meeting Helen for lunch, then she's going to paint until dinnertime, and all day tomorrow, and all day every day until she's finished. That's what she said this morning, anyhow."

I shrugged at Grace, and she at me. We'd found out what we wanted to know. When we got back in the car, I got out my map, the large one that shows every road in the county. We located the church, located the arroyo, then backtracked the road there until we found where it joined the highway. Grace took a red pencil out of her purse and marked the route, and I followed it.

The road came into the arroyo at its widest point, where it spilled out onto the prairie, an old arroyo, cut millenia ago by big floods, then cut deeper by smaller ones, leaving wide shelves halfway up the sides, the western one broad enough for a row of scattered houses and the narrow road. The lower arroyo was bare and sandy, obviously still washed out every few years, but the higher slopes were gentle and overgrown with sparse grass and a few piñons and ancient clumps of silvery bony choya, which even in full bloom looks like the skeleton of something else.

We stopped where the mailbox said GARVEY. When we opened the car doors, we heard piano music, the thunder of tiny fingers, as Jacob had used to say. I thought it was Chopin, and skillfully played, though the total effect was anything but musical. The piano was sadly out of tune.

I knocked on the door once, then more loudly. Feet came pattering, the door jerked open, and a bright voice said, "Thank God you're here. I couldn't stand five more minutes of it." Then the person caught sight of Grace.

"You're not the piano tuner," she challenged.

"Miss Garvey?" I asked. "Millicent?"

"Millibelle Garvey," she said. "I had a fanciful mother."

She was in her mid-seventies, bright as a new penny, cheeks pink and white hair fluffed. I introduced myself and Grace as friends of Ernie's half brother. I explained about his mother, and said we were making certain inquiries, could she help us?

"Oh, my dear boy, my dear girl, I do doubt it. Indeed I do. I knew very little of the Reverend Quivada and wished to know less. Indeed, had my need not been so very great, I would have done anything rather than sit through those really quite dreadful sermons. I used to sit there with my ear plugs in and think of Beethoven."

"Your need?" prompted Grace, with a straight face.

"For a piano. An instrument. My piano, the one my father gave me when I was merely a girl, was crushed when my roof fell in. It rained, you see. For days. We all say it doesn't rain in Santa Fe, and of course it doesn't, except occasionally. This was such an occasion. The roof is earthen, of course, and quite unknown to me, the coating on it leaked, so the rain came into the roof, which became heavier and heavier until it fell in with a great squooshing noise, like a dinosaur settling into a swamp. The insurance fixed the house, but it would not stretch to a new piano."

"So you consented to play for the church up the slope there."

"With great trepidation. Which was entirely warranted. I dislike these cults that presume to count God among their personal friends. I dislike ministers who presume to instruct God in His duties. But without a piano, time lay so heavily upon my hands. . . ."

Another car drove up and stopped. A stooped, gray-haired gentleman got out, carrying a small bag. "Now there's the piano tuner," said Millibelle Garvey. "Let me just get him started."

When a steady *plink-twang, plink-twang* told us he was started, she came out once more, gesturing to a bench beneath an old cottonwood. We sat there, side by side, while Grace perched on a low table I identified as a cable spool doing duty as picnic furniture.

"How did you end up with Ernie's piano?" I asked. "I presume that is Ernie's piano."

"It's the piano from the church," she said. "I obtained it by signing a paper saying I forfeited all property rights in the congregation if I could have the piano."

"Who proposed this deal?" I asked.

"Mr. Bobbison," she said promptly. "He had the paper all written up. And his wife witnessed it."

"Well, well, well," said Grace, rising and brushing off her trousers. "Thank you, Ms. Garvey. I hope you enjoy your new instrument. I hope it tunes well."

I stood also, shaking the older woman's hand as we said goodbye.

"Oh, by the way," she said, interrupting our farewells. "When I went to the church to supervise the moving of the piano, I returned the hatchet."

Which explained, I supposed, why I had not seen it there before. I thanked her again, and we departed to the *plink, plink, plink* of the piano tuner and the sound of birds in the big old tree behind us.

Grace said she was starving, so after dropping the animals off at the ranch, we headed in the direction of Santa Fe. We were just approaching the military cemetary at the northern outskirts when she asked, "Who's Helen?"

"What?"

"Felicia said her mother's having lunch with Helen. Who's Helen?"

I told her about Helen, which led me to the subject of Warren Chamberlain, neither of whom I'd mentioned in my earlier version of recent events.

"Um," she said when I had finished. "When I was eighteen, I used to date a guy who was gay. I knew he was gay, but I liked going out with him. He was good-looking and fun, but there was no hassle, you know. He went off to New York, but I still get a Christmas card from him every year."

"I think that's how Helen felt," I said. "She appreciated the no-hassle aspects of the relationship."

"What was it Ernie wanted?" she asked next.

"When?" I asked, lost.

"When you told me about yesterday's conversation with the Bobbisons, you said Dwight Bobbison said Ernie called and wanted something. Or was it his wife who said it? And they took him something? What did they take?"

"I don't know. Getting information from that assemblage is like trying to sort out static."

"We ought to find out," said Grace. "It's important to know why they went over there that afternoon."

"We can go ask them. We probably won't learn a thing. Or we can talk to Ricardo and Lourdes," I said. "They were there."

"Right," she said. "When are we going to eat?"

I told her as soon as she decided where she wanted to go. She picked the Old Mexico Grill, where I watched in my usual bemusement while she ate enough fajitas to have satisfied any five ordinary men.

"I thought you liked Casa Sena," I murmured as she was wiping up her plate with the tattered remnant of her last tortilla.

"Saving it for tonight," she said.

"It's a Saturday during tourist season. It'll be mobbed."

"So, we'll eat early," she said cheerfully. "Or late."

"Or both," I said in a sarcastic voice.

"That would be nice," she sighed, patting her mouth delicately with her napkin. "One of the nicest things about you, Jason, you can afford to feed me. What do you suppose they have for dessert?"

After lunch, even though I felt I'd never be hungry again, I phoned Casa Sena for reservations, then Grace wanted to stroll, so we drove up to Canyon Road, found a place to park, left the car, and strolled. Every other tourist in Santa Fe was also strolling. We looked at art. We looked at glass, and hand weaving, and santos, and pottery—including a marvelous painted and partially glazed pottery Noah standing bemused among his animals, which I coveted but had no earthly use for. We looked at paintings, including Howell's of hair and Gorman's of crouched women, two artists who had succeeded in becoming clichés during their lifetime as "tourist" artists are wont to do. I saw nothing that even approached the style or elegance or emotional impact of Margaret's painting. I said so.

"She's got you wondering, doesn't she?" asked Grace, giving me a long, level look.

This was so accurate, I flushed. "I guess that's it," I said. "She's . . . she's different."

"Um," she said. "I can't wait to meet her."

"We'll go over in the morning," I promised. "That might be a good time to catch Lourdes, anyhow."

It was a little after four. Since it had been at least two and a half hours since she'd last eaten, Grace began sniffing the air. El Farol's bar was open and they offered tapas at four-thirty. We had tapas, and a drink, and more tapas. Some with chiles and some with sausage and some with shrimp. A good thing, Grace said, since we couldn't get into Casa Sena until after nine. Oh, absolutely, I replied, easing my belt a notch wider.

We went back to the ranch and walked the animals and had a nap. Sort of, while Critter stood outside the bedroom door and made tomcat noises. He has a *rowr-rowr-rowr* that would put any operatic baritone to shame. Fortunately, he does not usually mark territory unless there's another tom cat around, though I'd noticed Grace trotting around with paper towels a couple of times since she'd arrived, erasing Critter's aromatic evidence of himself. Evidently he considered Schnitz an interloper.

When we finally let him in, he settled down between us on the bed, his head between our heads, giving each of us in turn his amber-eyed stare. My arm hung off the side of the bed, and Schnitz sneaked under my hand and rubbed his back against my fingers for reassurance. I gave him a skull rub to indicate he was not being replaced.

"I missed you," murmured Grace between Critter's ears. "When you're there, I wonder about you, but when you're gone, I really miss you."

"Absence," I remarked, yawning. "Making the heart grow fonder."

"No. It's not fonder," she said. "It's clearer. Like I can see you clearer when you're not right there next to me, breathing in my ear."

"Who wants to see clearly during heavy breathing." It was a purely rhetorical question.

"So we have to figure out this business and get you back home."

I lied a little. "That's been my intention. I've been waiting for Lieutenant Snitel down in Tulsa to call me and say they've caught Boomer. Even though slashing a throat doesn't sound like his style."

"I've been thinking about that," she said. "About the weapon. I'm surprised the hatchet is still there. I should have thought the police would have taken it."

"The hatchet? It wasn't there. Millibelle brought it back."

"You don't know whether it was there Sunday or not. In the first place, it shouldn't be there at all."

"It shouldn't?" I sat up and frowned at her.

"Of course not. It's mid-summer. You don't need a wood stove in midsummer. Even when you do need a woodstove, you don't leave your hatchet out in the rain to get all rusty."

"But Ms. Garvey said she returned it."

"She herself wouldn't have left it outside to get all rusty. She's not that kind of person. Not that it rains that much down here, but as she pointed out, it does occasionally. It has recently. So, the hatchet was rusty, but not that rusty."

"What do you mean, that rusty?"

"I mean it was rusty, like it had been left out for a while, but not rusty enough for it to have been outside since last winter. So what was it doing there at all? And why did she have it, and when did she return it, and why was it outside?"

I shook my head, trying to remember if I'd ever used a hatchet in my life. An ax, yes. "Where did you learn about hatchets?"

"My Uncle Bern—I've mentioned him to you?—lived out in the country, in Minnesota. We used to go visiting. He and Aunt Tilde still heated with wood stoves. One time Ron and I stayed with them for several months when my mother was sick. Church twice a week and three times on Sunday. I was about ten, I think, not old enough to use the ax to split wood, but old enough to use the hatchet and make kindling. The hatchet and the ax both lived on nails beside the back door, under the porch roof, and if you wanted a whalloping, just leave one of them out to get rusty."

"Could someone slash a throat with a hatchet?"

She thought about it. "I shouldn't think so," she said. "Not unless it was sharp as a razor. The one there at the church wasn't that sharp."

I tried to summon up a picture of the hatchet as I had seen it when she called my attention to it. "It wasn't shiny," I said at last.

"The only part that gets really shiny is the edge," she said. "Just after it's sharpened. Uncle Bern kept his ax painted, even the head. He painted all his tools bright yellow, like a school bus, so he could find them if he dropped them in the woods or in weeds or stuff."

"Why do you think it's important?" I asked.

She shrugged. "Just because it doesn't belong there. I'm surprised nobody's walked off with it. It looked like a perfectly good hatchet to me. All it needs is cleaning up."

"On the way into town this evening, we'll stop and get it," I murmured sleepily. "Maybe it's evidence."

"Can we stop and talk to Mr. Fortunato's person, too. Lourdes, did you say?"

"Um," I said, giving up all pretense of following the conversation.

When one is with Grace, if there is a meal in the offing, one need not worry about oversleeping. I was wakened in good time. We stopped at the church and found the hatchet, which was still lying half under the front steps. Grace picked it up with a forefinger at each end and placed it in the trunk, wrapped in an old newspaper she'd brought for the purpose. We drove to Xavier's, where, as luck would have it, Lourdes herself answered the gate bell. I introduced her to Grace, and Grace asked about their visit to the church two weeks before.

"Did either of the people who came in have anything with them?"

"Have anything?"

"Were they carrying anything, Lourdes?"

She furrowed her brow in an effort to remember. "The fat

woman was carrying one little boy. The other one was running aroun outside. We saw him when we came out."

"What about Dwight? Was he carrying anything?"

She shook her head slowly. "He was behin her. She's so big, you know, an he's a little man. But I didn' like them yelling that way, so I wen out bery quick, but Ricardo, he was still in there. Maybe he knows."

"Would you ask him, Lourdes? It's important."

"When he comes home, sure."

"I'll come over in the morning," I said. "If it's not inconvenient."

She shrugged. "Don Xavier and me, we go to early mass. 'Cep for that, we be here all day."

"And I still haven't met Margaret," mused Grace as we turned away.

"Maybe tomorrow," I said. "She's got this show coming up, and she's working. I think it means more to her than anything else in the world."

"More than her family . . . well, her daughter?"

"Well, once she knew she was going to have a show, she told the Bobbisons she couldn't take care of them anymore. And commenting on that, Xavier Fortunato said, 'She'd only do that for her art, not for anything or anyone else.' Or words to that effect."

"I knew someone like that. When I was in high school. This kid who was a pianist. He wasn't just good, you know. He was something extraspecial. You see his name all the time now, on TV. He writes the music for this show or that. We used to kid him because he never let anything interfere with his music. He had a girlfriend . . . can't remember her name. Anyhow, they were close, but they broke up when he skipped prom night because there was a concert he wanted to go to."

There was something a little stressed in this retelling, as though she still found her memory hard to believe or in some way reprehensible. Perhaps she had been the girl in question. Certainly, in Grace's book, people would always take precedence over almost everything else. It was one of the things that made her lovable, and infuriating.

When we arrived in town, the closest place to park was the parking garage, and we were a few minutes early, so we strolled once more, looking in windows, commenting on tourists.

"Now there," said Grace. "There's your Santa Fe style!"

I followed her gaze to a couple standing with their backs to us, across the Plaza, in front of the Palace of the Governors. She was leaning against a post, and as the man turned toward her, I said, "It's Warren Chamberlain." He was wearing another one of his extravagant outfits, this one with a fringed leather jacket.

"And is that Helen?"

"It is."

"So he's got his dear girl back," murmured Grace. "Jason, has it occurred to you she's probably a lesbian."

The word took me totally by surprise. My immediate reaction was no, not at all, she wasn't, she couldn't be. Her father would know. Wouldn't he?

But why would he? I said, more forcefully than I'd intended, "It didn't occur to me, Grace. Warren said he thought she was asexual. I thought of repression, of course, maybe she'd had an unhappy experience in childhood or early adolescence."

Grace took a deep breath. "Jason, has it occurred to you that Margaret is probably a lesbian too."

For some reason I was glaring at her, fury boiling away at me, angrier than I could remember being recently. "Margaret?"

She put her fingers over my lips, and I realized I'd shouted. Across the plaza, Helen had heard me. She glanced across Warren's shoulder at me, then away. She didn't know me. Only the name had caught her attention.

Grace took my rigid arm, shook it until it moved, and urged me along the south side of the Plaza toward the twin towers of the Cathedral, jutting black against the darkening sky. She pulled me close and murmured, "Suppose Ernie's accusation was true! Maybe he walked in on Joy and Margaret together and had good reason to know it was true! He made the accusation to Joy, but also to Boomer, a man who could not, would not ever accept that he was married to a lesbian! He couldn't accept it because his masculine ego was at stake. So he turned the accusation around, accused Margaret of being the perverted one and told Ernie to get her out of town. Then he beat on him until he did.

"But even though he denied the accusation, it made him hateful and suspicious and more violent than he probably always had been. After that, he watched Joy like a hawk!

"Meantime, here in Santa Fe, after a while Margaret found a new friend, Helen. Also a lesbian. Because she's under Mother's thumb, however, Helen did what Mama wanted and tried marriage, which did not work. And back she came to Margaret."

I struggled to find words. "So all this business, this strangeness of Ernie's, the Bobbisons, all that. . . ."

"All these were Ernie's tactics for disrupting Margaret's relationship. Frankly, Jason, despite all your descriptions, I don't get a very clear picture of Ernie. My bet would be he didn't understand sexuality at all."

My words came out in a strangled voice I didn't recognize as my own. "He didn't understand *any* human reactions and relationships, including his own to other people. Satan was mixed into most human relationships."

"You'll agree what I suggest is a possibility?" She gave me a worried look.

"Why wouldn't I?" That same strangled voice.

"I thought, maybe . . . you were very attracted to her."

"To Margaret?"

She nodded.

I took a deep breath, then another, forcing calm and good sense and all that, refusing to be carried away on waves of denial and countercharge, though I much wanted to. Margaret had kissed me. Why had she kissed me if . . .

Because she was expressing gratitude. And I had chosen to think it was . . . perhaps hope it was . . . something else.

I said only, "There's something about her that's intensely attractive. I'm not at all sure that it isn't her very remoteness. A kind of unattainability."

"It's a challenge," she said softly. "Some women feel that way about gay men."

"I know." I managed a rather hollow laugh, remembering something Mark had said about that. He'd given up living at home years before, because his parents kept conniving with "acceptable" young women who thought they could convert him to heterosexuality. Had I had any such thought about Margaret, even subconsciously?

"I'm not sure all this has anything to do with what we're actually looking for," I said, trying not to sound annoyed. I was annoyed. Or hurt. Or . . . embarrassed. The whole thing was going in a direction I found intensely uncomfortable.

"I think so," she said as we turned left to pass Packard's and the Kiva on our way to the La Fonda corner. "Jason, I think it does."

"Let's let it lie for tonight," I said, managing, so I thought, not to sound angry. "I promise to let you examine my psyche in the morning, okay?"

She swung me around to face her, reached up to touch my jaw, which was clenched. "Hey, Jason."

I swallowed and took a deep breath. "Tomorrow. Tonight we just . . . eat, okay."

"That's always okay," she said, swiveling me around the corner. She tugged me across the street between two opposing currents of automobiles toward the covered alleyway that led to Casa Sena, while I tried to forget about Margaret Quivada and concentrate on feeling hungry.

Seven

SUNDAY MORNING. Two weeks since Ernie had died. Bruce marked the occasion by forgetting the two-hour time difference and calling at the crack of dawn to ask if I'd found out who'd done it yet. His mother, he said, was fretting.

During the night, I'd more or less come to terms with Grace's analysis of the Quivadas' sexual situation. I hadn't fully accepted it, but I wasn't fighting it any longer. Bruce had interrupted a tender moment. I started to tell him so, then stopped. It was hardly the thing to say to a man who was inquiring about a murder, and I certainly didn't want him quoting me to his mother. She'd think I didn't have my mind on my work.

"Soon if at all," I said. "There's very little unplowed ground to look at, Bruce. We've asked most of the questions that are askable."

"What about the Oklahoma stuff?"

"Still waiting for a call from the police."

He understood. He'd called only because his mother had asked him to. We muttered mutual conciliations and hung up.

Grace came to the door, grabbed me by the hand, and was tugging me back toward the bedroom when the phone rang again.

"Shit," she hissed, between clenched teeth.

I gave her an apologetic look and picked it up.

"Jason Lynx?"

"Speaking."

"Jack Snitel, Tulsa Homicide. I thought you'd like to know we picked up the Shepherd boys."

"When! Where?"

"Early this morning. I mean earlier. I forget you're an hour behind us. Buster got drunk at some little tavern over on the Missouri border, got in a fight, got arrested. His brother went along to arrange bail, somebody there had his wits about him and recognized the name. We had them both back here by five this morning."

"Have they said anything?"

"Boomer hasn't. Not about either killing. Buster has. Said Joy was an accident. Pretty much what you said happened. His brother just hit her once too often."

"What about Ernie?"

"Buster denies being anywhere near New Mexico two weeks ago. Said he and Boomer were in Santa Fe a month ago, on business, but two weeks ago they picked up with some other good old boys and went hunting—poaching deer is what they actually did. He says he didn't intend to shoot at anything except varmints. We can't charge him for just walking around in the woods, and he knows it."

"But he gave you names."

"Oh, indeedy he did. Including one ex–county judge and a district attorney. The one man I've got hold of so far says yeah, sure, the Shepherds were there. He also denies having any unlawful intent, of course. Just a bunch of the fellows goin' through some male bonding ritual."

I laughed, it was so unexpected. "I didn't expect pop-psych out of you, Jack!"

"Oh, hell," he said. "It was on TV. Burt Reynolds and his friends sittin nekkid around a campfire. My neighbor's doin it, too. Lolloping through the trees, dong floppin, beatin tom-toms. He invited me. Told him I was bonded enough."

I thanked him, he thanked me. Grace had gone back to the bedroom, and when I got there, she was half dressed.

"Are you going to call Bruce and report?" she demanded in a slightly hostile tone.

"Didn't think I would." I gave her a rueful look. No point trying to get back where we'd been fifteen minutes earlier. Obviously, Grace was on the move.

"You told Lourdes we'd be over this morning," she said.

"I didn't say at the crack of dawn," I objected.

"By the time we drive into town and have breakfast, it won't be the crack of dawn!"

"Where do you suggest we have breakfast at six in the morning."

"It isn't six, it's six-twenty. By the time you have a shower and shave, it'll be six-forty. By the time we get to Santa Fe, it will be seven. Dona Elena opens at seven. Tortilla Flats opens at seven. The Inn of the Anasazi opens at seven." She was tapping her foot. "The Petroglyph opens at six-thirty!"

Grace learns the opening hours of restaurants the way some kids pick up Nintendo. By osmosis. I'd rather had my mind set on brunch at Bishop's Lodge, but there was no arguing with her. Her clock had switched from sex to food, and only food would do. Without further demur, I got into the shower.

We went to Dona Elena's. Grace ate huevos rancheros and drank a gallon of orange juice. I had a breakfast burrito and coffee. After three cups, the day did seem to brighten. I bought a Sunday paper. The place wasn't crowded, so we lingered. By eight-thirty, when trade was beginning to pick up, we'd both had enough.

"What time is early mass?" she wondered. "Do you suppose Lourdes is back by now?"

"Let's just go on over there," I suggested. "Maybe you can meet Margaret and see if your suspicions are justified."

"Oh, they have to be," she said comfortably. "It's the only scenario that fits the facts."

We drove on over to Xavier's in Sunday morning quiet. There was little traffic. High overhead a cluster of eight or ten hot air balloons, like brightly painted lanterns, moved steadily toward the northwest mountains, all of them at the same altitude, moved by the same wind. At the surface, the air was completely still though not yet hot.

We turned into Xavier's road, surprising a coyote who was sitting on the verge, scratching himself. He watched the car pass, unwilling to move unless it was necessary. A bit farther on, I slowed to let a bright pink snake cross the road, which it did in one continuous whiplash of movement, vanishing almost before I was sure I had seen it. It had been at least six feet long.

"That snake was pink!" I gasped.

"Coachwhip," she said. "I think sometimes they're called Red Racers. They're harmless."

"If one were drunk, one might think otherwise."

"That's only elephants, isn't it?"

"Did you learn about coachwhip snakes at Uncle Bern's, also?"

"They're a Southern snake." She frowned, trying to remember where she'd learned of them. "Can't remember. Maybe I just read about them."

We turned the last corner and pulled up in front of Xavier's place. The new garage walls were already about four feet high. The gate stood slightly ajar, and we heard voices coming from inside the courtyard. Margaret's contralto, Felicia's soprano, Xavier's tenor. Plus a baritone rumble, which turned out to be Ricardo, who was just setting a laden tray on a stand beside the festively set table. Flowers, water goblets, slices of melon decorated with curls of lime. Lourdes had made Sunday breakfast an occasion.

"Are we interrupting?" I called.

Xavier beckoned. "Come in, come in. Join us."

Felicia got up and came toward us. I introduced her to Grace, and then Grace to the others. Both of us refused a second breakfast though Grace accepted a slice of melon and we both had coffee. We sat nearby while they ate. Margaret was in high spirits, because, so she said, she'd done some good work in the past few days.

"I saw your former houseguests yesterday," I told her. "They've moved into the house, along with Ernie's grandparents."

"We know," Felicia said, nodding over a mouthful of muffin. "Mom got a call from the gas company asking if it was okay to turn the gas back on."

"How did they know where you were?" I asked Margaret.

"I'd called and left this number on my account," she replied. "I told them I wouldn't be responsible for any more bills. Ernie's father left him a paid-up insurance policy, and Ernie's grandparents were the beneficiaries, so they can afford to pay their own utility bills."

"Did you know about the piano?" asked Grace.

When they looked at her blankly, she told them what Millibelle Garvey had told us about getting the piano in return for signing away a possible "share" in the congregation.

"I don't even care," said Margaret firmly. "I've resolved to stop caring." She shared a conspiratorial glance with Xavier, who nodded at her like a parent approving the actions of his favorite child.

"Well, I certainly don't care," added Felicia. "I hated that house and I have no use for a piano."

"Can we see the work you've been doing?" Grace asked Margaret. "Or would you rather we didn't."

"You can see," she cried, as though surprised by the question. "I'd love to show you."

She jumped up, patting her mouth with a napkin and leaving her breakfast unfinished. She took Grace's hand firmly in her own and dragged her off toward the guest quarters.

Xavier shook his head. "She would rather paint than eat. She would rather paint than breathe, if she could figure out how."

"Will she mind if I tag along?"

"No, no, go! By all means, go!"

I followed in their wake, through the open door, down a corridor, and into a sun-drenched room that faced out, across the arroyo. Halfway down the opposite side of the declivity stood a dotted line of houses, eight or ten of them, and I searched for the tree under which we had sat with Millibelle. It was there, a puff of green against the ashen slopes behind it, fed, no doubt, by the leaching field of the house plumbing. When I pulled my gaze from the outside world, it turned to paintings—paintings everywhere, standing against chair backs, against the wall, on the sofa back, and one in progress upon the easel: a picture of Eusequio, hunched beside the fishpool in Xavier's courtyard. Margaret was already standing before it. She fished the palette knife out of her jeans pocket, scraped up a touch of ochre, and scraped the color down the inside edge of a wall, making it glow with sunlight.

Grace walked among the other paintings, staring, moving, staring again. One of them was a portrait of Helen, seen from three-quarters back, head turned over her shoulder, heavy-lidded eyes half open in an expression indescribably erotic. Grace looked at the painting, then at me, then winked a salacious wink. Proof positive, her smile said as she jerked her head at me, saying silently, *Get out of here. Leave me to make womentalk.*

I murmured something and went. Besides, I wanted to talk to Ricardo.

I found him in the kitchen, on a stool beside the sink, peeling charred skin from a pile of chiles. *"Poblanos,"* he said. "Lourdes makes *chiles rellenos con queso* today. Some for el Señor, and some for the family."

I asked him the question I had asked his wife the day before. "When you were at the church that Sunday afternoon, did Dwight Bobbison carry anything in? Did he have anything in his hands?"

"He has *la hacheta,"* said Ricardo. "He wave it at me, and I tell him put it down or I make him eat it."

"The hatchet?"

"Sí. I look for it when we go there again, three, four days after, I think mebbe this is how he is cut, you know? No *hacheta.* It is not there. Then, when I go by again, I see it outside. It is *mohosa* . . . you say, moldy."

"Rusty?"

"Sí, Rusty."

"Dwight picked it up from outside and brought it into the church?" I mused, trying to make sense of that.

"No, no," said Ricardo. "My boy, Eusequio, he is outside. He says the man brings *la hacheta* in his car."

Why? To cut up the painting? To chop it to kindling? Because Grandma hadn't liked it?

"Did they say anything? About the hatchet?"

He shrugged. "Yelling only, at Lourdes an me."

I thanked Ricardo. Then I went back to Xavier.

"If Ernie had threatened Ricardo, do you think Ricardo would have attacked him?"

Xavier gave me a long look, trouble at the back of it. "I think not unless the threat was immediate, serious. Ricardo is a big man, but he is slow to anger."

"What if Ernie threatened to destroy the painting?"

"Ricardo would not attack a man over a painting."

"Do you know if he carries a knife?"

"To my knowledge, Ricardo does not and has never carried a knife."

Grace returned from the nether regions. We thanked Xavier for his always gracious hospitality, then she and I went out the gate, closing it carefully behind us.

"Dwight Bobbison brought Ernie the hatchet," I said without preamble. "Ricardo's boy was outside, he saw him take it out of their car."

"No mistake?"

"Dwight was waving it at Ricardo, and Ricardo told him to put it down or he'd make him eat it. I thought maybe Ernie intended to chop up the painting, because of Grandma's attitude toward it. She had time to give him an earful when he drove her and the others home after services that morning."

"He dropped the Bobbisons off at his house, why not pick the hatchet up then?"

"Maybe because he hadn't decided to do it then."

She mused, "If not then, how and when did he tell Dwight to bring it?"

"Dwight said Ernie called. There's a phone booth outside the tourist office," I said. "Ernie could have called home, told Dwight to bring the hatchet over, he was going to bash up the painting."

"That doesn't have the right feel to it," she said. "Considering Ernie's propensity for public display, wouldn't he want to do it when Margaret was there? To show her how unacceptable it was?"

"All right. Say he drops off the Bobbisons, gets an earful from Grandma, then he goes back to the church and prays about it. He decides to chop up the painting, it's an idol, it doesn't belong in his church. He goes over and calls Dwight, then he drives over here to Xavier's, where Margaret is painting in the garage, and tells her there is an important matter that needs her presence at the church. . . ."

"But she wasn't at the church."

"Wait a minute. So she says, I'm not finished, I'll walk over when I'm finished."

"Walk over! That's miles."

"It isn't. You can see the tree we sat under at Millibelle's house from the windows at Xavier's place. Felicia says it's only five minutes across the arroyo. It would be more than that for me. Part of the trip is climbing down, then up. So Ernie goes back to the church and walks in on Ricardo and Lourdes. Then Dwight and Vera arrive. There is a confrontation. Then everybody departs but Ernie."

"And what happens to Margaret?"

"Gets so involved in her work she forgets to go there—maybe never intended to. You saw how she was this morning. And Xavier says she'd rather paint than breathe. So, she doesn't think of it until she gets home and realizes Ernie is still at the church. So she goes there and finds him dead."

"Which leaves you right where you were when I got here," she said in exasperation. "Come on, Jason. Suppose she doesn't get all involved in her work and forget. Suppose she goes on over. And Ernie says he's going to destroy the painting. It's an offense. He's been preaching on getting rid of offenses, chopping them off and plucking them out. And she says, not my painting you don't, and they struggle over the hatchet, and . . ."

Her voice trailed away.

"And he accidentally gets his throat slit?" I said. "And she leaves the hatchet there, and Millibelle Garvey comes by and borrows it. . . ."

"For God's sake, Jason, the least we can do is take the damned hatchet to a lab somewhere and see if it has human blood on it! There's no water in that church building. No way to wash it, and wiping would never get it clean."

"We'll take it to the pueblo police," I said. "And we'll do it now. I'm sure they have access to lab facilities."

Grace told me she wanted to do it herself. At the police office in the shopping center she identified herself as a friend of the

victim's family, a police colleague who was asking for a professional courtesy in order to set the family's mind at rest. She got a
receipt for the hatchet and made it clear, in a pleasant way, that
she'd be following up.

"Where'd you find this?" the stocky man behind the counter
asked. His name tag identified him as Gary Vigil.

She pointed toward the dilapidated little church, which could
be seen from the front windows. "Half under the front steps."

"You think it was there when he was killed."

"We have a witness who saw it there the afternoon he was
killed, yes."

The man's face became intensely concentrated. "I was there
that evening," he said. "I didn't see it. If I'd seen it, I'd have
brought it in."

Grace cocked her head. "When were you there?"

"When the victim's wife came running over, around six, six-
fifteen. Joe Martinez and I went over there. I came back and got
the camera and took the pictures. Joe and I both went in and out
six or seven times. It was a long time before dark, but I didn't see
this hatchet. Didn't see any hatchet."

Grace and I shared a look. Either it had been there and he'd
missed it . . . or it hadn't been there. In which case, where the
hell had it been?

"Lab we use isn't open today," he said. "You want to call me
tomorrow afternoon sometime."

He was talking to her, not to me. I stared out the window at
the church, wondering what had gone on. Suppose Ernie had
threatened somebody with the hatchet. And that person had
taken it away from him and gone off with it. Then, later, they'd
brought it back. Or brought another one back.

When we went out the front door, I said, "Grace, how do we
know this hatchet is the same one Dwight had?"

"I didn't question it until a few minutes ago," she said.
"Maybe we could ask Margaret or Felicia if they can describe the
hatchet they had at their house. You said there was a wood stove
in that chapel place, so they probably had one. There's a circular
burn on the handle of this one, and some dark green paint left on
both handle and head. We can call from the ranch. I thought

we'd go back there and lie in the sun and splash in the pool a little. I have to drive back to Denver this afternoon."

"Today!"

"Well, Jason, I was doing pretty good to get two days off."

"I know. I just . . ."

"Me too," she said. "This thing gets curioser and curioser, doesn't it. I'd like somebody to say definitely the hatchet we've got is the one Dwight brought to the church."

When we got back to the ranch, while Grace was changing into her swimsuit, I called Xavier's place, got Felicia, and asked her if she remembered having a hatchet at the house.

"I haven't lived there for a long while, Jason!"

"I know. Do you suppose your mom would remember?"

"I can ask her. Hang on." There were going-away noises, the sound of distant voices, the crow of a distant rooster. After what seemed a very long time, she came back. "Mom says there was one. It had a place on the handle where a coal had landed and burned a round spot. And it had been painted dark green."

"One mystery solved," I said as Grace came out of the bedroom, sleek as a pigeon in a turquoise bikini. "The hatchet we took to the police is the one from Ernie's house. Now we ask Dwight where he got the one he took to the church."

"You go ask him," she said, her hand on the door. "I'm going to swim and then slosh sunscreen all over me and snooze. You won't be able to sit still until you find out, so go ahead."

I took a detour on my way to the Quivadas', hoping to find Millibelle Garvey at home. The Chopin flowing into the Sunday morning quiet told me she was. I knocked, then more loudly, then yelled.

"It's Jason Lynx, Ms. Garvey. Can you answer a question for me."

The music faltered, and in a moment she came to the door. "Mr. Lynx. How nice. Did you say you had a question?"

"You said you returned the hatchet to the church. What did you mean?"

"I found it," she said. "When I went up to supervise moving the piano, there it was at the top of the arroyo. I knew it belonged to the church, because when I was practicing last winter,

I'd used it several times to chop kindling for the stove. It was rusty, though, so I left it outside."

I frowned, trying to make sense of it.

"Was that all?"

I tried to think if there was anything else she might know that I did not. Nothing came to mind, so I thanked her and turned to go. Then I had a sudden thought. There was one thing, probably totally irrelevant, something Grace had said.

"Would you happen to remember what the text was for the last service you attended?"

"Text?"

"Mark 9:43–48. Do you know the reference?"

"The text?" She came out onto her tiny porch and stood very still, staring over the arroyo walls. "Oh, yes." She folded her hands in front of her and became a child, her face very calm.

"Mark 9:43:

" 'And if thy hand offend thee, cut it off: it is better for thee to enter into life maimed, than having two hands to go into hell, into the fire that never shall be quenched.'

"Verse 44: 'Where their worm dieth not, and the fire is not quenched.'

"Verse 45: 'And if thy foot offend thee, cut it off: it is better for thee to enter halt into life, than having two feet to be cast into hell, into the fire that never shall be quenched.' "

She sighed. "King James Version, of course. As a wee girl, when I attended vacation Bible School each summer, I always won first prize for memorizing Scripture. There's more. Do you want the rest of it?"

I felt the scriptural reference had struck entirely too close to home. I grinned ruefully. "I didn't like the first part."

"It goes on about plucking out eyes," she said. "Not one of my favorite passages. One inconsistent with my idea of the Christian message, which is more of the 'Let him who is without sin' variety. No, all the chopping and plucking is an interpolation, I think. By some revisionist and fanatical scribe who came along later."

"This was the subject of the sermon?" I asked her.

"My dear boy, I didn't listen. I assume it was, but the scriptural selection was quite bad enough without fundamentalist embroidery." She shook her head sadly.

I bade her goodbye and drove off, hearing the music resume behind me. It was only a fifteen-minute drive to the Quivada house. The people looked as though they hadn't moved since the day before. Same location. Same clothes. Same curlers in Vera's hair. I asked for Dwight; she bellowed, he came out, once more lifting his sagging suspenders onto his shoulders.

I thought he might limit the bluster if I talked to him halfway privately, so I met him near the house and asked, "Where did you get the hatchet you took down to the church two weeks ago?"

He turned white, then red, then white again. "Who says I . . . I didn't . . . if they say . . . what . . ."

"Look, Dwight," I said softly. "I don't care. Just tell me where you got it."

"He got it in here," said a voice from the door: Bobbi Kay, very self-important as she pointed into the room behind her. "Where the stove is, for wintertime. Because Reverend Quivada needed it. To lop off ungodliness."

Heaven help me, I was halfway back to the ranch before an understanding of what the child had said came to me as a sudden revelation, and with it an understanding of what I had not seen or had refused to see since I'd been here. I felt the sweat start out on my forehead, felt the knotting in my belly, that cold chill that comes with stomach-wrenching nausea. I pulled the car over to the side of the road and just sat there, breathing through my mouth. All the pieces fell into place, one by one, with self-satisfied little thunks. I belong here, and I belong here, and how stupid of you, Jason, not to have seen it before.

I hadn't seen it before. I wished I'd gone home and not seen it ever.

When I got back to the ranch, I didn't go out to the pool. I could see Grace supine beneath an umbrella, a book lying open on her stomach. Critter was curled up under the chair. No reason to destroy their peace.

I needed to make one very private phone call, to an artist

friend of mine in Denver. He told me what I wanted to know readily enough, but then he wanted to know why, which led to some exclamations and joshing and one thing and another. Then I sat down in the dim living room and didn't do anything for about an hour. Outside, the leaves rustled in the noonday wind. Grace wandered in, dropped a kiss on my head, and went into the bathroom. I heard the shower running. After a while she came out, a towel wrapped around her, and sat down next to me.

"What?" she asked. "Something's the matter."

"Mark 9, verse 43," I croaked.

She was puzzled.

"I saw it. The text for Ernie's sermon. It took me right back to Lutheran Sunday school in Minnesota, all that hand-lopping stuff. I forgot something about Ernie. He was very literal-minded."

She looked at me in dawning horror. "He didn't. That wasn't . . ."

"It was. He told Margaret to come to the church. He told Dwight to bring him the hatchet. He intended to lop off the offense. The cause of her behavior. Her painting."

"Her hand?" she choked. "Jason, not her hand!"

Grace got up, looking sick. I knew how she felt. In this day of gross-out movies and TV shows, the thought of a lopped hand shouldn't bother us, should it? Ho, ho, ho, look at the blood, the gore. Look at the funny man without a hand. Or better yet, sci-fi, we lop it off and build a new one.

And yet, when the hand belongs to a violinist, say, or a great surgeon, or an artist? Or to someone we love.

"She *did* come to the church. My God, she could have bled to death!" Grace cried.

She could have, of course. Perhaps he had planned on first aid. Perhaps he had even planned on a tourniquet first. Margaret had said he'd worked as an ambulance driver. Surely he'd had some kind of training. . . .

"They struggled over the hatchet?" she asked. "And it really was the weapon?"

I shook my head. "She had a knife."

"Margaret?"

"She usually has a knife. In her front pocket. Her jeans are cut to ribbons there."

She thought for a moment. "It's a painter's knife! A, what you call it, a palette knife!"

"According to an artist friend of mine in Denver, if you have a good one, a long one, it can get as sharp as a scalpel just being stropped across the canvas and dragged across the palette. It's like stropping a razor. I cut myself on the one Margaret uses. It's sharp."

"Then it wasn't murder."

"It was self-defense."

"But she never said a word! Never."

"She took the hatchet and dropped it on the trail down into the arroyo. She went on back to her painting. She had a show to put on. She didn't have time to deal with laws, or police, or even family. A little time for Helen, maybe. A few hours for Felicia. Xavier told me the other day he had to threaten her to get her to take time to buy a dress."

We sat staring at one another. "What are you going to do?" she asked.

"I don't know," I said. "I hope you don't feel called upon to do anything professional."

She shook her head. "Not if you're right about that bastard," she said. "Do you suppose Boomer told him to do it?"

I hadn't thought about it, but that could have been the gist of Boomer's message, when he came up from Oklahoma. Boomer was from Bible Belt country. Perhaps he, too, could call selectively upon Scripture.

I considered suggesting this fact to Lieutenant Snitel. It might serve to jostle Boomer's memory.

"If Boomer didn't suggest cutting off her hand, he may have suggested some kind of assault. If Buster heard him do it, Buster may tell Snitel. I can suggest it."

It was the measure of Grace's nausea and anguish over the whole matter that she did not want lunch. Needless to say, nor did I. When she and Critter left me about two for the drive back to Denver, she kissed me and told me she'd call when she got home. I said so far as I knew, I'd be right where she left me.

By ten, when Grace called to report her safe arrival, I had decided that duty and ethics required me only to prove the theory she and I had agreed was likely. I'd thrashed this out with myself during a very long walk down the river bottom, all the way to the Rio Grande and back. I had to carry Schnitz the last few miles. He wasn't used to that much exercise, and no more was I. After a bite of supper, I fell heavily into bed, propped myself up on the pillows, and reviewed the decision. If we were right, justice had more or less been served. If we were wrong, then . . . perhaps someone had to do something. Someone would have to do something about Bruce's mother, of course. She couldn't be left hanging, worrying, feeling guilty. . . .

I wondered how much the Quivadas knew. Nothing more than they'd hinted at already, probably. Margaret hadn't been there when the Bobbisons got to the church, and they couldn't prove she'd ever been there. Margaret hadn't told Felicia, either. Had she told Helen? Had she told Joy? Was that one reason for Joy's worry and concern when I saw her?

The only one who knew for sure was Margaret herself. So I thought.

Monday morning I left the animals in the run and went to the Fortunato house. It was almost as though I'd been expected. Lourdes met me at the gate and said Xavier wanted to see me.

He sat in his dim, lovely living room, surrounded by beautiful things, hands folded on top of his cane. He let me seat myself across from him, meantime giving me a hawkish, dark-eyed stare. He spoke of the weather, which was hot. Lourdes brought in coffee, which was also hot. When she had gone, shutting the door firmly behind her, he spoke of more important things.

"Ricardo says he told you about the hatchet. I had not thought to tell him not to mention it."

"You knew?" I gasped. I don't know why it surprised me, except that everything about him surprised me. He was so in command of his life, in command of his surroundings. Rare in any age. Particularly rare today.

"Of course I knew," he murmured. He sat back and weighed

me with another look, nodding to himself, seeming to come to some decision.

Finally, he said, "It was to me she came when she returned from there, shaking like a young tree in the wind, horrified as much at what she had done as at what he had threatened to do. You know what he threatened to do?"

"I guessed," I said. "Putting two and two together. He was going to cut off her hand."

"Lop off one hand," he said. "Pluck out both eyes."

I simply sat there with my mouth open. Of course. Scripture was Scripture. A woman with one hand could still cook and wash. A blind woman could still do lots of things. But she couldn't paint.

"Visualize it," he whispered to me. "The man standing behind his lectern, the Bible open upon it. He does not need to read the verses. He knows them by heart. But he reads them, nonetheless, lingering over the words, holding her close. She has caused trouble with her selfish desires, he says. She has ruined a family in Oklahoma with her perverted ways. She is ruining his family here in New Mexico. The hatchet rests above the book. When he has finished, he grasps her firmly with one hand, takes up the hatchet in the other. He says she must put her right hand upon the pulpit, the eyes will come later. He does not seem to see her. His gaze is fixed on some other place, some other world.

"She is terrified. Her right hand touches the palette knife in her pocket. She grasps it. He starts to pull her close. She lashes out with the knife! It is the only weapon she has. She has no idea what it will do!

"It slices through him, she tells me. His chin falls forward, as though he is puzzled. He raises his head. The red flood rushes down the front of him, onto her, her hand, her arm. He drops her arm. He slumps. He falls. She picks up the hatchet, stands there looking at him, thrusts the knife back in the pocket where it always is, then runs away, horrified. Is he dead? How can he not be?

"She drops the hatchet somewhere near the arroyo. She flees to me, like a child to a parent, for have I not been a parent to her? Her mentor, her helper, her support and comfort? I take the shirt and the jeans and the knife to be burned. She has a shower in my bathroom, to wash away the blood. She has other clothes here, clean ones, ones she keeps here to change into if she gets herself, as she says, messed up. I tell her to go back to her work, as though nothing has happened. Later I will find his body. She says no. No, she will go there, if he does not come home for supper. *If,* she says, still not believing what has happened. Already, in her eyes, I can see the forgetting going on."

He sat back. Quietly. An old eagle, resting. "We are going to be married. Margaret and I. It is decided."

I gaped at him. "But she's . . ."

"In my case, does it matter what she is? I was married. I had children. Two have died. Two still live. They are successful, well provided for. My grandchildren are numerous, all well set up in life. Why should I not . . . provide for a great artist. Why should she not provide for me."

"Provide . . ."

"Interest. Amusement. Someone for me to admire and encourage."

"There's no reason why not," I said at last. "No reason I can think of."

The Señora would be Fortunato indeed. I remembered how Bruce and Lindsay had worried over her. Wondering how she would live, how Felicia would live.

I sighed.

"What is it?" he asked.

"Ernie's mother. If she knew this . . ."

"But why should she ever know this? Why should she not enjoy her former daughter-in-law, her granddaughter, without taint. Surely she can be told . . . something more acceptable."

"Like?"

"His mother knows her son was a thorn in the flesh of the people at the pueblo. Suppose we say everything that we know, except one thing. He stayed at the church. He phoned to have the hatchet brought to him. He argued with Ricardo and Lourdes. We know his attitude toward the painting: obviously he was going to chop it up! But then someone else came, someone who confronted him or argued with him. He had the hatchet in his hands, and he probably waved it in a threatening manner, frightening the unknown person, who struck out with his knife. Then the person fled. We even know which way he went, along the edge of the arroyo, for that is where the hatchet was found.

"Who is to say it did not happen in that fashion?"

I thought about it. "Phyllis Norman would accept that. Is that going to be our theory of what happened? We can't prove it, of course."

He smiled a bleak, old-man smile. "It is a theory with some substantiation. Already there are rumors of this one or that one from the pueblo. Persons who have, so to speak, disappeared. Who have not been seen for some time. The killing was almost an accident, so we believe. Will Margaret's mother-in-law insist upon finding the person who did this thing?"

"You're an old fox," I grated, half admiringly.

"I'm old," he said, suddenly looking incredibly so. "I have seen most of this century. I am no longer sure what justice is, but I know it has little to do with the law. Once the law served justice, but now it is only a game attorneys play, where the greatest skill lies in playing by the rules, no matter what injustice results.

"As for me, I still venerate justice, and it is justice that Margaret should have some peace."

I stayed awhile longer, but we had said everything there was to say. I didn't ask to see Margaret. He did not offer. She was in good hands and, as he had said, already she was forgetting. She was wiping it out. I hoped I'd manage that myself. Every time I thought of that scene in the church, I started to sweat all over again.

Just before I left, I gave him the papers I'd found in my jacket pocket that morning, the ones I'd picked up at Ernie's house. The settlement and deed to the house. In the name of the congregation.

I didn't call Lieutenant Snitel. I didn't call Bill Reiserling. I didn't call Warren Chamberlain. By two, I had my things packed and my animals in the car. I thanked Phil for his hospitality, gave him the case of beer I'd picked up at Kokomans in Pojoaque (best liquor and wine shop in or near Santa Fe), paid the rent on the house over Phil's protests—Mike had offered it freebies—and started the trip back. Bela lay on the backseat, watching me, not the traffic. He was worried about me.

He had reason to be. I was jittery, uncertain, in an evil temper. It wasn't the first time I'd gotten myself into this situation, knowing more than was good for me, required to keep some ugly secret. At least in this case, I wouldn't be running into people every few months whom I needed to keep secrets from. Bruce and Lindsay and Bruce's mother were safely ensconced on the East Coast, where I would be unlikely to see them oftener than every ten years or so. If then.

But still. I had known Ernie since I was a young man. I felt I had known Bruce all my life. We'd gotten drunk together and shared midnight confidences, we'd bailed one another out of trouble and laughed together at the world's oddities, among whom we included Ernie Quivada. We'd shaken our heads and wondered what he'd do next, and we'd stayed away from him, mostly, because he was uncomfortable to be around.

We'd seen him, we'd known him, but we hadn't really seen him or known him. Grace's words kept coming back to me, her comment about going to see the aardvark. She'd seen something breathing, but she had not seen the beast itself. Bruce and I had also seen something breathing, but we had not sensed old earth pig himself, rising up out of the darkness with his huge sharp claws that could disembowel a man as easily as they could move tons of earth in a night. We had not seen the aardvark himself for what the aardvark actually was; he was in the dark, where no one who lived in daylight could ever see.

Margaret had seen the aardvark. Joy had seen the aardvark, over and over again, up to the end, when he struck the blow that killed her.

"What they do to us," Margaret had said, meaning men, some men. "What they do to us."

What they have always done.

Oh God, please, I thought, let Grace marry me. Let us live together as aspiring humans, conscious of the creature breathing in the dark. Let us have children; let us warn them about the aardvark.

Let us do everything we can to keep the beast at bay.